Prol

Saturday 3rd June 2023

It was the night of the strawberry moon, a fact that he neither knew nor cared about, but he was grateful for the moonlight flooding the landing through an open doorway. A gentle snoring was coming from the master bedroom, its door ajar behind him as he moved stealthily towards the smallest bedroom at the front of the three-bedroom semi. Its door too was ajar, and he pushed quietly into the room. A nightlight, shaped like a child's drawing of the sun, cast a pale yellow glow over the baby asleep in his cot. It lit the jungle scene pasted on the wall behind the cot, the remaining three walls a pale leafy green decorated with framed prints of characters from *The Jungle Book*.

The child lay on his back, clothed in a blue and green Hey Duggee onesie, a green blanket flung aside, arms stretched out, a dummy discarded on the sheet nearby. His cherubic face was capped with a mop of untidy fair hair, and he snuffled slightly as he dreamt the dreams of the innocent.

First, he carefully switched off the baby monitor. Then he took the dummy and dipped it into the small plastic container he'd brought with him. Honey for sweetness with a drop of highly diluted morphine, the dose carefully calculated not to harm the child. Gingerly, he eased the dummy into the child's mouth, relaxing only when the child started sucking without even waking. After a couple of minutes, he lifted the now sedated baby and gently placed him into the black sports bag, already lined with a blanket. He retrieved a well-sucked blue-coated rabbit from the cot and placed it at the child's feet. Then he closed the zip, leaving a couple of inches open to allow air to circulate. Stealthily, he made his way down the moonlit staircase and silently let himself out of the front door. He walked casually down the road, alert to his surroundings, confident that no one was watching. When he reached the waiting car, he used a seat belt to fasten the sports bag onto the back seat, before climbing into the front passenger seat.

'Will he be all right like that?' whispered the driver.

'For now,' he grunted in reply. 'It's a necessary precaution, just in case the fuzz pulls us over.' She nodded before starting the engine and pulling away into the night.

✿

Mia woke to sunlight streaming in through her pastel pink curtains. She rolled onto her side and gazed at the sleeping form of her boyfriend, Vikram, admiring his smooth brown skin and well-toned muscles, drinking in his warm muskiness. For a moment, she was so content, so happy to have this wonderful new man in her life.

He seemed to sense her watching him, stirring and opening his eyes before twisting his head to return her gaze. 'Good morning, my darling,' he murmured softly. 'It seems as though your sweet little boy has finally consented to let us have a weekend lie-in.'

At that, her sleepy brain was alerted by a twinge of uneasiness. The sun was shining directly into their room, implying it was much later than her son's usual ungodly hour of awakening. And there was no sound from the baby monitor, not even a whimper. But she was usually woken up by him screaming for his first feed of the day. And she felt surprisingly refreshed considering they'd not gone to bed until after midnight. She sat up, suddenly wide awake and alarmed.

'Whatever's the matter?' Vikram soothed. 'Come and lie down with me while we have the chance.'

'Noah!' was her panicked reply as she snatched her phone from the bedside locker and saw the time. Nearly half past nine!

Before Vikram could speak, she was out of bed and flinging open the bedroom door in her haste to get to her

Acknowledgements

A huge thank you to everyone who read my second novel, *The Mystery of the Missing Wallet*, especially those who took the time to leave a review. It was universally adjudged to have been better than my first book, which puts a lot of pressure on this third in the series! I just hope it lives up to your expectations.

My grateful thanks again to all the people at The Choir Press for guiding me through the publication process, especially to David and Rachel for all their support, and to my lovely copy editor, Ann-Marie.

A special thank you to my friend Dawn, who has become my mentor and de facto developmental editor. Your feedback and encouragement are invaluable! And thank you, Heather, once again, for your beautiful artwork. I think you've surpassed yourself this time!

To my wonderful husband: thank you for your continued support and patience, especially on the days when I am shut in my writing room (aka the spare bedroom) for hours at a time. Just keep those cups of tea coming, please!

Finally, I want to give a shout-out to Chris and Helen who have just taken on the role of designing a new website for me and taking over my social media posting. I look forward to exciting times ahead.

I dedicate this book to you all!

The Mystery of the Missing Child

The Salisbury Murders:
Book 3

by

WENDY BOYNTON

THE CHOIR PRESS

First published in the United Kingdom in 2025 by
The Choir Press

ISBN 978-1-78963-576-8

This book is a fictional story set in the beautiful and very real city of Salisbury in Wiltshire. I lived in the Salisbury area for many years and still return regularly to visit family and friends there.

Whilst I have tried to stay faithful to the real locations, I have altered or invented certain aspects for the sake of the story. For instance, there is no care home called Britford Lodge, nor do Cathedral Accountants, Linda's Lunches or The Hanging Man pub exist. All the characters in this book are entirely the products of my imagination, and any similarity to real people, living or deceased, is coincidental.

This publication contains language and themes that reflect the attitudes of a particular time and of certain characters in the storyline, which some readers may find offensive. They are included intentionally as part of the story and not to endorse such views, and they do not represent the author's personal opinions.

son. On the landing, she saw that his door was wide open and gasped a strangled 'no' as icy hands twisted her stomach. She forced herself into her son's room to look into his cot, fearful of what she might see. It was empty. The bottom suddenly dropped out of her world, and she cried out like a wounded animal.

Chapter One

Margaret Thornton, better known as Meg to staff and residents alike, was sitting at her favourite spot in the day room, an old gate-legged table positioned near a window overlooking the car park. She was indulging in her favourite pastime, working on a jigsaw puzzle with her dear friend Jeannie Lewis. They made quite an incongruous pair; Meg verging on the statuesque, with warm brown eyes and a crown of glossy grey curls framing her intelligent face; Jeannie petite, almost pitifully thin, with a wizened face and wispy white hair. They worked in companionable silence amid the background noises of the television in the far corner, sporadic muted conversation and a variety of snores from somnolent residents.

Meg kept glancing at her phone. She was expecting – or at least hoping for – a text message from Lauren. She'd been metaphorically keeping her fingers crossed for the last hour because Lauren Peachy, the twenty-year-old carer who'd become her close friend, was taking her driving test that morning. But still no news. Was that good or bad?

The answer finally came as an old but remarkably well-kept black Peugeot 206 swept triumphantly into the car park. It was Lauren's new car. And she was alone, which could only mean one thing.

Jeannie looked up and smiled. 'I told you she'd pass first time.'

Meg acknowledged her friend with a broad grin as she rose from her chair and hurried to meet Lauren at the front doors to Britford Lodge Care Home.

'Congratulations, my dear!' Meg, now eighty-two years old, hugged her friend.

1

'Oh, my goodness me, I was so nervous,' Lauren gasped, eyes gleaming brightly. 'But I only had one minor fault!' she exclaimed.

'That's excellent news. I see you've ditched both your L-plates and your boyfriend?' Meg enquired with a twinkle.

'Don't need L-plates anymore,' Lauren chuckled, 'and of course I've not ditched Viv! He's gone back to work, over the moon that he no longer has to accompany me everywhere. Don't get me wrong, I'm very grateful he let me practise my driving for the last few weeks, but I am so happy to finally be free and independent.'

'Yes, I bet you are. But what now? You're far too early for the start of your shift! Are you going home and coming back again?'

'Actually, I thought perhaps we could go down to the farm shop café together to celebrate. For lunch, my treat.'

'I would love to have lunch with you, but I insist it's my treat. You have a car to maintain and pay for now, and they don't come cheap.'

'That's true enough; the insurance alone cost an arm and a leg! But Viv's given me some money so that we can celebrate, so technically it's actually his treat.'

'In that case, I'll have a quick word with Maureen to let her know I'm going out, and then I'll get my handbag and a cardigan.' Maureen was the care manager who, among her many tasks managing the home, kept a log of the residents' comings and goings.

'I doubt you'll need a cardigan; it's really hot outside today,' Lauren commented.

'You forget, us elderly folk feel even the slightest breeze.'

As it happens, Lauren was right; it was much hotter outside than Meg had realised, and she ended up carrying her cardigan as they strolled down Lower Road to Britford Farm. A retired schoolteacher, she was wearing a floral print dress that she'd bought years ago from M&S and comfortable sandals. Lauren was wearing cropped leggings and a sleeveless turquoise T-shirt that showed off her slender figure and accentuated her aquamarine blue eyes. With her short pixie-cut blonde hair, she was a very attractive young woman, as attested to by a wolf whistle from a farm labourer mending the fence in the adjacent field.

'Why do men have to do that?' Lauren grumbled. 'It's so demeaning.'

'Take it as a compliment,' suggested Meg. 'When I was young, we felt put out if we *didn't* get any wolf whistles.'

Lauren tilted her head to one side as she thought about that. It was certainly a more positive slant on things. And today, she was feeling very positive. She lightened her step and held her chin up, feeling good about herself. The last year had been a tough one, with her mum's cancer diagnosis coming whilst she was still grieving for her dad, killed in a car accident three years earlier; finishing college and job hunting, only to lose her first job after just five weeks; working for the agency and dating David, which had turned out to be a huge mistake. Not to mention the trauma of the events at The Cedars last September and again in January, when she'd been attacked not once but twice! But now, her nightmares were all behind her and life was good. She had a steady job, which she was enjoying. She had a steady boyfriend, whom she loved to bits. And her mum was now officially cancer-free and back at work full time. And today, she'd passed her driving test. Yippee!

Meg and Lauren enjoyed their Wiltshire ham salads and indulgent cakes, before strolling back up to Britford Lodge to find that the sun had got even hotter during their time inside the café. Lauren skipped off to get changed for her late shift, seemingly not feeling the heat, whilst Meg decided to have a post-lunch lie-down on her bed, after downing a full glass of refreshing water.

She was roused from her snooze about half an hour later by a military knock on her door. 'Come in,' she called out drowsily, pushing herself up onto one elbow to see Albert entering her room, a little hesitantly.

'I say, old gal, are you feeling under the weather? We missed you at lunch.'

'I'm so sorry, Albert, I should have told you. Lauren passed her driving test this morning, so we went down to the café for a celebratory lunch.'

Albert looked put out. 'You could've invited me,' he grumbled. Captain Albert Grimshaw, Royal Navy retired, looked every inch an old sailor with his proud bearing, bald head and comic-book beard and moustache. Five years older than Meg, and half a head taller, he had first met her when she moved into The Cedars a year ago. Meg's deductive thinking had impressed him and, truth be told, he had a huge soft spot for this indomitable lady. So, he couldn't stay offended for long.

'How about a game of rummy?' he suggested.

Meg was still a bit tired, but she didn't want to disappoint him twice in one day. She agreed to follow him downstairs in a moment or two.

They had played several hands of rummy when Lauren arrived with the tea trolley.

'I hear congratulations are in order?' boomed Albert.

'Thank you, yes. I'm a fully fledged driver now,' beamed Lauren as she handed him his mug of milky sweet tea.

'Well, you take care, young lady,' he warned. 'There's a lot of idiotic drivers on the roads these days.'

'Oh, and how would you know that?' Lauren bantered cheekily.

'Harrumph!' snorted Albert. 'You only have to watch the news to see how many accidents there are nowadays. And nearly all caused by drivers going too fast, texting or talking on their phones, or ignoring the weather conditions.'

'He has a point,' agreed Meg, putting a hand on Albert's arm to prevent him from carrying on with his tirade. 'Please be careful when you're driving.'

'You too? Well, don't worry. Viv's already given me the same lecture, and my mum.'

'It just goes to show how much we all love you,' Meg soothed.

'I suppose,' relented Lauren.

She moved on to the next group of residents, chatting here and there as she made her way round the day room, before taking the trolley back to the kitchen. She parked it up in its usual place just inside the kitchen door and was putting the milk away in the large refrigerator when one of the sous-chefs, Sanjeev, approached.

'Would it be possible to speak with you, if you have the time?' he asked, very politely, a worried frown on his face.

'Of course, is there a problem?'

'I'm very much afraid there is,' he replied seriously.

'Is it one of the residents?' asked Lauren, puzzled by his tone.

'No, I'm afraid it is not a problem concerning anyone in this care home. It is another matter which I wish to ask for your help with.'

'What's it about?' exclaimed Lauren, now mystified.

'It is about a man accused of a crime he did not commit.'

Chapter Two

Lauren's mouth gaped open; had she just heard him correctly?

'What the heck?' she gasped.

'I'm sorry to bother you, but I know that you helped to solve that murder here in January. And I know that if anyone can help my cousin, it's you, Lauren.'

'You'd better tell me all about it.'

'I want to, but I can't right now.' He glanced around nervously. 'I have a lot of work to do this afternoon, and Stuart will be back from his cigarette break any moment now.'

'What do you suggest?'

'Could you come to the kitchen after dinner this evening? I will be on my own then, so it will be easier to talk.'

Just then, the bulky frame of head chef Stuart Nokes appeared in the open back door, and Sanjeev moved hastily away from Lauren.

'That's fine, Sanjeev,' she called out brightly, 'no problem at all.'

Leaving the kitchen, she wondered what on earth this could be about. She immediately returned to the day room to consult with Meg.

'I would suggest you listen to what he has to tell you before making any commitment to help,' advised Meg.

'I wouldn't get involved at all, if I were you,' growled Albert.

'And why is that?' Meg asked with a warning look.

'Well, umm, you know. He's a young chap and a foreigner to boot. Not sure Lauren should be meeting him on her own. There's no telling what he has in mind.'

'Albert!' the two of them chorused disapprovingly.

'What? What?' he spluttered in indignation before taking

note of their horrified expressions. 'I didn't mean ... umm, well ...' His voice trailed off as he realised that he'd put his foot in it again.

'I'm quite capable of looking after myself,' asserted Lauren.

'Umm, of course you are, m'dear,' soothed Albert, not sure how to extricate himself from his blunder. To his surprise, Meg wasn't ready with one of her tongue-lashings.

'Actually, Albert has a point,' she said to a surprised Lauren. 'Not anything to do with Sanjeev's ethnicity, which is neither here nor there, nor with his intentions, which I seriously doubt are anything other than honest. But if there is a problem to be solved, then two heads will be better than one.'

'That's a good idea,' agreed Lauren with a glint in her eye. 'It would be a great help if you'd come with me to hear what Sanjeev has to say.' Just as Meg was about to commend her on her good sense, Lauren added, 'It'll save me from having to repeat it all to you later!'

Albert guffawed loudly then turned it into a cough when Meg glared at him.

The two of them made their plans and then Lauren scuttled off to get on with her work.

❖

Sanjeev was clearly on edge throughout dinner that evening. Twice he dropped a utensil and several times he got muddled up with his orders. Meg watched him discreetly whilst eating her dinner as slowly as she could, at the same time as maintaining a conversation with Albert, Jeannie and another friend, the plump and motherly Betty. The four nearly always sat at the same table for meals.

Lauren was in and out of the dining room, but it was Sue who was supervising the residents whilst they ate. Sue Barclay, a matronly woman in her mid-fifties, had been promoted to senior care assistant after her predecessor was arrested in January and was now full of her own importance. She was in charge of the late shift, and Meg wondered if Lauren would be able to slip away for long enough to hear what Sanjeev had to say. She needn't have worried; Lauren had that one covered.

When all the other residents had left the dining room, Meg watched as Sanjeev cleared the last of the food from the hot buffet before wiping down and disappearing into the kitchen. Sue was clearly impatient for her to leave the dining room.

'Is there a problem, Meg?' she asked haughtily. 'It's not like you to be so slow.'

'I think I may have eaten too much at lunch,' Meg apologised.

'Oh yes, I saw that you'd gone out to lunch. With Lauren, I presume?' She sniffed her disapproval. Meg took no notice, knowing that the care manager, Maureen Wilkinson, was fine about the two of them being good friends, so long as it didn't interfere with Lauren's work. Which, she thought with a twinge of guilt, it just might this evening.

When she was sure that Sanjeev had finished in the dining room, Meg made her way out to the hall and paused near the door to the kitchen, looking around for Lauren. A moment passed, then her young friend appeared from the treatment room opposite. 'Let's go in quickly, before bossy Barclay sees me,' urged Lauren quietly.

'What if she notices your absence?' Meg whispered back.

'Kayla's going to cover for me,' Lauren hissed as she slipped into the kitchen. Kayla Higginbotham was only a couple of years older than Lauren and, after Meg had helped her to escape from her abusive boyfriend, she had become positively friendly towards them both. She was now living in a rented flat and blossoming with her independence.

Sanjeev started to smile when he saw Lauren, which broadened into a grin when Meg appeared behind her. 'I am honoured to have you come with Lauren,' he said; as always, very polite. 'Please, there are two stools here, if you would both sit. I will stand while I tell you about the problem.'

Meg and Lauren settled themselves onto the stools and looked at Sanjeev expectantly.

'I am very worried about my cousin Vikram,' he began.

'I didn't know you had family in the country,' interrupted Lauren.

'Then permit me to tell you a little about my family first, so that you will understand. If that will not bore you too much?'

'Please do, that will be very helpful,' encouraged Meg.

'Very well. My parents came to England nearly thirty years ago and settled in Bradford, where my father is a GP. My mother is a nurse, so it was easy for her to find work too. My eldest brother was born in India, but myself and my other brother and sister were all born in Bradford, so I am British, you see.'

'That's why your English is so good.' Meg nodded to herself.

'Yes, indeed. I was brought up speaking English first and Marathi second. That's the state language of Mumbai, where my parents are from. I also speak a little Hindi.'

Lauren was amazed. 'Did your parents speak English before they came to England?'

'Yes, indeed. It was necessary for them to be multilingual, working in the hospital in Mumbai. And they spoke English at home with us, to prepare us for school in this country. My parents wanted us to be integrated into British society, but that is an ideal that is not always possible.'

'And not your fault, I'm sure,' Meg said with sympathy. 'It is a sad truth that not all British people accept those perceived as foreign, whether or not they were born here.'

'That is very true. But let me get back to my story. Although my immediate family are settled in this country, I have many aunts, uncles and cousins still living back in India. My cousin Vikram was one. His father and my father are brothers. He was raised in Mumbai, but at eighteen he came to England to study at university here. You may not know it, but Mumbai is considered by many to be the financial capital of India. Vikram's parents are both accountants, and they were keen for him to come to this country, where it is possible to earn a much better income than in India. He spent three years at university in Leeds, where it was not too great a distance for him to come to Bradford for the holidays. He graduated with a first-class honours degree in Business Economics and then studied in London with one of your top accountancy firms, Deloitte, to become a chartered accountant. Three years ago, he came to Salisbury, where he has a good job, many friends and a beautiful girlfriend. I'm telling you all this because I want you to know that he is a good person, an intelligent person. He simply would not have done what he has been accused of doing.'

'And what's that?' asked Meg gently.

'They say that he has abducted and murdered a child!'

Chapter Three

'What?' exploded Lauren. 'Whose child? And why was your cousin accused?'

'I suspect it is the child that was in the papers recently and on the local news. I think his name was Noah?' Meg asked gently.

'His name *is* Noah,' confirmed Sanjeev. 'I cannot, I will not, believe that he is dead.'

'They haven't found him yet?' asked Meg. She could see that Sanjeev was getting emotional.

'No, and I think the police have stopped looking. But I swear to you, it was not Vikram who took Noah. And, most certainly, he could not have murdered him.'

'I know a little about the case,' Meg said with a nod. 'Are you aware of it, Lauren?'

'Sorry, no, not really. I think I've heard the name, now you've said it, but I don't remember any of the details.'

'That is okay, I will tell you,' Sanjeev said eagerly. 'My cousin Vikram Chopra lives with his girlfriend, Mia Jenkins, in a house they are renting together in the Laverstock area of Salisbury. Noah is Mia's son by another man, but he has her surname, so he is Noah Jenkins. They met last year – Mia works in the sandwich shop in town, where Vikram buys his lunch most days – but they only started dating on Valentine's Day this year. To cut a very long story short, they fell in love and, about a month ago, they moved in together. Noah adores Vikram … and Vikram treated him like his own son.'

'But then Noah was kidnapped?' prompted Meg.

'Yes, he was taken from his cot in the middle of the night on the third of this month. Police started a major search. There were appeals on the radio, on television, in the newspapers and all over social media. But baby Noah could not be found.'

'How old was … is he?' asked Lauren.

'He was one on the twenty-ninth of March, so nearly fifteen months old now,' replied Sanjeev. 'I was at his birthday party. He is such a bright, lively little boy, into everything and walking very well for his age. What has happened to him is terrible. Absolutely terrible.'

'Yes, indeed,' agreed Meg, 'but why do the police think that Vikram is responsible?'

'There were no signs that their house was broken into so, from the very beginning, the police were convinced that either Mia or Vikram had to be responsible or had helped whoever took Noah. They questioned them both for hours but got nothing, because they are both innocent. They appealed for witnesses, and one of the neighbours came forward to say they'd seen Vikram leaving the house at about one-thirty in the morning, carrying a black sports bag. Vikram swears this was not him, but the police don't believe him.'

'Is that it?' asked Lauren, incredulously.

'They say that Noah was likely smothered in his cot. Otherwise, he would have cried out and Mia would've heard. They say that Vikram put the child's body in the sports bag and took it out to dispose of it somewhere. This is simply not true! The police have no proof of this, but they have made up their minds that Vikram is guilty.'

'Do you know if this is one of Dan's cases?' Lauren asked Meg with a frown.

Dan, who Meg regarded as her honorary grandson, was a good friend and frequent visitor of hers. He was also a detective inspector with Salisbury Police and Lauren's boyfriend's boss.

'No, unfortunately it isn't. I'm sure he wouldn't have arrested someone on such flimsy evidence. That is, if you really have told us everything, Sanjeev?'

'I have told you what I know and what I believe. I'm sorry but I cannot be sure that I have all the details.'

'What about Mia? Does she think that Vikram did this?' demanded Lauren.

'No, she is as adamant as I am that Vikram could not

have done this. She is distraught. Not only is her baby still missing, but now she is all alone because they have arrested Vikram and put him in prison.'

'And the poor lad has been missing for – what? About two and a half weeks?' Meg pulled a grim face, knowing that the likelihood of a good outcome was falling with every day that passed. 'Did the police ever have any other suspects?'

'At first, they questioned Noah's birth father, but they soon discounted him because he has an alibi. Mia thought it had to be him, but now she doesn't know what to think.'

'Do you know if Vikram has been formally charged? And, if so, what with?' enquired Meg. As the widow of a former detective chief inspector, she knew that this detail was important.

'I believe they have charged him with child abduction,' Sanjeev replied mournfully.

'But they haven't charged him with murder?' Meg checked.

'No, I do not think so. Mia says the police are now searching for Noah's body. They say, when they have that, they will charge Vikram with murder.'

'There must be some doubt, then,' Meg said thoughtfully, 'or, at the very least, they have insufficient evidence. Otherwise, they would have charged him already.'

'Does that mean he's innocent?' asked Lauren.

'Not necessarily, but there is definitely room for doubt. Listen, Sanjeev, if Lauren and I were to investigate this, we would do so with an open mind. I cannot promise to clear your cousin if he is, in fact, guilty.'

'I understand,' Sanjeev nodded earnestly, 'but I guarantee, you will find that he is innocent.'

'What makes you so sure?'

'Because he is a devout Hindu.'

Lauren looked at Meg, puzzled.

'I'm sorry,' Meg shook her head, 'but being religious does not preclude a person from doing bad things. Sadly, many crimes are committed every year in the name of religion.'

'No, you do not understand,' Sanjeev argued. 'Hinduism is not just a religion. It is as much about a way of life. It is our culture, if you like. It is everything we are brought up to believe in.'

'It's not that I don't believe you,' Meg said firmly, 'but in every religion, there are people who fail to follow the tenets of their faith, believing that they have sufficient justification for doing something prohibited.'

'I do know that. But I am telling you, Vikram is not like that. He believes in samsara, karma, atman—'

'Wait a moment,' Lauren interrupted. 'Sanjeev, I'm sorry, but I know next to nothing about Hinduism. I've heard of karma, of course, but sams ... sama ...'

'Samsara,' Sanjeev corrected her. 'It is belief in the continuous cycle of life, death and reincarnation.'

'Oh.'

'And atman is our word for the soul. We believe that all living things have a soul; not just humans, but animals too. It is forbidden to take a life, any life. That would be totally against everything we believe.'

'In that respect, it is not so very different from many other religions,' agreed Meg, 'but unfortunately, that still doesn't prove that Vikram is innocent.'

'But we are going to investigate!' Lauren sounded indignant.

'Oh yes, we will investigate.'

'Thank you so much, Meg. Thank you, Lauren. You are both so kind and so clever. I know you will be able to get Vikram released.'

'We can't make any promises,' warned Meg. 'We'll do what we can, but we are not the police. And we can only find whatever evidence is there to be found, which may or may not be enough.'

'I understand. But at least you were good enough to listen to me.' Sanjeev was fervently shaking hands with first Lauren and then Meg and then Lauren again when there was a knock on the door and Kayla's head appeared.

'Quick, Lauren, old bossy Barclay is on the warpath, wanting to know where you are. I told her you've been helping me and have just nipped to the loo, but you'd better come and join me in Jeffrey's room, quick as you can, before she comes back again.'

'Thanks for that,' gasped Lauren. She quickly said goodbye to Meg and Sanjeev and followed Kayla. Meg hoped that she wouldn't get into trouble.

✲

When Lauren had gone, Meg withdrew a notebook and pen from her cardigan pocket, which she'd brought with her, just in case.

'Now then, Sanjeev, I need some details, please.'

'Yes, of course, whatever you need. So long as I know it, I will tell you.'

Meg jotted down various details about Mia, Vikram and Noah before asking what Sanjeev knew about Noah's birth father, which turned out to be not a lot.

She moved on. 'Do you know when Vikram was arrested?'

'On Friday.'

Hmm, four days ago. He must have been charged already and refused bail. Meg studied her notes, wondering what else she needed to ask.

'Do you perhaps have a mobile phone?' asked Sanjeev.

'Yes, I do.'

'Then will you permit me to put your number into my phone, and I will put mine into yours, so that we might text each other if there are other questions you need answered?' he suggested.

'That's a very helpful idea,' approved Meg, handing over her phone immediately.

Chapter Four

The next day was slightly cooler, much to Meg's relief, although the intermittent cloud cover was probably less helpful to the crowds gathered at Stonehenge for the summer solstice. To be fair, Meg had no idea what the weather had been like at dawn. Like most sensible people, she'd been asleep in her bed when the sun had crept over the horizon. As it was, she had risen earlier than usual this morning and eaten a light breakfast so that she could meet up with Lauren to discuss their new case.

When she arrived at the farm, Lauren was already parked there, waiting. She got out and bounced over to Meg to greet her warmly. 'Isn't this exciting?'

'I'm not sure Mia or Vikram would agree with you,' said Meg dryly.

'No, of course not. It must be dreadful for them. I can't imagine someone taking your baby away from you. Nor being wrongly accused of something you didn't do.'

'Be careful of making assumptions,' warned Meg. 'We need to go into this investigation with an open mind. I hope, for Sanjeev's sake, that he is right, and his cousin is innocent. But we need to follow wherever the evidence takes us.'

'Yes, of course,' Lauren nodded, recognising the truth in Meg's words. 'You take a seat, and I'll go and order. I assume you want a pot of tea?'

Meg thanked her and took a seat at their favourite table, tucked in a corner of the café, slightly apart from the other tables. Lauren returned from placing their order at the counter and drew her notebook out of her large shoulder bag. 'Right, I started doing some research on the people involved. I was able to confirm what Sanjeev told us. Vikram Chopra was born in India in 1995 and came to England in 2013. He spent three years at Leeds University, four years working for Deloitte in London, and has been with Cathedral Accountants in Salisbury since October 2020. I had a quick look at their website, and he's listed as one of the junior partners. There's a photo and a mini biography of him here, if you'd like to have a look at it.' She turned the screen around for Meg to see.

Meg studied the photo of Vikram. He had shortly cropped black hair and a neatly trimmed beard and moustache. He wore glasses and looked both handsome and intelligent. It was impossible to tell how tall he was, as he was sitting behind a desk, but he appeared to have a well-toned body. A man who liked to work out, perhaps? He certainly looked like a nice young man, but looks could be deceiving.

She read the biography with interest; it seemed Vikram had done well in his studies and was highly thought of by his senior partners, with phrases like 'promising future' and 'highly commendable work ethic' featuring in their description. But then, they'd hardly portray him in a negative light if they wanted to attract business to the firm, would they?

The now familiar waitress arrived at that moment with their order, so Meg moved the computer to one side and beamed at her. 'Hello again, how are you today?'

'I'm very well, thank you, and grateful it's not as hot as yesterday. It's nice to see you both again so soon. You're getting to be two of my best regulars.'

Meg explained that she lived at Britford Lodge.

'I thought you probably did. We get quite a bit of custom from there, particularly at the weekend when families are visiting and like to take their loved ones out for a treat. Not so much during the week, though. Is this your granddaughter?'

'Oh no, Lauren is a very dear friend.'

'Oh, that's nice for you.' She moved away to clear a couple of tables before returning to the kitchen.

'Seems like you now have an honorary granddaughter,' Lauren teased cheekily, 'to go with your honorary grandson.'

'I never had children,' Meg said a little wistfully, 'but if I had, I suppose they'd be well into their fifties by now, meaning you could indeed be my granddaughter.'

'Yeah, isn't that weird?' replied Lauren. 'But I'd rather stick to calling you Meg, not Granny, if that's okay with you?' Meg nodded as she poured her tea. 'Talking of Dan, are you going to tell him about our investigation?' Lauren was referring to DI Daniel Bywater, who had become close friends with Meg after they had been involved in two cases together.

'Not just yet,' said Meg. 'I'm not sure how well he'll take the idea of us investigating a police matter that is, when all's said and done, none of our business. I'd like to wait and see what we turn up, first. If we find that the police are probably right to have arrested Vikram, then I see no need to upset the apple cart.'

'Yeah, I suppose he might see it as a criticism of his colleagues, even if he wasn't the investigating officer.'

'Exactly.'

'Now, I've not had time to get much information on anyone else, but I'm not sure that the internet's going to tell us a lot until we know what we're looking for. I think we'd be better off talking to people directly, to begin with.'

'I agree,' said Meg. 'Why don't you put that computer away? I've got my notebook here' – she withdrew a spiral-bound paper pad from her handbag – 'with the details Sanjeev gave me last night. I think the first person we need to talk to is Mia. Sanjeev said he would phone her last night to tell her that we've agreed to investigate, so hopefully she'll be expecting us to get in contact.'

'Good idea, but doesn't she work?'

'Yes, she works part time in a sandwich shop on Castle Street. Now that you've got your driving licence, I wondered if you'd be up for taking me for a little trip into town?'

'What, right now?'

'Well, after we've finished our drinks. There's no rush, but it would be nice to meet Mia and arrange a better time to talk to her properly.'

'Do you think she'll be at work today, with everything that's happening?'

'Sanjeev said that she can't afford to keep taking time off. She works ten to three every weekday, so she should be at work by the time we get there.'

Lauren checked her watch. It was five to ten. Perfect. She drank her coffee as quickly as she could and then waited impatiently for Meg to finish her tea.

❁

Lauren drove into Salisbury and parked in the central car park near Avon Approach so that they wouldn't have too far to walk. Meg was quietly impressed with Lauren's driving; she'd expected her to be more nervous than she was. Lauren was confident and precise; anyone would think she'd been driving for a lot longer than she had! But then, she'd been taught by her boyfriend, DS Vivian Williams, who held an advanced driving certificate with the police.

They easily found the sandwich shop, called Linda's Lunches, next to an estate agent's. The shop looked empty. The door was locked when they tried it, and there was no answer when they knocked.

'What time do they open?' wondered Meg.

'Eleven o'clock,' Lauren replied, studying the sign in the window, 'but if Mia starts work at ten, she should be here.'

'She could be working out the back,' Meg suggested. 'Perhaps it would be better if I tried her phone, so she knows it's us knocking.'

Lauren waited as Meg rummaged for her phone in her handbag and made the call.

'Mia? It's Meg Thornton here, I don't know if Sanjeev ... 'There was a pause as Meg listened. 'Yes, that's right. I'm with Lauren now. We wondered if we might be able to talk to you?' There was another pause. 'Yes, right now, if that's not too inconvenient. We're just outside the shop door ... Yes, it was us knocking.'

After a further pause, Meg said goodbye and ended the call. 'She's agreed to let us in.'

19

Chapter Five

Sure enough, a young woman appeared from a doorway behind the counter. She was about average height, curvaceous rather than plump, with long brown hair tied back in a ponytail that was stuffed inside the food hygiene net covering her head. Her face looked pale and drawn, and her eyes were appraising them anxiously as she unlocked the door. She was wearing jeans and a black T-shirt with a bibbed white apron over the top.

'Meg? Lauren?' She glanced at the two of them nervously.

'Yes, I'm sorry to surprise you like this. With hindsight, I should have phoned ahead and asked if it was all right for us to come and visit you at work.' Meg looked apologetic.

'No, it's okay. Do you mind coming through to the kitchen with me?'

They agreed and quickly followed her inside.

'I'm not supposed to allow members of the public back here,' she said awkwardly, 'but there's a couple of chairs over there, if you don't mind sitting out of the way while I carry on with the food prep. Linda's not here, so I'm on my own. She usually comes in about half past ten but she's going to be late today. I don't suppose it will do any harm for you to be here, so long as I get my work done.'

Meg reassured her that they were more than happy to keep out of the way, 'If you don't mind talking while you're working?' she checked.

'No, it's fine. I'm happier if I've got something to do with my hands anyway.' She picked up a knife and carried on slicing the tomatoes that were sitting on a chopping board on the pristine metal worktop. Meg and Lauren settled themselves into two old wooden kitchen chairs by a desk at one side of the kitchen.

'What do you need to ask me?' Mia asked, biting her bottom lip and looking tense.

'Well, it might help us if we knew a little bit more about you and your background first,' Meg suggested, trying to put her at ease.

'Yeah, okay. I was born in Salisbury, and I've lived here all my life. Don't really know anywhere else, to be honest. My mum came from Swindon and my dad from Devizes, so I've got grandparents in both those places, and a couple of aunts and uncles around the county. But Mum and Dad moved to Salisbury, like, ages ago. They've lived in Laverstock since before I was born. That's why Vikram and I rented the house we live in, because it's close to Mum. She usually has Noah for me while I'm at work.' Mia swallowed hard as a wave of emotion washed over her face. She turned away to put the storage container, now full of sliced tomatoes, in the fridge and brought out some other salad vegetables for chopping.

'Do you have any brothers or sisters?' Meg asked, trying to keep her talking.

'No, it's just me,' she replied thickly as she expertly sliced a couple of cucumbers.

'Just like me,' Lauren chipped in. 'I'm an only child too.'

'You're from Salisbury too?' asked Mia, looking at Lauren properly for the first time. She wrinkled her face. 'Do I know you from somewhere?'

'Yeah, possibly,' Lauren agreed. 'Did you go to St Edmund's?' She was referring to the girls' secondary school in Laverstock that had been amalgamated with the boys' school next door during her time there, to form the Wyvern St Edmund's Academy.

'Yeah, I was at St Edmund's for five years. Left after my GCSEs in 2015.'

'We must've just crossed over,' exclaimed Lauren. 'You would've been four years above me. I'm twenty now.'

'I'm twenty-three,' replied Mia, 'but I'll be twenty-four next month, so yeah, four years above you. I thought your face was vaguely familiar.'

The two women started comparing memories from their school days, discussing teachers who'd taught them both.

But Meg was conscious of the time passing. 'I hate to interrupt,' she began.

'Yes, of course,' said Mia, pushing the sliced cucumbers to one side and starting on some vibrant red and green peppers. 'Please carry on with what you wanted to ask me.'

'When did you and Vikram move in together?' Meg asked, trying to remember what they'd already covered.

'About five – no – six weeks ago.'

'And where were you living before?'

'With my parents. You see, after me and Tyler – that's Noah's father – split up, I couldn't afford a place on my own. I'm really lucky that my parents were so supportive, but it wasn't ideal, moving back home again with a baby.'

'Were you with Tyler for long?' asked Lauren.

'About eighteen months.'

'How did you meet?'

'At The Bishop's Mill, it's a pub in Salisbury,' she explained for Meg's benefit. 'I was a chef there and Tyler worked behind the bar. We dated for about six months before I moved in with him. Biggest mistake of my life. I'd only seen the nice side of him before, but then he revealed his nasty side. Turns out he's a right bastard.'

'I'm sorry to hear that,' Meg said. 'Do you mind me asking, how was he nasty?'

'He's a bully and a thug, knocked me around a bit. And he was so possessive. Twice I tried to leave him, but he wasn't having it. It was like he thought he owned me. I put up with it because I didn't want to tell my parents how bad things were. Until I had Noah. But the thought of him taking his temper out on Noah ...' She broke off.

'So you went back to your parents,' Meg surmised.

'Yeah, when Noah was about six weeks old. But Tyler kept coming round, banging on the door and threatening us. Eventually, Dad had to get a court order to stop him from coming near us.'

'That must have been tough,' Meg empathised.

Mia shrugged as she returned all the chopped salads to the fridge. 'It went quiet for a while after that. I hoped I was rid of him.'

'Then what happened?' asked Lauren, as Mia started mixing up some tuna with mayonnaise, diced red onion and sweetcorn.

'When Noah was three months old, Mum offered to help babysit him so I could look for a part-time job to help with the finances. I got the job here, which is perfect. I couldn't have gone back to pub work, what with the long hours and late evenings. And Linda, who owns this place, has been such a good friend.'

'And when did you meet Vikram?' prompted Meg.

'He used to come into the shop nearly every day for his lunch, so I suppose you could say I've known him for about a year now. At first, he was a bit shy, didn't say much. But then we started chatting and he was just so different to Tyler. I had the biggest crush on him, but I thought he was never going to ask me out. Then, about a week before Valentine's Day, he asked if I'd got any plans. When I said no, he asked if he could take me out to dinner. It was so romantic.'

'You'd only been dating for a couple of months when you moved in together, then,' commented Meg, surprised.

'Yeah, I know,' replied Mia, getting the ingredients out to make coronation chicken. 'My parents were worried about that too but, as soon as they met Vikram, they understood. He's not a bit like Tyler was. He's so polite and kind; he never even swears. And he's always encouraging me to do what I want; he's not at all possessive. And he loves Noah like he's his own.' Her voice cracked and she looked like she was about to burst into tears.

'I'm sorry,' said Meg. 'This is obviously very painful for you. It really wasn't fair of me to ask you to talk while you're trying to work. I think perhaps we should go now. But it would be good if we can arrange another time to come and ask you some more questions, perhaps at your home?'

'Yeah, thanks. I think that'd be better,' agreed Mia, wiping her eyes with a tissue. 'It's just so hard, wondering where Noah is and what's happening to him.' She sobbed heart-wrenchingly for a moment before visibly pulling herself together. 'And Vikram too,' she said brokenly. 'I miss them both so much.'

As Lauren was on an early shift the next day, they suggested going to Mia's house after she finished work. 'We'll be with you about four o'clock, I expect,' said Lauren. 'That's great,' said Mia, 'I finish work at three, so I'll be home in plenty of time.' She showed them out of the front door, thanking them for agreeing to help her.

Chapter Six

Thursday 22nd June 2023

When Meg and Lauren arrived at Mia's home the following day, she was waiting to let them in. 'Come on through to the lounge,' she said, leading them through a door to their right. Meg looked around with interest, noting the modern furniture, some of it a little well worn but nevertheless spotlessly clean.

'I clean whenever I'm stressed,' said Mia, following Meg's gaze. 'I can't just sit down and do nothing. Take a seat and I'll get some coffee.'

'I'm sorry,' said Meg, a little awkwardly. 'I'm afraid I don't drink coffee. Never been able to stand the taste.'

'Oh,' said Mia, taken aback.

'I'd love a cup of tea, if that's possible?'

'Umm, I know we've got masala chai tea, because Vik drinks that, and we might have some green tea as well. I can go and have a look.'

'No, don't go to any trouble,' said Meg, inwardly shuddering at the thought of green tea. 'I'll just have a glass of tap water, please.'

'If you're sure that's okay. What about you, Lauren?' Mia asked.

'I'd love a coffee, please. Black, no sugar.'

Mia disappeared through an archway leading from the dining-room end of the open-plan living room, presumably into the kitchen. Meg sat on the comfortable cream leather settee and looked around with interest. The walls were painted magnolia, and the furniture was mostly dark brown and from Ikea, at a guess. Shelf units and bookcases lined almost all of the wall opposite the sofa and, apart from the large flatscreen TV, they were crammed with books and ornaments. There was a row of pull-out fabric boxes along the bottom level, visibly stuffed with children's toys. Several photos of Noah were framed and hung on the walls, and Meg got up to study, with interest, the chubby, smiling baby at various stages of his first year. He was a bonny, healthy-looking child, dressed nicely in clean clothes. She returned to the settee, which had most probably been acquired second-hand because it was clearly more worn than the other items, although well looked-after. A circular glass table and four modern chairs filled the dining end of the room, overlooking the small back garden. The table was topped with a scattering of paperwork, and a basket of dry washing stood on one of the chairs, the only items in the room not tidily put away. 'Excuse the mess,' apologised Mia, seeing Meg's gaze as she returned from the kitchen with a drink in each hand. 'I haven't had time to tidy up since I got in from work. I always like to have a shower and change first.'

That's quite all right,' smiled Meg, accepting her glass of water.

'Crikey,' said Lauren, 'if you think this is untidy, you should see my house!' She thanked Mia for her coffee and waited until she'd returned with her own drink. 'How long did you say you and Vikram have lived here?' she enquired.

'We moved in on the thirteenth of May, so nearly six weeks,' replied Mia. 'We were lucky because the previous tenant left the place in a good state, even down to the beautifully decorated nursery upstairs. According to the letting agent, they had a two-year-old boy and were expecting twins, so they've moved to somewhere bigger.'

'That was a bit of good luck for you,' grinned Lauren.

'Yeah, and my parents had Noah over the weekend we moved in, so we were able to get everything sorted out quickly. We bought that brand new,' she indicated the Ikea shelving units, 'and all of Noah's furniture too, but pretty much everything else came from Vik's old place.'

'Can we have a look upstairs?' asked Meg. 'Not right away,' she added, as Mia went to leap up. 'Finish your drink first. But it would really help us to see the whole house, particularly Noah's room.'

'Yeah, I thought you'd want to look around. Anything I can do to help you get Vik out of prison and my baby home.' A cloud passed across her face. 'I guess you want to know what happened?'

'Yes, I'm sorry to put you through it, but we need to know as much detail as you can tell us, please.'

'That's okay. I do nothing but think about what happened and who could have done it. I mean, who would want to do something like this to us?' Her face crumpled and tears flowed down her cheeks. She jumped up and grabbed a box of tissues from the small square coffee table and dabbed furiously at her eyes. 'Don't mind me,' she said, sitting down again. 'Just ask whatever you need to ask.'

Lauren edged a bit closer to Mia and took her hand sympathetically. 'Just tell us in your own way,' she said. 'We can always ask questions afterwards.'

Mia clung onto Lauren's hand as she spoke. 'Okay. Vik and I both work all week, so Friday night is our chill-out night. After we'd put Noah down, we had a takeaway and watched a couple of films, so we were quite late to bed. Vik checked that the front and back doors were locked, and all the downstairs windows were shut, same as he always does. I went upstairs to get ready for bed and looked in on Noah. He was sound asleep in his cot. Everything just seemed like normal.

'We went to sleep, somewhere around quarter past twelve, I think, and neither of us heard anything at all after that. It was only when I woke up that I became aware that something wasn't right. Usually, Noah wakes up somewhere between six and seven, screaming his head off. But he didn't wake us that morning. I was lying in bed and kind of gradually realised that it was later than usual. Then I panicked when I saw the time. It was half past nine. He's never slept that late, so I just knew straight away that something was wrong. I ran to his room, worried that perhaps he was ill … or … something.' She gulped. 'But he wasn't there!' She took her hand out of Lauren's and reached for her tissue again, sobbing.

Meg and Lauren gave her a moment to pull herself together, both feeling desperately sorry for her. Then Meg asked if they could look round the house now and ask questions as they went. Mia stood up and led the way into the kitchen.

The kitchen wasn't too small, and it was well laid out, being fitted with a dishwasher and a washing machine next to the sink, an electric cooker with a ceramic hob in the corner, and a large fridge-freezer next to the back door. Like the living room, it was spotlessly clean and tidy. Meg tried the back door handle, but it was locked. Mia immediately leant round her and turned the key in the lock.

They wandered out into the garden. Clearly, the young couple weren't gardeners. It was mostly laid to lawn and surrounded by high fences, apart from a small paved area outside the back door. A brightly coloured plastic slide took centre place on the overgrown lawn.

Meg walked around the fences, feeling to see how strong they were and whether there were any signs of anyone having climbed over them. They all backed onto other gardens, and she very much doubted anyone could have come in that way.

'There's a gate at the side that leads to the drive, but we keep that locked because of Noah.' Mia pointed to a tall wrought iron gate, secured with a sturdy padlock, filling the gap between the house and the garage. 'The police checked everywhere outside, and they even sent one of those CSI people like you see on the telly. They said there was no sign of anyone getting in anywhere.'

Meg agreed; it seemed unlikely. She led the way back inside, waiting for Mia and Lauren to pass her, then she closed and locked the back door, examining the mechanism thoroughly.

'The CSI woman examined that too and said it hadn't been interfered with,' said Mia.

'Are you sure Vikram locked it before you went to bed?' Meg enquired.

'He swears blind that he did,' Mia replied earnestly, 'and I believe him.'

Chapter Seven

They made their way round the rest of the downstairs, with Meg checking all the windows and the front door. Again, Mia insisted that Vik had locked everything properly. 'He always does. And the police are adamant that there were no signs of a break-in. I just don't understand it, I mean, someone must have broken in.'

Or someone inside the house either let the kidnapper in or was responsible themselves, thought Meg.

'Does anyone else have a key to the house?' she asked.

'My parents do,' replied Mia, 'but they wouldn't have done this. You can't think that, surely?' She looked at them anxiously.

'No, of course not,' Meg reassured her, despite a slight twinge of doubt. After all, they had to suspect everybody at this stage.

They all filed upstairs.

The first room off the landing was Mia and Vikram's, painted in pale pink with one wall a strong magenta colour that wouldn't have suited Meg at all. But each to their own taste. Then there was a fair-sized bathroom in white, with patterned grey tiles.

The second bedroom looked out to the front, decorated in pale blue and currently used as a study-cum-storage room. Beside the desk, there was a chest of drawers topped with a large tray holding a small statue, incense sticks, a bell, a couple of small pots and a bowl of water. It was decorated with artificial flowers and tealight candles in pretty jars.

'It's a Hindu shrine,' explained Mia. 'Vik prays here every day.'

'He doesn't go to a temple or something?' Lauren asked with curiosity.

'No, apparently Hindus quite often worship at home. It's a good job too, because the nearest temple to here is in Southampton. Vik goes there occasionally, for festivals and holy days, that kind of thing.'

'He's very devout, then?' Meg commented.

'Yes and no. I mean, he prays every day, and he believes in living a good life. He's really into karma and all that. But he's never tried to force his religion onto me.'

'Yes, I believe that's the Hindu way,' replied Meg.

'That's why I'm so sure Vik couldn't have done this. He's so kind. And gentle. I mean, he literally wouldn't hurt a fly. I hate spiders but he wouldn't kill one for me, only catch it and let it go again outside. He says all living things have a soul, and to kill anything is like killing a part of God. Honestly, he would never in a million years have hurt Noah.'

Meg nodded. 'I understand that it would have been out of character for him to have harmed Noah ...'

'I'm telling you; he didn't do this!' Mia protested firmly.

'I know you believe that. But do you think he could have wanted Noah out of the way for some reason? I mean, Noah was another man's child. Do you think he could have taken Noah ...'

'How can you even suggest that?' Mia wailed.

'I'm sorry but I have to ask,' Meg replied calmly, her heart wanting so much to believe that Vikram was innocent, if only for Mia's sake. 'Even if he wouldn't have hurt Noah, could he have taken him somewhere else?'

Mia took a deep breath. 'Vikram was happy to be Noah's dad; he even talked about adopting him. I am absolutely certain that there is no way that Vikram either abducted or harmed Noah, or colluded in any way with anyone else. And I told the police that too.'

Meg just hoped that Mia's faith in Vikram wasn't misplaced.

'What about anyone else? Can you think of anyone who might have wanted to take Noah? Or perhaps someone who might have wanted to hurt either you or Vikram?'

'Oh, that's easy,' Mia replied immediately. 'Noah's birth father, Tyler Ford. He fought for custody and was bitter about losing. And he hated that his son was living with Vikram. He's a thug and a racist, as I discovered to my cost. As soon as I discovered that Noah was missing, I suspected Tyler. But the police have assured me that he has a solid alibi and can't have done it. Which is baffling, but I suppose they must have checked that thoroughly.'

Meg thought that she would be checking it as well, for Tyler certainly sounded like a strong suspect.

They went through to the smallest bedroom, also at the front of the house. As Mia had said, it was beautifully decorated. Meg looked at the cot and the chest of drawers and the abundance of cuddly toys in the corner. 'Was anything else taken with Noah?' she asked.

'Yeah, his favourite cuddly is missing.'

'What is it?' asked Lauren.

'It's a Peter Rabbit in a little blue coat that my parents bought for him when he was born. He loves sucking on its ears. And he never goes to sleep without it. Oh yeah, and his dummy is missing too.'

Meg thought that significant. Why bother taking the two things that would comfort a baby if he was already dead? The news gave her a glimmer of hope, but she didn't say anything.

'Is that a baby monitor?' asked Lauren.

'Yeah. That was strange, 'n' all. I'm sure it was on when we went to bed, but it was switched off in the morning.'

'Did you tell the police that?'

'Yeah, and that CSI woman checked it for fingerprints. But she said there wasn't any.'

Meg and Lauren looked at each other. Logically, it should have had Mia's prints on it, and possibly Vikram's. 'No prints at all?' checked Meg. Mia confirmed that's what she'd been told, shrugging it off.

'What kind of monitor is it?' asked Lauren, peering at the device.

'It's sound and video,' Mia demonstrated. 'We take our part of the monitor downstairs in the evening when we put Noah to bed and then bring it back up to our bedroom when we come to bed. We don't really need the audio on at night, as we'd probably hear him from our room anyway. But the video is useful. If he's just babbling, we can see if he's happy on his own or not.'

Meg shook her head in wonder at modern technology. 'Does it record the video?' she asked hopefully.

'No, it's not that fancy,' Mia sighed. 'And, in any case, whoever took my baby must've turned the monitor off.'

'Were the bedroom doors open or closed?' Meg asked next.

'We always leave both our door and Noah's pulled to but not properly closed at night. It's quieter to move about without disturbing him.'

'If you don't mind, I'd like to try an experiment,' Meg announced.

'What kind of experiment?' Mia asked suspiciously.

'I'm wondering how easy it would have been for someone to sneak up the stairs without you hearing them,' Meg replied.

Chapter Eight

Meg explained what she wanted the two younger women to do, and they agreed and left the room. Meg turned towards the window and studied the road outside, noting that several neighbouring houses overlooked the front of this house. She heard Lauren clattering downstairs and then the house fell silent. 'Ready,' called Mia from her bedroom, where she had gone to lie on her bed, the door ajar just as it had been on that fateful night.

Meg strained her ears and thought that she could just make out the occasional creak on the stairs. She waited and heard no more sounds of movement; perhaps she had been mistaken? Then, to her surprise, Lauren pushed open Noah's door and was standing beside her. She signalled to Lauren to turn around, and they went into Mia's room.

'How much did you hear?' Meg asked.

'I think I heard Lauren creeping up the stairs, but only 'cos I was listening for her. I didn't hear her at all on the landing until she pushed Noah's door open, and I don't think I would've heard that if I'd been asleep.'

'Very well.' Meg nodded thoughtfully. 'That confirms someone *could* have crept upstairs and into Noah's room if they were careful. Next question: would Noah have woken up when they opened his door?'

'No, that's why we leave it ajar,' said Mia.

'Whoever it was must then have switched the baby monitor off, to reduce the likelihood of you seeing or hearing anything. Does it make a beep when you turn it off?'

'No.'

'Is it possible to lift Noah from his cot without waking him?'

'Vik and I can, but I'm not sure about a stranger.'

'What if they put the dummy in his mouth?'

'Possibly,' Mia said with a shrug. 'He might have settled back to sleep in their arms if they were gentle with him, I guess. But I can't believe they could have taken him out of the house without him crying at all.'

Meg ignored that, thinking that someone who knew how to handle a baby, someone like the baby's own father, could have done that easily enough.

'Didn't Sanjeev say that Vikram was seen leaving the house with a black sports bag?' Lauren enquired. 'Could he have carried Noah out in that?'

'That's a lie!' protested Mia, becoming agitated again. 'He didn't leave the house that night!'

'Perhaps it wasn't Vikram who was seen,' said Meg, keen to keep Mia calm. 'What I'm more curious to know is, could you carry a baby in a sports bag and not wake him up?'

Lauren looked doubtful, and Mia shook her head adamantly.

'I don't suppose you know which of your neighbours reported seeing Vikram?' Lauren asked.

'They wouldn't tell me, but I'd bet anything it was old nosy Norman, at number eleven,' replied Mia. 'He's always twitching his curtains and staring out of his windows. Like, every time I walk past! Gives me the creeps! And he was so rude about Vik when we first moved in.'

'How so?' asked Meg.

'He told me he didn't mind having me as his neighbour, but he didn't want "the likes of him" living here.' She made quote marks with her fingers and curled her lip in disgust.

Meg decided the neighbour might be worth investigating. Lauren must have read her mind because she suggested the very same thing. 'What about your other neighbours?' she added.

'I haven't really had a chance to meet most of them,' Mia said, shaking her head. 'There's a couple next door, Philippa and Ian, she's quite chatty. She's the one who warned me about nosy Norman. But I don't really know anyone else.'

'What about the black sports bag?' enquired Meg. 'Does Vikram even have one?'

'Yes,' admitted Mia, 'he goes to the gym a couple of times a week before work, so he usually keeps it in his car.'

'Is that his car in the drive?'

'Yeah, and you're welcome to have a look, if you like. But the police have been all over it.'

'Was the sports bag in the car when the police looked?'

'Yes, it was in the boot, where it always is. But I can't show you; the police took it away with them.'

Meg suspected that they would have done forensic tests to see if there was any trace of Noah inside the bag. How she'd love to know if they'd found anything.

She thought that Vikram's arrest would almost certainly only have come after the police had received the results of all the forensic tests. What had they found that had led to Vikram's arrest?

'Do you know if the police charged Vikram on the same day that they arrested him?'

'Yes, that inspector came to see me in the evening. He said that they'd charged him with child abduction and were keeping him in custody on suspicion of murdering Noah too. Which is just plain ridiculous! For a start, Vikram didn't do this. And Noah can't be …' she choked. 'I'm his mother, I'd know if he was …' she wailed.

'Do you know if Vikram has appeared before the magistrate yet?' asked Meg. 'I think he should have, by now.'

'Yeah, on Saturday morning. It was just a bail hearing.'

And obviously he didn't get bail. Meg wondered why. She reassured Mia as best she could and promised they would do their best to investigate, giving her the same warnings she'd given to Sanjeev.

'I get it,' replied Mia, 'but at least you're going to investigate. The police seem to have given up since they arrested Vik.'

Meg seriously doubted that; she knew what a huge amount of work went on behind the scenes after an arrest was made, from talking with her late husband, DCI Grant Thornton of Bournemouth CID.

They made their way downstairs and said goodbye to Mia at the front door, after she and Lauren had exchanged mobile numbers and promised to keep in touch.

Once she'd closed the door, Lauren turned to Meg and asked if they should start knocking on the neighbours' doors straight away. Meg checked her watch and was amazed to find that it was already gone half past five.

'I think you'd better take me back to Britford Lodge,' she said, shaking her head. 'I really don't think I should miss dinner without having told anyone in advance.'

Lauren chuckled. 'It's Brandon in charge this evening. He won't mind.'

'No, but Albert will!'

They both chuckled as they got into Lauren's car. 'What do you think?' asked Lauren as she navigated the back streets of Salisbury, keen to avoid the bypass that was usually as congested as hell during rush hour.

'There's a few interesting points,' said Meg thoughtfully. 'It's easy to understand why the police thought either Mia or Vik had to have been involved, because there were no signs of a break-in. But I honestly can't see Mia kidnapping her own baby. And if Vik had done it, why would he then insist that he'd locked all the doors and windows?'

'Oh, of course! It would have been more believable that someone else could have broken into the house if he'd admitted to leaving one of them open!' Lauren exclaimed.

'Exactly. I think that argues against it being Vikram. Which leaves us with the conundrum of how someone else got into the house without leaving any signs of a break-in.'

'Perhaps they had a key?' Lauren suggested.

'That's logical, but I don't like where this might be taking us,' Meg replied grimly. After all, Mia had insisted that the only other people with a key were her own parents.

Chapter Nine

Lauren thought about that for a moment and then said quietly, 'We're going to have to investigate Mia's parents, aren't we?'

'I'm afraid so,' Meg agreed, pleased that Lauren had come to the same conclusion.

'And we need to check out Tyler's alibi too,' Lauren reminded her. 'He's obviously the prime suspect, so I can't help wondering how solid this alibi of his actually is.'

'Yes, I thought exactly the same thing myself,' Meg confirmed.

'It's not looking good that Noah is still missing this long after he was taken, is it?' Lauren asked miserably.

'Usually, I'd say no. But there's the dummy and the Peter Rabbit toy.'

'What about them?'

'Well, if you smothered Noah first before taking him from his cot, as the police have suggested, then why take his favourite toy and his dummy?'

'I hadn't thought about that.'

'They're the two things you would need to comfort a *living* baby,' Meg pointed out. 'I could just about buy someone wanting to lay Noah to rest with his favourite toy. But why take the dummy too?'

'Yes, that is odd,' agreed Lauren.

'What I find interesting is the lack of fingerprints on the baby monitor. We need to find a way of double-checking that, but if Mia was telling us the truth, that surely indicates a third party. Neither Mia nor Vikram would have needed to wipe their prints.'

'No, of course not,' Lauren agreed. 'What about the statement the neighbour made?'

'Yes, we need to investigate that too. It could be true, or partially true, in that the neighbour saw *someone* leaving with a black bag, not necessarily Vikram. Or it could be a lie; in which case, why lie to the police?'

'Either because you were guilty and trying to put the blame on someone else,' said Lauren, thinking it through, 'or because you wanted to get Vikram into trouble.'

'Yes, those were my thoughts exactly. I'd also be interested to know whether the streetlights stay on all night or whether the council turns them off and, if so, at what time. Just how easy would it have been to see someone's face at that time of night?'

'Ooh, good thinking,' said Lauren, shooting across a traffic light as it turned amber.

'I should be able to look that up online.'

'Thank you.'

'Where do we go from here?'

'What are your shifts over the next few days?'

'I've got the next two days off,' grinned Lauren, 'then I'm back on a late on Sunday.'

Meg grimaced. 'Unfortunately, I have an optician's appointment in the morning, so I won't be able to do anything with you until after lunch.'

Lauren risked a sideways glance. 'No problem,' she said. 'I can do a little investigating on my own, if you don't mind. Where do you want me to start?'

'Do you think you could visit the sandwich shop again and talk to Mia's boss, Linda? And then see if you can find a way to talk to some of Vikram's colleagues at Cathedral Accountants. That will give us an insight into what other people think of our couple.'

'That should be easy enough. I'll get all the addresses and all the background info I can off the internet tonight, then I'll go sleuthing tomorrow morning. How about we meet up at the café in the afternoon so I can tell you what I've found out?'

Meg approved. 'An excellent idea, though I will probably have to bring Albert with me, as he hates being left out.'

'Briefing at two-thirty?' suggested Lauren.

'The police lingo's rubbing off on you,' teased Meg.

'Hmm, I wonder if I should tell Viv what we're up to.'

'That's up to you, my dear. It doesn't do to keep secrets in a relationship, but he may not approve.'

Lauren was quiet for a while, thinking about that.

After Lauren had dropped Meg back at Britford Lodge, she drove home deep in thought. Should she tell Viv or not? Ditto, her mum?

Only six months ago she'd been attacked while helping Meg to investigate a dangerous murderer, and the two people she cared about the most had begged her never to put herself in the same position again. But this wasn't a murder case, she reasoned. It was a missing baby. And, if she told them, maybe their perspectives on the case would be helpful?

But what if they told her not to get involved? What would she do then?

She was still preoccupied when she walked in through her front door. She flung her car keys onto the hall table and was about to head into the kitchen, when her mum called out from the lounge. 'We're in here, Lauren. You've got a visitor.'

She went into the lounge to find Viv and her mum side by side on the sofa, poring over a photo album she'd not seen before. 'What's going on here?'

'I was just showing Viv my honeymoon snaps,' replied Bekka. 'Remember me telling you that your dad and I went to Jamaica?'

'Oh yeah. And I remember you promising to show me those photos as well, so how come Viv gets to see them first?' She slipped onto the sofa next to Viv as she was talking, and he squeezed her hand.

'Hey, gorgeous. You're not jealous, are you?' he teased.

'Of course I am, coming home to find you cosying up to my mum!' The glint in Lauren's eye belied her words and the couple kissed.

'Oi, you two, I'm still here, you know?' protested Bekka.

'Sorry, Mrs Peachy, but your daughter is just so damn irresistible.' They all laughed.

'For that, you can go and make us a cup of tea,' said Bekka with mock sternness, 'while I warn my daughter about the dangers of smooth-talking handsome young men.'

'Coffee for me, please,' said Lauren as Viv stood up. She slid across to her mother and looked at the photo album with interest.

Whilst Viv made them hot drinks, Bekka showed her the photos. Two things struck her: just what a good-looking couple her parents had been when they were younger, and just how beautiful Jamaica was. She touched a photo of her dad posing on a beach with a pang of grief. 'I still miss him so much,' she whispered.

'So do I, dear.' Bekka gave her daughter a comforting hug.

Viv returned and handed out the drinks before sitting next to Lauren and putting his own black coffee onto the side table at the end of the settee.

'How come you're so late home from work today?' he asked. 'I finally got to finish work early for once and came to spend some precious time with you, only to find you weren't here.'

'Ah,' said Lauren, realising that she had no choice but to tell him what she and Meg had been up to. Either that or lie, which was not something she felt comfortable doing.

She took a deep breath. 'I've got something to tell you both,' she said. 'And I know you're probably not going to like it but, please, hear me out before you say anything.'

To their credit, neither Bekka nor Viv interrupted Lauren and, when she'd finished, there was a stunned silence.

Chapter Ten

'Let me get this right,' Viv said slowly, 'you and Meg have agreed to investigate a police matter that has nothing whatsoever to do with you? I mean, I get that it was hard for you not to be involved with the murders at The Cedars and again at Britford Lodge when you were working in those places. Even though running around investigating put you and Meg in the way of danger. But this? Why do you need to get involved at all? It's got nothing to do with you!'

'Because I can't stand by and allow a possible miscarriage of justice,' Lauren replied.

'But you promised not to put yourself in danger again,' protested Bekka.

'Mum, this is a missing child, not a murder,' reasoned Lauren. 'I'm sure there's no danger. Anyway, if Meg and I are wrong and the police are right, then the guilty person is already in prison. So, where's the risk?'

'Then why bother to investigate?' countered Viv.

'Because Sanjeev and Mia are both convinced that Vikram couldn't have done this. And, since we've spoken to Mia, both Meg and I feel that there are some unanswered questions that the police appear to be ignoring.'

'How do you know what the police are or aren't doing?' demanded Viv hotly. 'Do you even know who the senior investigating officer is? Or what his team has been doing? No, you don't. If this Mia is still a suspect, it stands to reason the police won't have told her everything.'

'How is Mia a suspect when they've arrested Vikram?' protested Lauren.

'She's his partner. She could have assisted him or been complicit. You have no idea what the situation really is.'

'No, I don't,' said Lauren fiercely, 'and that's exactly why I want to find out more!'

'You do know that an investigation doesn't end just because a suspect has been arrested, don't you? The team will be working hard. They have to gather sufficient evidence for the Crown Prosecution Service to agree to proceed. If the case is too weak, it will be thrown out before it even gets to court. If this guy is as innocent as you seem to think, that will come to light. Why can't you just leave it to the professionals?'

'And what if baby Noah is still alive and the police have stopped looking for him?' Lauren argued. 'What about him?'

Viv paused and took a deep breath. His face looked like thunder, but he was clearly trying to get his anger under control.

'How do you know that the police aren't looking for him? Eh?'

That brought Lauren up with a jerk. It was true; she had no idea what the police were or weren't doing. She only had what Sanjeev and Mia had told her.

'Could you just find out a few facts for me? Please?' she begged.

'Like what?' Viv's voice was dangerously quiet.

'Who is the SIO? What evidence do they have against Vikram? And what are they doing to find baby Noah?'

'You don't want much, do you?' Viv gave a hollow laugh. 'You do realise, I could upset quite a few people by sticking my nose into another team's case? I could even lose my job. Is that what you want?'

'Of course not!'

'Listen, I'll make a few discreet enquiries, but ...'

'Thank you!' Lauren flung herself at Viv, glad that he had seen reason. He pushed her away and grabbed her arms.

'Let me finish, will you?' he ground out. 'I'll make a few enquiries *if* you promise to stop investigating.'

Lauren stared at him in disbelief, feeling on the verge of tears. Could she really just stop investigating? What would Meg say to that? And Sanjeev? And Mia? She'd be letting them all down.

She shook her head. 'No, I'm sorry, Viv, I can't promise not to investigate.'

'What the …!' It was his turn to stare incredulously.

'But I do promise to be very careful and to keep you informed of where I am and who I'm talking to at all times. That way, you'll know I'm safe.'

'In case I have to come dashing to the rescue, I suppose,' Viv spat out angrily.

'That's not what I meant!'

'Well, I don't like this.' Viv stood up. 'If you're going to keep interfering in police matters, it's going to put me in a very difficult position at work. I wish you'd just listen to reason.'

'And I wish you'd listen to me,' snapped Lauren, standing up to glare at him.

'Hey, stop this, you two,' intervened a concerned Bekka. 'Don't throw away a good relationship because of one difference of opinion. You both need to take a deep breath and calm down.'

'Yeah, perhaps I'd better go and do just that,' muttered Viv, stalking out of the room and slamming the front door on his way out.

Lauren burst into tears and stormed up to her room. What the hell was she going to do now?

❂

After Lauren had cried out her anger and frustration, she lay on her bed, thinking. Was this case worth risking her relationship with Viv? She certainly couldn't bear the thought of him not being in her life. But when she thought about Mia's distress and the possibility that baby Noah was alive out there, somewhere, waiting to be found, she just had to investigate! Her emotions felt tied up in knots.

A tap on the door interrupted her conflicting thoughts.

'Hey,' said Bekka softly, 'I've brought you a strawberry smoothie. Thought you might need someone to talk to?'

'Thanks, Mum.' Lauren smiled weakly, sitting up.

Bekka came in and sat on the edge of Lauren's bed, handing the glass to her. She took an appreciative sip.

'You already know that I don't like the idea of you investigating crimes because I worry about what danger it might put you in,' Bekka said gently. 'But I also want you to know that I wouldn't want to stop you living your life the way you want to live it.'

'I know.'

'I also hate to see you this upset.'

Lauren threw her hands up in despair. 'I just don't know what to do. I love Viv and I hate that we've just argued. But I can't let Mia down now that I've promised to help her. I just can't!'

'That's quite a dilemma,' agreed her mother. 'My advice, for what it's worth: don't let the sun go down on an argument. Contact Viv, tell him you love him. Then sleep on it and see how you feel about everything in the morning.'

Lauren knew that was good advice, but she resented the idea of apologising to Viv. The argument was as much his fault as hers, surely? And he was the one who'd stormed out!

'I'll think about it, Mum,' she whispered.

'Okay, dear. Why don't you come downstairs with me, and we'll have some dinner and watch a film? It might be good to take your mind off it for a while.'

'Give me a few minutes,' Lauren replied.

Her mum hugged her and left her to her thoughts.

Later that evening, having spent a couple of hours downstairs with her mum, Lauren lay in bed trying to compose a text to Viv. She made several attempts, furiously deleting each one before finally hitting send.

Hey, I h8 that we argued. Love u xxx

Barely a minute later, her phone pinged with a reply. *Love u 2 sorry if I was insensitive*

Lauren: *Me 2*

Viv: *I'm gonna talk to Dan in the morning. Get his advice.*

Lauren: *If u think that's best. I don't want u to get into trouble.*

Viv: *Sleep well*

Lauren: *I will xxx*

Lauren felt a hint of that warm fuzzy feeling she usually got inside when she and Viv messaged each other. She let out a sigh of relief that at least he was still talking to her.

She was just drifting off to sleep when her phone pinged again. She picked it up, surprised to see that it was from Mia.

Can't tell you how grateful I am that you've promised to help. I miss Noah and Vik so much it physically hurts. It was like no one was listening to me. But u did, so thank u for that.

The message tugged at Lauren's heartstrings and sent her spiralling right back into the dilemma she was facing. It took a long time for her to get to sleep that night.

Chapter Eleven

Friday 23rd June 2023

Viv was feeling overtired and disgruntled during his drive into work the following morning. He'd found it impossible to get to sleep, the whole argument replaying on a continuous loop in his mind.

He was angry that Lauren was poking her nose in where it didn't belong. What the hell did she think she was doing? Did she even realise what a difficult position she was putting him in?

But, at the same time, he felt that perhaps he hadn't handled it as well as he could have done. Losing his temper probably hadn't helped the situation. And walking out had been a mistake; he knew that.

He also hadn't been entirely honest with her. He knew very well who the SIO on the abduction case was. Everyone in the station did. It was Billy Barnes, a DI coming up to retirement who was inclined to look for the easiest solution to any case. Could it be possible that he was mishandling this investigation? Unfortunately, the answer was yes. The question was, what could he do about it? It wasn't his case!

Another thing was bothering him. Although baby Noah hadn't been found yet, the truth was that the search *had* been scaled right back on the assumption that the child was probably dead. The first twenty-four hours in a missing child case were crucial, and each hour after that reduced the chances of a successful outcome. And Noah had been missing … what? At least two weeks now. Maybe longer.

And it wasn't your typical kidnapping case, not that you saw many of those in Salisbury. There'd been no ransom demand. Nothing to suggest that he was still alive. The outlook for Noah wasn't good, but did that mean it was okay to give up on him?

Viv knew the answer to that in his heart. If it was his case, he'd still be out there, turning over every stone in his search for Noah Jenkins.

And that was the problem. A small part of him acknowledged that Lauren was right to have concerns over the handling of this case. Not that he'd ever tell her that in a million years. It had been drummed into him during his initial training and repeated at just about every course he'd been on since: you don't share details of a case with a member of the public.

A little voice in the back of his head was whispering, *But Lauren is your girlfriend*.

And there it was; he still wanted Lauren in his life. Dammit, it was more than that! He loved her.

He was conflicted, unsure of which way to turn. And that was why he had decided to talk to Dan about it all. Dan was his immediate boss, after all.

But he still wished she hadn't put him in this position in the first place.

❖

Sometime later, Lauren woke up feeling groggy, but a shower and two cups of coffee revived her. She didn't want to go against Viv, but she'd come to the decision that she needed to carry on with the investigation. She'd promised Sanjeev and Mia, and she didn't break her promises if she could help it.

She hopped into her little black car and set off for Salisbury. First stop, Cathedral Accountants. She'd had a quick look on their website and there appeared to be four partners – two senior and two junior – plus several other aooountanto, olcrks and secretaries. Their offices were in Castle Street, a little further out of town than Linda's Lunches, so she parked in the central car park again.

Cathedral Accountants were on the second floor of a featureless modern office block. Lauren took the lift from the sterile lobby, emerging into a much plusher environment with carpet, pot plants and modern wall art. She approached the reception desk in trepidation. 'Can I help you?' asked the blonde-haired, heavily made-up receptionist with bright scarlet nail polish.

'Umm, yes. I'm a friend of Vikram's.'

'I'm sorry, Mr Chopra is not available at the moment.'

'I know. I wanted to talk to some of his work colleagues about his current situation. You see, I don't believe that he's done what the police say he's done.'

'What are you? A journalist?' The receptionist sniffed disapprovingly. 'We have no comment for the press. I wish you people would just leave us alone.'

'No, I'm not a journalist,' Lauren hastened to reassure her. 'I'm working on behalf of his partner, Mia, to investigate Noah's disappearance.'

'You're a private investigator?'

'Sort of, yes.'

The receptionist hesitated. Lauren feared that she was about to be given the brush-off when a door opened and a middle-aged man with silver streaks in his full head of chestnut hair looked out. 'Is there a problem, Kirsty?' he asked.

'Not at all, Mr Bebbington, I was just about to ask this young lady to leave.'

'Oh?'

'I wanted to talk to some of Vikram's work colleagues,' jumped in Lauren hastily. 'I'm trying to prove that he's innocent of child abduction.'

'Are you police? Or press?' he demanded.

'Neither. I'm a friend.'

'I've got fifteen minutes to spare before my next client arrives, come in.'

Feeling the receptionist's astonished stare burning into her back, Lauren followed him into his office. He gestured for her to take a seat on one side of a large desk as he moved round to the other and lowered himself into an expensive-looking black leather chair. 'Charles Bebbington, one of the senior partners,' he said. 'Please explain who you are.'

Lauren introduced herself and succinctly outlined the situation.

'Well, I'm glad someone is bothering to do their due diligence,' he said. 'The police haven't deigned to visit us yet. I was expecting a visit but, apparently, they aren't interested in our opinions.'

'Which are?' asked Lauren.

'I've worked with Vikram Chopra for just over two and a half years. I and our other senior partner, Miles Whitney, interviewed him and offered him the junior partnership here. He was by far the best candidate who applied, and we haven't regretted our decision one iota. He is diligent, hard-working, polite, respectful and always willing to help others. He is universally liked by his colleagues, not one of whom believes he could have done the things we've read about in the local press.'

'That's extremely good to hear,' said Lauren. 'Would you mind if I take some notes?'

'Feel free. But you've got a mobile phone on you, I presume?'

'Yes,' said Lauren, puzzled.

'Well, why don't you use it to record our conversation? It's much more convenient than for me to have to keep stopping while you write things down.'

Lauren mentally kicked herself for not thinking of this herself. She thanked him profusely and got out her phone. Having set up the record function, she laid it on the desk and asked Charles again for his opinions of Vikram Chopra.

Chapter Twelve

Whilst Lauren was getting more co-operation than she could have hoped for from Cathedral Accountants, Meg had just returned to Britford Lodge from her optician's appointment. It hadn't taken too long, fortunately, although she was facing a hefty bill for her new varifocals. Oh, the joys of getting older!

To her surprise, she found Dan waiting for her in the foyer.

'To what do I owe this pleasure?' she asked, having a suspicious feeling that she might know.

Dan studied her face. 'Viv came and had a chat with me this morning,' he said.

'Ah. No doubt Lauren told him about our latest investigation. I wondered if she would.'

'Yes, she has. And she's put Viv in a very difficult position. You do realise that you two shouldn't even be investigating this case?'

'You're telling us to back off?' asked Meg, understanding why Dan had to do this but not liking it.

'Officially, yes.'

She looked at him in surprise. 'And unofficially?'

'Look, this is strictly between you and me, not to be repeated to anyone other than Lauren. Do you understand?' He looked at her intently.

'Yes, of course,' Meg agreed, wondering what was coming next.

'The thing is, there are a few of us at the station who are having doubts over the handling of this case. That's not to say that Vikram Chopra is innocent,' he warned hastily as Meg was about to speak. 'Let me explain. When uniforms attended the triple nine call and established it was a child abduction, they immediately called in the duty CID team, as per protocol. The DI on call that weekend was Billy Barnes.

Now, Billy's a good man but he's nearing retirement and he's not … how shall I put it? He's not as on the ball as he used to be. Let's just say, Billy usually gets the less sensitive cases to investigate, so everyone was expecting that the case would get passed on to my team on the Monday morning. That happens sometimes.'

'But it wasn't passed on?' guessed Meg.

'Exactly. Billy managed to persuade the superintendent that he could put the case to bed quickly, and she allowed him to run with it. He concluded that it had to have been either the baby's mother or her partner or someone known to them, which wasn't unreasonable given there was absolutely no evidence of a break-in.'

'And the obvious choice was the foreign boyfriend who'd only recently moved in with Mia and Noah!' Meg interrupted scathingly.

'I don't think for one second there's anything racist behind Billy's decision to arrest Vikram,' Dan replied hastily. 'But yes, Vikram was the more likely suspect.'

'But what evidence is there?'

'You know I can't tell you the details,' said Dan, 'but I will say that it's mostly circumstantial.'

'Do you have doubts about Barnes' decision to arrest Vikram?'

'Not exactly. I can't quite put my finger on it.' Dan hesitated. 'To be honest, Viv and I are tied up on a complicated fraud case at the moment, and I suspect that's why the super didn't want to pass this on to us. The main concern around the station is the fact that Billy has stopped the active search for Noah. While, sadly, the odds are that he isn't going to turn up alive, there's also no evidence that he was killed at the house. In fact, there *is* evidence that he was more likely to have been taken alive.'

'The cuddly toy and the dummy,' supplied Meg.

'Yes, you're quick off the mark, as usual.'

'We spoke to Mia yesterday.'

'How was she with you?'

'Distressed, obviously. But grateful we had agreed to investigate, and very co-operative. It turns out that she and

Lauren went to the same school, although not in the same year group. I think the two of them got on quite well together.'

'Well, I would suggest she needs a friend right now, and if Lauren can be that friend it puts her in a good position to monitor the situation.'

'Is that your way of saying we can continue to investigate?'

'It's my way of saying that I won't stop you doing what you're doing, so long as you are discreet, and you don't interfere with the police investigation.'

'I understand.' Meg smiled at Dan's subtle way of giving them the go-ahead.

He ended with a warning. 'And for goodness' sake, don't go putting yourself at any risk. If you find out anything pertinent, please pass it on to the police and let them follow up on it.'

※

When Dan had gone, Meg wandered into the day room, where she was immediately pounced upon by Albert.

'I say, bit unusual for DI Dan to come visiting mid-morning,' he exclaimed, raising an eyebrow at her in expectation.

Meg sighed. Albert was a dear friend, but he couldn't always be trusted to keep his mouth shut. She'd have to be very careful what she told him.

'Yes. Why don't we go and sit down over there?' She led him to a secluded corner.

'Come on then, old gal. Spit it out,' he encouraged enthusiastically.

'You know I told you last night that Sanjeev had asked Lauren and me to investigate his cousin's arrest?'

'Yes.'

'Well, Dan wanted to talk to me about that.'

'Is it his case, then?' asked Albert. 'Does he need your help again to solve it?'

'Not exactly, no,' said Meg evasively.

'Well, what then?'

'It's not Dan's case, so he can't ask for our help even if he wanted to, which I'm sure he wouldn't. Look, this is very hush, hush.'

Albert's eyes gleamed. 'Nod, nod, wink, wink,' he said, tapping the side of his nose.

'Well, that's just it. I can't tell you,' Meg apologised.

'What!' exploded Albert indignantly.

'Shh!' hushed Meg, knowing that she'd offended him. 'I can't tell you what Dan said, but that doesn't stop you being involved in this case, if you want to be.' She winced as she said it, knowing he'd be more of a hindrance than a help. But he had saved her life, twice, back in January, and she owed him that much.

'Only too willing to help, m'dear, you know that. What's this case all about then?'

Just as she'd expected, he hadn't listened to a word she'd said yesterday evening. 'The missing baby … Noah?' she reminded him.

'Ah yes, mother has a Paki boyfriend who's done the baby in and hidden the body.'

'Albert!' Meg exclaimed, appalled. 'For a start, Vikram is Indian, not Pakistani …'

'Same thing,' muttered Albert truculently.

'No, it is not!' she scolded. 'And don't you ever use that awful word in front of me again!'

Albert had the grace to look abashed. It wasn't the first time Meg had told him off for his racist views, but he couldn't help the way he'd been brought up, could he?

'Sorry, old gal. Put my foot in it again, haven't I?'

'Yes, you jolly well have. And you've got the case all wrong.' Meg was fuming.

'Will you explain it to me again?' asked Albert contritely. 'And I promise to listen properly and not say a word.'

Not that Meg believed him, but she told him the outline of the case so far.

Lauren almost skipped along Castle Street, heading from Cathedral Accountants to Linda's Lunches. She couldn't believe that it was already nearly lunchtime, but her morning at Vikram's place of work had certainly paid dividends. She could appreciate that both Sanjeev and Mia were biased when it came to Vikram, but for every single one of his work colleagues to have supported the view that he was innocent? That spoke volumes!

Chapter Thirteen

Lauren pushed open the door to the sandwich shop and saw immediately that trade was already brisk. Mia was serving one customer and another three were queueing, so she stood to one side and quietly studied the large blackboard menu. Just as her stomach was rumbling from so many tempting combinations, Mia dashed over and touched her arm. 'Please tell me you've found Noah!' she whispered breathlessly.

Lauren felt a stab of guilt; she hadn't thought that her visit might get Mia's hopes up unnecessarily. She quickly explained that she had simply come to talk to Linda.

Mia's face fell but she nodded her understanding.

'I'm sorry,' whispered Lauren, aware of the growing queue in the little shop, 'these things take time, but we are working on it, I promise you.'

Mia went to the kitchen door to call for Linda to come out front, before hurrying back, full of apologies, to serve the next customer.

Linda reluctantly invited Lauren through to the kitchen, so as not to distract Mia. 'You'd better make it quick,' she warned. 'I'm just waiting for these cookies to come out of the oven, and then I'll probably need to go and help Mia serving.'

The delicious aroma of cookies baking only caused Lauren's stomach to rumble more.

She quickly explained why she was there. 'Can you tell me what you think of Vikram?' she enquired.

'There's no way he did this,' asserted Linda firmly.

'What makes you say that?' Lauren asked.

'Look, I know I haven't known him for long, but I only had to meet Vikram once to see what a genuinely nice guy he is. And believe me, I was pretty sceptical when I first heard that he'd asked her out. I was worried she wouldn't cope with another relationship after the way Tyler treated her, and I certainly didn't want to see her make the same mistake twice. There are some women that do that, aren't there? For some unfathomable reason, they keep dating the same kind of scumbags. But that's not the case with Mia and Vikram. He's totally besotted with her and she with him. And he's the total opposite of Tyler.'

Lauren wasn't convinced; just being a nice guy didn't make him innocent. Linda must've read her mind.

'Before they were going out, Mia told me she was terrified of telling Vikram she had a son, worrying that it might put him off. On the day that he asked her out the first time, she told him about Noah, and it didn't faze him one little bit. If anything, it made him even more interested. He told her, straight off, that he's always wanted children. Then I met him properly at Noah's birthday party and, I'm telling you, watching him playing with Noah, it was like watching a father with his son. I wasn't at all surprised when Mia told me, a little while later, that Vikram had asked if he could perhaps one day adopt Noah.'

'If it wasn't Vikram—' Lauren began.

'It wasn't!' snapped Linda, just as the oven timer started beeping. She donned large oven mitts and started pulling trays of cookies out of the oven, expertly sliding them onto large cooling racks. The smell was making Lauren's mouth water.

'Right, they need five minutes to cool before I can stack them.' Linda indicated that Lauren should sit down, before taking the other kitchen chair.

'I was going to ask, if it wasn't Vikram, then who do you think might have abducted Noah?' Lauren asked.

'Tyler Ford,' was Linda's immediate response.

'But he's got an alibi,' Lauren pointed out.

'I wouldn't trust that as far as I could throw the bastard,' Linda declared. She followed that up with a very strongly worded tirade expressing her opinion of Tyler Ford.

'Have you talked to him yet?' she eventually challenged Lauren.

'No, not yet,' Lauren admitted.

'Well, get yourself over to B&Q. That's where he works.'

Lauren reassured her that she would do just that. 'But first, can I just ask if you think there's any way Mia might have been involved in this?'

Linda's response was as forthright as her views on Tyler; there was no way Mia would've done anything to risk harming her son.

Lauren thanked Linda and decided it was time she left. But not before buying herself a doorstopper of a sandwich stuffed with Italian meats, rocket and sun-dried tomato chutney. And a couple of cookies for later. She also arranged to pop round to Mia's that evening for a drink; she looked like she could do with some company.

❁

Lauren drove to the large B&Q on Southampton Road and ate her sandwich sitting in her car whilst she googled Tyler Ford on her phone. She wasn't all that delighted with what she found. Apparently, he was the leader of a far-right neo-Nazi group called Radical Action Salisbury. And from a quick look at their social media, they were both racist and anti-immigration. That certainly explained why Mia had described him as a thug and a racist. He must have hated the fact that his son was living with an immigrant, and a successful one at that. She wondered briefly why Mia hadn't mentioned this group to her but then supposed it hadn't been relevant at the time.

The one good thing was that she'd found Tyler's photo online, so at least she now knew who she was looking for. She finished her lunch and headed for the store entrance.

She checked the tills first and then wandered around the vast store, but there was no sign of anyone looking like Tyler. Perhaps he wasn't at work today?

Eventually, she stopped a skinny lad in the store's uniform, who barely looked sixteen, and asked him if he knew if Tyler Ford was at work today.

'He works outside,' was the lad's brief reply. 'Can't imagine what you'd want with him, though,' he added darkly. It wasn't exactly comforting.

She found Tyler driving a small forklift truck, moving a pallet of paving slabs from a warehouse into the garden centre area. She watched until he'd skilfully lowered the pallet into a gap in the display, before hopping down to replace the price label in front of the stone squares.

'Excuse me,' Lauren said, with a little trepidation chipping away at her usual confidence. This guy was built like the proverbial brick outhouse – broad shouldered, bulging muscles and legs like tree trunks. But that wasn't the scary part; the skinhead haircut and arms plastered in repulsive tattoos, along with the scowl he threw at her when she spoke, were intimidating, to say the least.

'Yeah?' he grunted. Obviously, customer service wasn't his forte.

'Are you Tyler Ford, by any chance?'

'What the …? Who are you?' The scowl grew deeper.

Lauren introduced herself as a friend of Mia's.

'That slut!' he exploded.

'Excuse me?' Lauren was taken aback by the venom in his voice. A moment later, when Tyler went off into a rant, she wished she hadn't asked. His opinion of Mia was bad enough and centred mostly around the fact that she had deserted him and taken Noah with her. But his opinion of Vikram was loathsome and completely unrepeatable. He made no secret of how much he hated the fact that Vikram got to live with his son and play at being his dad, whilst *he*, Noah's real dad, didn't even have access.

Lauren's emotions were in turmoil. On the one hand, his vile rant was making her blood boil, and she longed to give him a piece of her mind. But she recognised that perhaps introducing herself as Mia's friend hadn't been the best approach, and she was certain that both Viv and her mother would consider any further confrontation with Tyler to be extremely unwise.

She put up her hands in a conciliatory gesture as she backed off. 'Look, I'm sorry to have bothered you. I was going to ask if you had heard anything about Noah, but I can see that you're busy right now. I'll leave you to get on with your work.'

'I haven't got the foggiest idea where my son is,' Tyler spat out angrily. 'Why don't you try asking that boyfriend of hers … oh, you can't, can you? The pigs have already nicked him, haven't they?'

There was something about the way he spoke that left Lauren feeling distinctly uneasy. She couldn't quite put her finger on it, but it was as if he was mocking her.

She beat a hasty retreat to her car.

Chapter Fourteen

Meg was still having qualms about including Albert when they strolled down to the farm shop café after lunch to meet Lauren. Her Peugeot was already parked in the farmyard when they arrived, so they went into the café to find her cradling a black Americano in both hands and looking decidedly glum.

'No luck, then?' surmised Meg.

'Oh no, I've got plenty to tell you.' Lauren brightened up as they joined her at their usual table. 'Come and sit down and tell me what you want. I'll go and order for you.'

'No need for that,' Albert replied defensively. 'You stay where you are; I'm quite capable of ordering. Tea for you, Meg?'

Meg agreed and thanked him, as she sat next to Lauren. She took advantage of his absence to quickly tell Lauren about Dan's visit.

'Dan and Viv are okay with us investigating?' Lauren whispered, wide-eyed.

'I can't speak for Viv, but that's what Dan implied.'

A weight seemed to lift from Lauren's shoulders. The situation with Viv wouldn't be half so difficult if Dan had, albeit indirectly, given his approval for them to continue investigating.

Just then, Albert rejoined them. 'I've taken the liberty of ordering us all some scones,' he announced. 'They look rather tasty, what!'

'We've only just finished lunch,' protested Meg, 'and I'm not sure I need a scone.' Then she relented at Albert's crestfallen expression. 'But I shall enjoy it very much all the same, thank you.'

Lauren decided not to mention that she had two cookies waiting for her in the car. She'd take them home and share them with her mum later.

'You're welcome,' Albert said expansively as he sat down. 'Now, do tell. What have you been up to, eh, Lauren?'

Lauren glanced at Meg, who gave an almost imperceptible nod.

'Well, I've spoken to several people at Cathedral Accountants. That's where Vikram works,' she explained for Albert's benefit.

'Oh, is he a cleaner, or something like that?' he asked.

'No, he's a chartered accountant. He's a junior partner in the firm,' Lauren explained. Meg glowered at him, and he mimed zipping his mouth shut.

'I've got most of what they said recorded,' Lauren continued, 'but to cut a long story short, no one there thinks that Vikram could have been responsible for abducting Noah, and they certainly can't believe that he could have murdered anyone. They all commented on how kind and considerate he is. Wouldn't hurt a fly, just like Mia said. He's even a vegetarian.'

'What's that got to do with it?' exploded Albert, unable to keep his mouth zipped.

'It goes to show how committed he is to respecting all living things,' explained Meg.

'I thought being a vegetarian was just a fad,' grumbled Albert.

'It might be for some people,' she instructed in her best schoolteacher's voice, 'but for most people it's a decision based on religious, moral or ethical grounds. In Vikram's case, it's most likely because he's a Hindu.'

'I thought they were all Muslim over there?' Albert replied, digging his hole even deeper.

'No, they are not,' Meg snapped.

He saw the look on her face and decided it was time to shut up. Meg gathered her thoughts and then asked Lauren to oontinuo.

'Umm, yes. Well, apparently, he went into work on the Monday after Noah was abducted, to hand over some urgent client files. He was taking some compassionate leave so he could help in the search for Noah and be with

61

Mia. Anyway, everyone who saw him that day said how genuinely upset he was. They told me that he doted on Noah and was already talking about adopting him, if he and Mia ever got married.'

'He was pretty serious about his relationship then,' remarked Meg.

'Yes, I got that impression too.'

'How many people did you speak to there?' she enquired.

'About a dozen. They couldn't have been more helpful.'

'That's good. I take it you've been there all morning?' There was a pause as the waitress arrived with their tea and scones and stopped to exchange pleasantries.

'No,' said Lauren, once the waitress had gone. 'I finished there just before midday and walked down the road to Linda's Lunches.'

Meg explained to Albert that that was where Mia worked. 'Go on, my dear. Did you manage to speak to Linda?'

'Yes, I spoke to both Mia and Linda. Mia was pleased to see me. I think she thought we'd solved the case already! But I explained that these things take time. I'm going to go round this evening,' added Lauren, 'just for a drink and a chat. She's so lonely.'

'That's good, I'm sure she needs a friend right now,' Meg said with a nod, 'and she might remember something she didn't mention to us yesterday.'

'That's what I thought. Anyway, then I went through to the kitchen to talk with Linda. She was adamant that Vikram wouldn't have hurt Noah. She went to Noah's first birthday party, like Sanjeev, and she told me how he treated Noah like he was his own son. She was just as insistent that Mia couldn't have been involved, either.'

'Well, that's good to hear.' Meg poured her tea before it got too strong and added a dash of milk. 'I assume, after all of that, you didn't have time to go anywhere else?'

'I managed to squeeze in one more visit, although I kind of wish I hadn't, now.'

'Oh?' Meg looked at her quizzically.

'Linda suggested I go and talk to Tyler Ford. He's her

prime suspect, alibi or not. She told me he works at B&Q, so I went there to look for him.'

'And did you find him?' put in Albert.

'Yeah, unfortunately I did.' Lauren wrinkled her nose in disgust.

'Why? What's he like?' Meg sounded concerned.

'A thug,' replied Lauren instantly. 'I mean, I know you shouldn't make snap judgements, but with some people you can just tell, can't you?'

'I think I know,' smiled Meg, 'but explain it to me.'

'Well, he's big and broad and tough-looking. He's got a skinhead haircut, and his arms are plastered in tattoos. Not that I've got anything against tattoos,' she added. 'I've got a couple myself.' Meg was surprised because she hadn't seen any. But then, perhaps it was better not to ask, as they were obviously well hidden.

'But it was more his manner,' Lauren continued. 'He was totally snarky and aggressive. He called Mia a little slut who didn't deserve to have sole custody, Noah was his kid too, blah, blah, blah. And he said he was pleased the police had nicked that … well, I won't repeat what he called Vikram, but it wasn't very nice.'

'Unfortunately, there will always be people with racist views,' said Meg, looking pointedly at Albert.

'It was more than just racist,' replied Lauren. 'It was hateful and vicious. He went off on a rant that made me feel quite sick. Couldn't wait to get away from him, to be honest.'

Meg sympathised. She could see that Lauren was shaken by her experience.

'That confirms what we already thought: Tyler had a very strong motive to abduct Noah.'

'I agree,' nodded Albert, eager to join in.

'Yeah, I'd agree too,' said Lauren, 'if it wasn't for his alibi.'

'I think this alibi needs to be thoroughly checked out,' Meg said darkly.

'The rozzers will have done that, won't they, old gal?' chipped in Albert.

'You'd certainly hope so,' Meg said enigmatically. She paused. 'I'd also like to know why Mia was granted sole custody,' she added thoughtfully.

'Yes, I thought that was a bit odd. I thought most dads got joint custody or visiting rights, or something. I was going to ask Mia about that this evening,' Lauren said.

'Good idea, but don't inundate her with too many questions,' advised Meg. 'Just try and gently steer the conversation in the right direction, if you see what I mean.'

'What do you take me for?' demanded Lauren, rolling her eyes then grinning cheekily to show she wasn't offended.

Chapter Fifteen

There was a lull in their conversation as Meg and Albert finished off their scones.

'Right,' said Meg, topping up her teapot with hot water. 'We need to plan what to do this afternoon. I thought perhaps we could visit Mia's parents.'

'I thought that too,' Lauren replied, 'but Mia said they'll be out. They always do the weekly shopping on a Friday afternoon. She's going to arrange for us to call on them tomorrow morning, if you're up to it, or I can go on my own if you prefer.'

'No, I'd like to come with you,' replied Meg firmly. She'd already been forced to miss out on that morning's investigating; she didn't want to miss anything else.

'I'll come too,' announced Albert.

'No, you won't,' said Meg firmly. 'This needs to be handled delicately.'

Albert looked about to argue then shrugged his shoulders and didn't press the point. Meg was relieved as she really couldn't trust Albert to keep his prejudices to himself. She was still regretting suggesting he could help with this investigation.

They chattered some more about the case, and then Lauren drove Meg and Albert the short distance back to Britford Lodge to save them walking up the hill.

Lauren then headed home to Downton, pleased that she'd have time to do a bit more research into Tyler Ford and this group he belonged to.

As she parked on the road outside her house, to her surprise, she spotted Viv's blue Vauxhall Astra. Her stomach lurched, and she wasn't sure whether she was excited or nervous to see him after the way he'd left yesterday.

'Hello,' she called out as she went in through the front door, wondering why he was here so early in the afternoon.

'Hi, gorgeous,' said Viv, a little sheepishly, coming out of the living room to meet her. He held out a bunch of pink and purple carnations. 'Truce?'

'Yeah, I'd like that,' muttered Lauren, tears unexpectedly pricking her eyes. She buried her face into the flowers and inhaled their fragrant scent.

'Can I get you a coffee?' he offered.

'Thanks.' She followed him into the kitchen to put her flowers into water. For a moment, neither spoke. Then they both started to say 'I'm sorry' at the same time and stopped again, each waiting for the other. Viv put his hands loosely either side of Lauren's waist and held her at arm's length. 'Listen,' he said, studying her face. 'I'm sorry I left the way I did yesterday, but I didn't want to risk saying something I'd later regret. I was only mad at you because you mean the world to me. Back in January, when I heard what had happened ...'

'But I wasn't seriously hurt,' pointed out Lauren quietly.

'I know. But it made me realise just how much I love you.'

Lauren's heart did an almighty somersault. She leant forward and kissed the end of his nose. 'I love you too,' she said. Then she pulled back, looking strained. 'But you can't protect me from everything in life,' she said. 'I don't want a relationship where you make all the decisions and tell me what I can and can't do.'

'I get that,' Viv nodded, 'and I don't want that either.'

'Good.' She allowed him to pull her in for a more passionate embrace.

'Oh, my goodness, you two!' exclaimed Bekka coming in from the dining room. They pulled apart, slightly embarrassed. 'Don't mind me,' she chuckled, 'I'm just glad to see that you've made up.'

'Cup of tea?' Viv asked as the kettle conveniently came to the boil.

'Yes, please,' replied Bekka. 'Now, Lauren, come through to the lounge and tell me what's happening with this poor

66

missing baby. I've been reading in yesterday's *Salisbury Journal* that he still hasn't been found. It's just awful.'

Viv made their drinks, and he and Lauren settled on the settee, her mum taking the armchair this time so she could look at them both.

'You go first,' Lauren told Viv, still not quite sure what his feelings were about her investigating.

'Okay. I had a chat with Dan about it this morning. As you know, it's not our case, so we can't be involved. Not officially anyway.'

'What does that mean?' demanded Lauren.

'Just what I said. *We* – as in Dan and I – can't poke our noses into another team's case. Having said that, there are a few concerns around the station that … umm … well, that perhaps the investigation isn't being handled as thoroughly as it could be.'

'What are you saying?'

'Well, if two members of the public were to go investigating off their own backs, that isn't our responsibility, is it?'

'You're saying we can carry on with the investigation?'

'Officially, no. But we can't stop you, can we? Particularly if we don't "know",' he made air quote marks with his fingers, 'what you're up to. Officially. If you see what I mean.'

'I think so,' said Lauren doubtfully.

'Look, I don't like the idea of you putting yourself in any kind of possible danger,' explained Viv, 'but I also realise that I don't have any right to tell you what you can and can't do. And, in this particular case, Dan feels that it might be useful to have someone doing their own bit of amateur sleuthing. You and Meg, you're both observant, and you added a lot to our investigations at The Cedars and Britford Lodge. If you were to ask a few questions, chat to Noah's mother, that kind of thing, and come up with some evidence as to what happened … without putting yourselves at risk …'

'So, officially, we can't investigate, but, unofficially, we can,' Lauren summed up.

'Yes. But promise me, as soon as you uncover anything significant, you go straight to the station and report it to DI Barnes and his team? No delving in deeper and getting yourselves into trouble.'

'Yeah, yeah, I get it,' Lauren reluctantly agreed.

'What's your progress with this case, so far?' Bekka asked, when the young couple fell into a slightly awkward silence.

Lauren told them both about their visit to Mia the previous day, and her visits to Cathedral Accountants and Linda's Lunches that morning.

'I can't believe Billy Barnes didn't even bother to interview anyone at Vikram's place of work!' exclaimed Viv. 'And did he interview this Linda, do you know?'

Lauren replied that she didn't think so.

Viv was appalled. Granted, anything Vikram's work colleagues said wasn't evidence of his guilt or otherwise. But it demonstrated the character of the suspect, which was important to consider. He began to wonder if perhaps Meg and Lauren were right to think that Vikram was innocent.

Lauren decided not to mention her encounter with Tyler Ford, worried that Viv would consider it irresponsible, especially if she told him just how vile the man was. For the moment, she just wanted to enjoy the fact that they were patching things up.

Chapter Sixteen

Saturday 24th June 2023

The next morning dawned bright and sunny. 'How are things with Viv?' asked Meg as she fastened her seatbelt in Lauren's car. Lauren had picked her up, as arranged, and they were expected at Mia's parents' at ten-thirty.

'Well, we've made up!' she grinned. 'He was kind of sweet, bought me flowers an' all. But I got the impression that he's still not totally comfortable that we're investigating.'

'He's concerned about you.'

'Yeah, that's what he keeps saying.' Lauren navigated her way out onto the Ringwood Road and headed towards Salisbury. Traffic was heavy, as it so often was on a Saturday morning.

'He was a bit miffed when I wouldn't go out with him last night, but I explained that I'd already promised Mia I'd go round hers for a drink.'

'Perhaps he was worried you were still mad at him after your argument?' Meg suggested.

'Hmm, I don't think it was that. But, in any case, we're going out tonight, so I can make it up to him then.'

Meg smiled. Lauren was a fiercely independent young woman who reminded her of herself at that age. She changed the subject. 'Tell me about your evening with Mia.'

'We had a few cans of cider together.' Lauren caught the look on Meg's face. 'Don't worry, I was drinking non-alcoholic. I took both, knowing I was driving.'

Meg smiled; Lauren was, in so many ways, quite mature for her age.

'We chatted about all sorts of things. And, no, I didn't inundate her with questions. She talked quite openly about herself, her relationship with Vikram and, of course, Noah.'

'That's good,' Meg said with a nod.

'And I found out why she was granted sole custody. It seems that Tyler's got quite the record for violence. You remember her mentioning that she'd tried to leave him a couple of times? Well, on one occasion, he grabbed her arm so violently that he broke her wrist!'

'What a nasty piece of work! Did you tell her you'd met him?'

'Yeah, I told her what happened. She said that was typical of Tyler. Apparently, he's got a right chip on his shoulder. Oh! And I forgot to tell you yesterday; I found out that he's a member of some far-right group that's anti-immigrants. You know the kind of thing. Britain is for white Brits only.'

'That hardly surprises me after what you've told me about him. We need to dig deeper into his alibi, but we don't even know what that is yet.'

'Ah, I think I do. Mia told me that Tyler regularly meets up with his far-right buddies at a pub called The Hanging Man on Friday nights. And that pub is renowned for having lock-ins.'

'What's a lock-in?' enquired Meg, puzzled.

'It's when the landlord locks the doors but carries on serving his customers past closing time. It's illegal, obviously. But it's just the sort of thing I can see Tyler and his buddies doing.'

'And, of course, they'd give him an alibi if he asked.'

'Yeah, that's what I thought,' Lauren nodded, as she negotiated yet another of Salisbury's roundabouts and joined a queue of slow-moving traffic heading down Southampton Road.

'We need to visit that pub,' Meg suggested, 'but preferably not on a Friday evening, when we'd stick out like a sore thumb.'

'We could call in for a drink after we've spoken to Mia's parents,' suggested Lauren, 'unless you need to get back to Britford Lodge in time for lunch?'

'No, I didn't know how long we'd be gone for, so I told Hazel I'd be out for lunch.'

'Great. We can grab a bite somewhere.'

'My treat this time,' Meg insisted.

Having navigated a back route through to Laverstock, Lauren found the house they were looking for and parked up outside. It was an older-style semi-detached, probably ex-council housing stock, Meg thought. But well looked after and, from the beautiful display of flowers in the front garden, it seemed that someone obviously enjoyed gardening. They walked up the path and Lauren pressed the doorbell. The door opened almost immediately, and a smiling woman in her mid-forties greeted them warmly.

'Hi, I'm Rachel, Mia's mum. She's told me all about you, and I'm just so glad you've agreed to help.' She ushered them into the lounge, where a taller man of a similar age stood up from the settee to shake hands with them both.

'Hugh Jenkins,' he said, gesturing for them to sit down.

'Welsh?' guessed Meg, from his name. Not that his accent betrayed anything.

'My parents were,' he said ruefully. 'The name's a bit of a giveaway, isn't it?'

Rachel fussed around, making sure they were comfortable and offering them tea or coffee. She was a slender woman, with shoulder-length brown hair and big brown eyes. Hugh, on the other hand, was quite heavily built, with receding blond hair and blue eyes. Once they all had drinks, Rachel's face became more serious, and a couple of worry lines showed across her forehead. 'Right then, what do you want to know?'

'Tell us about Mia and Vikram. What did you think of their relationship? And of them moving in together when they did?' Meg asked.

The couple looked at each other, and Hugh nodded for Rachel to speak. 'We were a bit worried,' she said carefully. 'I mean, you do worry about your daughter, don't you? Especially after that bastard Tylor and what he did to her. Not that she told us very much, but we could see that she was afraid of him. She changed so much while she was living with him, and there didn't seem to be anything we could do. When she finally left him and came back home to live, he used to come round in the evenings, hammering on the door, shouting threats and intimidating us. Hugh had to get an injunction to stop him coming near the house, you know. So, when Mia started dating Vikram, we were worried. Was she only dating a coloured guy to get back at Tyler? Was Vikram going to be as bad as Tyler had been? You read about women who always go for the same kind of man, don't you? But we couldn't have been more wrong. Vikram is the total opposite of Tyler … and I don't mean his colour.'

Hugh coughed. 'I don't like to think I'm racist,' he looked down at his feet in embarrassment, 'but I did have my doubts about Vikram.' He looked up and spoke directly to Meg. 'But Rachel's right, he's a stand-up guy, and he adores Mia and little Noah too. Even so, I wasn't happy when she announced they were going to rent somewhere together just a couple of months after they'd started dating.'

'You tried to talk her out of it,' Rachel interrupted, looking at him reproachfully.

'Yes, I'm afraid I did. I thought it was too soon. Especially after Tyler. And with her having the baby to look after.'

'But Vikram came round to speak with us,' continued Rachel. 'He told us that he wanted to give Mia all the support that she needs. That he loved her, and he wanted them to be a family. He said he hoped that their relationship would lead towards marriage, and even if that wasn't what Mia wanted, he'd like to be a father to Noah. He talked about adopting him. That's why the very idea of him doing anything bad to Noah is just so crazy!'

'And I must admit, I was wrong,' added Hugh. 'Even in the short time they've been living together, I can see that Vikram is good for Mia. It's been lovely to see her so happy again, and to watch her regain her confidence.'

'And now, that low-life Tyler has destroyed all of that,' spat Rachel furiously.

'You think he did this?' asked Lauren.

'I'd bet my life on it,' she stated. 'He didn't want Mia to leave him. He was fuming when she refused to register

Noah with his surname, even though they weren't married. And he made it clear that he wanted custody of Noah. What's more, he's an out-and-out racist, so he wouldn't have been able to stand the idea of Vikram being around his son.'

'Do you think Tyler would harm Noah, given that he is his son?' asked Meg.

'I ... 'Rachel broke off, a pained expression sweeping across her face. 'I don't know. Oh, God, I hope not.' Tears trickled down her cheeks. Hugh passed her a tissue and comforted her.

'I have to hope he wouldn't,' Hugh ground his words out, 'but I wouldn't trust him as far as I could throw him.'

The couple were visibly upset, so Meg and Lauren gave them a few moments to compose themselves.

Chapter Seventeen

When Rachel and Hugh had recovered their composure, Meg thought perhaps it might be an idea to give them something positive to hang on to. 'We do have reason to believe that whoever took Noah, took him alive.' Meg explained about Peter Rabbit and the dummy. 'But I don't want to get your hopes up too much.'

Rachel nodded furiously, a smile spreading across her tear-stained face.

'A question for you: do you think it's possible to put Noah into a sports bag and carry him away without waking him up?'

Rachel answered promptly, 'Yes, it's quite possible. We used to pick Noah up from his cot and put him in his car seat to go shopping quite regularly and he never woke up. If he did stir, you only had to pop his dummy into his mouth and that usually worked.'

'And how do you think someone broke into the house to get Noah?' asked Lauren.

'Well, we do have a theory about that,' explained Rachel, 'but that policeman who came round here asking loads of questions said that it was too far-fetched.'

'Why don't you try telling us?' suggested Meg gently.

'Mia still has a key for here, and she gave us a key to their place when they moved in. In case of emergencies, you know?'

Meg and Lauren nodded, listening to Rachel with interest.

'Well, I kept Mia's key in my handbag. On Friday afternoons, we'd take Noah straight back to her house after we'd finished the shopping, to save disturbing him twice. If Mia wasn't back from work when we got there, I had the key to let ourselves in, you see?'

'That makes sense,' commented Meg, wondering where this was going.

'Well, on the day before Noah was taken, we got to Mia's house, and she wasn't in. But I couldn't find her key anywhere in my handbag. We ended up waiting in the car for twenty minutes until she came home.'

'At that point, I just thought Rachel had mislaid it,' added Hugh. 'She can sometimes be a bit scatterbrained, so we weren't really all that worried.'

'But when Mia phoned the next morning to say Noah had been taken, we searched everywhere for that key. And it's gone missing.' Rachel put her hands over her face and sobbed. 'It's all my fault.'

Hugh comforted her. 'We don't know that the key isn't simply lost somewhere,' he said. 'You wait, one day it will turn up when we're not looking for it.'

'And even if your key was taken to let someone else get into Mia's house, that's hardly your fault,' Meg added.

'No, it's totally on them,' agreed Lauren firmly.

'But if I'd reported the key missing straight away …' choked Rachel.

'I doubt if it would have made any difference,' insisted Meg. 'Would Mia and Vikram have changed their locks immediately, just because you couldn't find your key? Of course not, they'd have given you time to look for it at home.'

'What do Mia and Vik think about it?' asked Lauren.

Rachel looked at Hugh guiltily. 'We haven't said anything to them. They were both so devastated by Noah being taken that I didn't like to mention it.'

'But you told the police?' confirmed Lauren.

'Yes, of course. Not that it did any good. That police inspector said it was irrelevant as Vikram had obviously taken Noah himself. He wasn't listening to a word we said.' Hugh spoke bitterly.

'Can you think of a time when someone could have stolen the key from your handbag?' Lauren looked at Rachel enquiringly.

'I've been racking my brains over that,' she replied. 'All I can think of is, I was in the market on Tuesday that week, and it was particularly crowded near that popular fruit and veg stall, and people were jostling against me. Then, when I went to pay for my veggies, I discovered that my handbag was open. I checked that my purse and phone were still in there, which they were, so I didn't think any more of it, at the time.'

'But how could anyone have known that Rachel had Mia's key in her handbag?' asked Hugh. 'It doesn't make sense, does it?'

Meg agreed; it was puzzling.

'Tell me, do you both work?' asked Lauren, changing the subject.

'I work Sundays to Wednesdays on nights,' said Hugh. 'I'm a foreman at a bakery factory near Warminster. I sleep until three or four, on the days after my shifts, but it means I get three days off at the weekend, which is nice.'

'Isn't it difficult having a baby here while you're trying to sleep?'

'It doesn't usually bother me,' he grinned. 'Rachel always says I could sleep through an earthquake!' They both chuckled.

'I used to work fulltime at the One Stop shop down the road,' said Rachel, 'but since I've been looking after Noah, I just work Sunday afternoons and the occasional evening, when they're short-staffed. I haven't known what to do with myself since Noah's been gone.'

Her face fell and she looked on the verge of tears again.

'We'll look into it as best we can,' Meg reassured them, 'but we can't make any promises.' She stood up and suggested it was time to go.

'Who's the gardener?' she asked, as they shook hands on the doorstep.

'Both of us,' replied Rachel. 'I do the flowers; Hugh does the veggies. We're outside every afternoon for an hour or two, if the weather's nice. It's a great way for me to unwind after looking after a toddler who's into everything, and it's good for Hugh to get some fresh air before he goes into work.'

That gave Meg an idea. 'Is there a way anyone could

have got into the house while you were both in the garden?'

'I never thought of that,' Rachel frowned. 'I suppose, if we were both busy, it's possible someone could slip inside without us noticing.'

Meg and Lauren said their goodbyes and were waved off by Rachel, who was still standing on the doorstep as they rounded the corner at the end of their cul-de-sac.

❁

'Do you think someone stole the key from inside the house?' Lauren asked, as she slowed to a halt in the next road.

'Not necessarily, but it's more likely than someone taking it from Rachel's handbag in the market square, don't you think?'

'Yeah, I suppose so. Where do you want to go next? Only, The Hanging Man is across the other side of town, and I wondered if you wanted to talk to anyone else in Laverstock before we go there?'

'Who did you have in mind?' Meg suppressed a smile.

'I thought perhaps we could call on nosy Norman at number eleven.'

'As long as you don't call him that to his face,' Meg grinned.

Chapter Eighteen

Lauren made her way to Birch Close and parked up out of sight of Mia's house, which was round a bend where the road forked. She locked her car, and they walked up the road to number eleven. They both noticed the net curtain in the front bay window twitch as they headed up a short path to the door.

'Let me handle this,' whispered Meg. Lauren nodded her agreement.

The door opened and a grumpy face looked at them suspiciously. 'What do you want? If you're Jehovah's Witnesses, you can beat it.'

'I assure you we're not from any religious sect,' Meg smiled sweetly. 'We're conducting an independent survey into the way the police conduct interviews with members of the public. We understand you recently gave a statement?'

'Yes, what about it?'

'Could we come in and ask you a few questions? It won't take long.'

'Very well.' He stood back and regarded them suspiciously as they entered the stale-smelling hall. 'First door on the left,' he grumbled, following them into an untidy living room. Books and letters were strewn about haphazardly, there were several mugs with dried-on coffee rings lying around, an ashtray with several discarded butts, a variety of screwdrivers and other tools and a thick layer of dust over everything. Like the hall, the room smelt stale and neglected, and the reek of cigarette smoke was almost overwhelming. The man, quite tall and in his seventies, with untidy white hair, didn't bother to offer them a seat.

'Go on then,' he demanded, looking them up and down in a discomforting way.

Meg turned on her charm as she sat carefully on the

edge of a tan-coloured sofa, signalling for Lauren to do the same. 'We're so sorry to take up your valuable time, and to call on you unannounced. It's very good of you to agree to talk to us.'

Begrudgingly, the man sank into one of a pair of dark green armchairs.

Meg took out her notebook and consulted it discreetly, not allowing the man to see the page. 'Now then, can you confirm your full name for me, just so that I know we've got the right person.'

'Harold Victor Norman.'

'And your date of birth?'

'Tenth of May 1946.'

'Thank you for confirming that. And we understand you gave a witness statement to the police regarding the abduction of the child of one of your neighbours?'

'That's right.'

'Did they come to you, or did you go to the police station?'

'They came here first, knocking on my door unannounced, just like you two. It were a couple of young coppers, in uniform. I didn't tell them anything 'cos I didn't know then what'd happened. But when I saw that appeal on *South Today* the day after – with that young couple – well, I put two and two together then. The mother, she were genuinely upset; you could see that. But he were just putting it on. I can tell, you see. These bloody foreigners think we can't read them, but I can.'

'I see, so you went to the police station to give a statement? I must say, that's very public-spirited of you.'

'Course I did. Well, I saw him, you see.' He stuck his jaw out defiantly.

'You saw Vikram Chopra?' Meg confirmed.

'Yes, I did.' She noticed he didn't look at her as he spoke.

'And when was that?'

'It were about half past one in the morning, and he were walking down the road carrying a big black sports bag. Very suspicious, he looked, I can tell you.'

'And you're sure about who you saw?'

'Bloody 'ell, I just told you, didn't I?' He sounded quite belligerent.

'And you saw him come from number twenty-five?'

'Yep.'

'And where did he go?'

'He got into a car parked just down the road, a tad closer than where you're parked now.'

'Was there anyone else inside the car?'

'I don't know. It were too bloody dark to tell, weren't it?'

'Tell me, Mr Norman, did the police officer taking your statement question your allegations?'

"Ere, what are you suggesting?'

'Nothing at all, I just need to ascertain whether the police officer followed the correct procedure.'

'Oh yeah, right. Well, he asked me if I was sure about what I'd seen, then he wanted a description of the man I saw, and I told him it were that Paki that was on the TV appeal. He asked about the car too, but I don't know much about cars. It were one of those big SUV things and it were a dark colour. Probably black.'

'Mr Norman, are you aware that Vikram Chopra is Indian, not Pakistani?'

'Nope, and I don't much care, either. He's the only wog living in this street, so it had to have been him.'

Meg cringed inwardly but carried on regardless. 'Did you notice which side of the car the man got into?'

'Eh? No, I didn't notice.'

'And where did he put the sports bag?'

'In the car, obviously.'

'In the boot?' Meg persisted.

'I dunno! What difference does it make?'

Quite a lot, Meg thought, but she carried on regardless. 'Did the officer taking your statement ask you where you were when you saw Mr Chopra?'

'I told him that at the start of the interview. I were upstairs in my bedroom, having a fag. I often look out of the window when I'm smoking; I likes to see what's going on in the area. Neighbourhood Watch, you see.'

Meg doubted whether this man had anything to do with

Neighbourhood Watch, but she wasn't going to argue with him. 'Can you tell me whether the streetlights were on or off, at the time?' she asked.

'What's that got to do with this survey of yours?' he demanded suspiciously. 'What organisation did you say you were from?'

'I noticed the police officer didn't mention the streetlights in your statement.' Meg ignored his question and metaphorically crossed her fingers. 'It's something he should've checked.'

'Oh well, I don't remember. But they must've been on, right? I saw that Paki's face!'

'Yes, of course. Thank you, Mr Norman, you've been so helpful. Do you have anything you'd like to add about the officer who took your statement?'

'He believed every word I said, not like you, questioning everything and making it sound like I don't know what I saw. And he showed me his ID. Where's your ID, then? You still haven't told me what organisation you're from.'

Meg put her notebook back in her handbag and made a show of searching for her ID. 'I'm so sorry, Mr Norman, I seem to have left it in the car. I can go and get it for you if you like?'

'Don't bother, just get out of here. I've had enough of your questions.' He stood up and strode to the front door, holding it open for them and immediately slamming it shut after them.

'Phew,' said Lauren, taking grateful breaths of fresh air as they paused on the pavement outside the house.

'Yes, it's a relief to be out of there,' agreed Meg. 'What did you make of our witness?'

'Witness?' scoffed Lauren. 'I'd be surprised if he actually saw anything.'

'I take it the streetlights weren't on, then?'

'No way, I checked. The streetlights in residential areas go off at midnight. It would've been too dark to see a face clearly.'

'Any other anomalies?' asked Meg, eager to see if Lauren had picked up on the same things she had.

'Well, *if* nosy Norman saw someone, there's no way he could've seen which house the person came from. You can't see Mia's house from here.'

Meg nodded.

'And then there's the inconsistencies in his story. How come he could see Vikram clearly, but it was too dark to see if there was anyone else in the car? And, if he was that observant, how come he had no idea which side of the car he got into?'

'Or exactly where he put the sports bag,' added Meg dryly.

'So that was all a pack of lies!'

'Being generous, it's possible he *might* have seen someone walking down the pavement. But I think that's about all,' Meg surmised.

'It's very thin evidence for arresting Vikram.'

'There are other circumstantial factors,' Meg pointed out, trying to keep an open mind.

'Yeah, whatever! I don't believe for one second that Vikram took Noah. We need to follow up Tyler's alibi next, see if it's as dodgy as nosy Norman's witness statement.'

'To the pub, then,' agreed Meg, hoping that The Hanging Man wasn't going to be quite as dismal as its name suggested.

Chapter Nineteen

Lauren made her way towards Bemerton Heath and skilfully negotiated a narrow lane beside The Hanging Man to the car park at the rear. There were a few cars parked, but it wasn't exactly busy. The pub was an old building badly in need of some repairs, and the entrance from the car park was hardly enticing. Lauren had a momentary doubt about taking Meg into such a dive. As if reading her mind, Meg quietly suggested that they need only have one drink and a quick chat with the landlord and then go somewhere else for lunch. Lauren nodded as she pushed open a panelled door to enter the main lounge.

Inside, the red carpet was faded and worn and sticky in places from spilled drinks, but the dark wooden tables and chairs looked clean and well polished. A middle-aged couple sat in one corner, eating something and chips, and a small group of young men were chatting noisily in another section, all with pints in front of them. Two other couples sat at tables across the other side, and there was an elderly man propping up one end of the bar. Lauren and Meg went up to the bar, nodding hello to the man, who acknowledged them with a grunt.

'What can I get for you?' asked a burly man appearing from a doorway behind the bar. His height and weight might have been intimidating, but his manner was friendly enough. His tousled black hair was streaked with grey, and Meg guessed he was probably in his early fifties.

'I'll have a small lemonade, please,' said Meg.

'Have you got any non-alcoholic ciders?' asked Lauren, standing on tiptoe trying to see what was behind the bar.

'I've got the Old Mout Berries and Cherries,' the landlord offered.

'Ooh, great,' replied Lauren, brightening up. 'I'll have one of those, please.'

'I don't think I've seen you in here before,' he remarked as he got their drinks.

'No,' replied Lauren, 'you haven't. A mate of mine mentioned coming here one evening, said it was heaving, so I thought I'd check it out.'

'Thank you. We're busy most evenings although it's always quieter at lunchtime.' The landlord passed Meg her lemonade and set about opening the bottle of cider. 'Do you want a glass and ice?' he asked Lauren, who replied yes.

He poured the drink and put it on the bar in front of Lauren before speaking again. 'We have a function room through there.' He pointed to a closed-off section on their right. 'Tuesdays is quiz night, Wednesdays is darts and Thursdays is bingo. And on Fridays, RAS meet here. Don't think that would be your cup of tea, though.'

'Oh, why's that?' asked Lauren, sipping her cider with relish.

'You don't look like the sort of person we get in on a Friday night. They're a bit rough and rowdy, to be honest. But they drink plenty of beer, so I can't grumble.'

'No, I guess you need all the business you can get after COVID?'

'Yeah, the pandemic nearly finished us off, but I just about held on and now things are beginning to pick up again. We've got karaoke tonight, if you're interested.'

'Thanks, but we've got something else on. By the way, what's RAS?'

'Radical Action Salisbury.'

'Not heard of that one before, is it an environmental group or something?' Lauren was putting on a good show of being naive. Meg watched the conversation with interest, even though she was longing to sit down.

'You've got to be joking!' chuckled the landlord. He shook his head and leant towards Lauren. 'Between you and me, I don't like their attitude or their politics, but you can't afford to be choosy when you're in business.'

'No, I suppose not,' sympathised Lauren.

'RAS is all anti-immigration, anti-foreigners, that sort of thing.'

'Oh, one of the women I work with was going out with someone like that,' Lauren exclaimed. 'He was a bit of a thug, knocked her around, I think. To be honest, I was happy when she left him. I think his name was Tyrone? Or Tyler?'

'That sounds like Tyler Ford,' he replied. 'Nasty piece of work, he is.'

'Then you might know my friend Mia?' Lauren said hopefully.

The landlord looked taken aback. 'I know Tyler lived with a girl called Mia for a while, but I don't think I ever met her. If it's the same one as your workmate, she's the one whose kid was kidnapped a couple of weeks ago, right?'

'Yeah, that's her,' said Lauren. 'It's been absolutely dreadful for her, as you can imagine.'

'They still haven't found the lad then?'

'No. And now the police have arrested her current boyfriend, she's at her wits' end.'

'I had the police in here, asking questions about Tyler, the day after that little boy was taken,' the landlord confided to her.

'Ooh, why?' asked Lauren, wide-eyed.

'They were asking if he was in here the evening before the kidnapping. The baby was his, but I expect you know that.'

Lauren nodded.

'I wouldn't have been at all surprised if he had done it,' the landlord sighed. 'But, unfortunately, he was here all evening.'

'I'm guessing Tyler wouldn't have been too happy that Mia's new boyfriend is Indian,' suggested Lauren.

'You've hit the nail on the head there,' he agreed. 'It really got up his nose that she left him and took up with an immigrant.'

'That explains why everyone I know is convinced that Tyler took Noah,' Lauren said. 'But you're sure he was here all evening?'

'Yes, he was. He and most of that crowd he hangs around with.'

'Wasn't the baby taken much later in the night?' asked Meg, chipping in for the first time. 'Surely your pub closes at eleven?'

'Well, normally it does.' The landlord looked around then leant towards her. 'But sometimes I stay open a bit later if there's a good crowd in and they bung me a bit extra.'

'Doesn't that get you into trouble with the police?' Meg asked innocently.

'It would do, if they knew about it,' he chuckled.

'But if you gave Tyler an alibi …' Meg looked puzzled.

'Well, to begin with, I told that copper that Tyler was here until closing time, which is true. He was sitting near the partition wall through to the other room, and I could hear his loud voice mouthing off about this and that from time to time, and I could see him, every time I glanced that way. Then the copper pressed me about what time Tyler *really* left. He said he didn't care if it was after last orders, said he'd turn a blind eye so long as I told the truth. So, I told him. Tyler and his mates didn't leave here until nearly two in the morning. And, by that time, they were far too drunk to be doing anything quietly, let alone sneaking a baby out of a house.'

'His alibi really is genuine,' sighed Lauren.

'Did Mia ask you to check it out?' he guessed.

'Yeah, sorry, she did. I hope you don't mind.'

'Not at all, I wish I could help her. I can't imagine what it's like for someone to take your child and not to know what's happened to them. I've got kids of my own, grown up now, of course. And I've got a grandson about the same age as Mia's little boy.'

Just then, a man came up to the bar and the landlord moved away to serve him.

Lauren looked at Meg. 'Would you like to go and sit down?'

'Yes, please,' Meg agreed gratefully. They took their drinks across to a small round table with a bench seat on one side and a carver-style chair on the other. Meg sank into the chair with a sigh.

'Are you feeling okay?' Lauren enquired, concern in her eyes.

'My joints don't like standing for that long,' Meg admitted, 'but I'll be fine once I've had a bit of a rest.'

'I'm sorry, that was really thoughtless of me.'

'Don't apologise, you handled that landlord very well and got exactly what we needed to know from him.'

'Even if it wasn't what I wanted to hear,' Lauren said grumpily. 'I was really hoping the police had made a mistake about Tyler's alibi.'

Just then, the elderly man who had been propping up the bar appeared at Meg's side.

'Sorry to interrupt,' he wheezed. 'I couldn't help overhearing your conversation with Greg ... mind if I join you for a moment?'

Chapter Twenty

Lauren shuffled up the bench and the old man sat down gingerly. 'I can't sit for long,' he explained, 'on account of a bad back.' Meg sympathised.

'You were asking about Tyler,' he said. 'Well, I know Tyler and that crowd. I'm in here most lunchtimes and evenings, just for a quick pint, like. It's better than being stuck at home all day on my own.'

Meg guessed from the redness of the man's nose, the veins across his cheeks and his sunken sallow-looking eyes that he was perhaps a bit of an alcoholic.

'I'm telling you; it's not just Tyler that copper should've been asking about,' he continued. 'He would've done anything to get his baby boy away from his missus and her new fella. And I reckon that includes getting that mate of his to do the job for him.'

Meg and Lauren looked at each other. 'Can you tell us more?' Lauren asked.

'I'd tell you what I know,' he croaked, 'if my throat wasn't so dry.'

Lauren took the hint. 'Can I get you another pint?' she offered. His eyes lit up and he beamed, showing crooked nicotine-stained teeth. 'A pint of best bitter, if you will.'

'What about you, Meg?'

'Umm, I don't know. What about lunch?' Meg looked up at Lauren questioningly.

'Would you like me to bring the menu back?' she suggested.

'Yes, please.'

'Greg does a proper nice ploughman's,' offered their new acquaintance.

'That sounds good. Can you order me a ploughman's and another lemonade then, Lauren? But, remember, this is my treat.'

Meg and the man sat talking about the shocking price of things these days until Lauren returned with the drinks. He took a long draught of his pint and sighed contentedly.

'Right, then. What was it I was going to tell you? Oh yes, about Tyler and his mate Hal.' He took another quick swig then set his glass reluctantly on the table. 'Those two, Tyler and Hal, they're as thick as thieves. In here with the rest of their Nazi chums every Friday. But sometimes they're here on other nights as well, just the two of them or sometimes with a couple of the others. Anyway, what was odd about that Friday you were asking about was that Tyler was here all right, but his second-in-command, Hal, wasn't. And, what's more, Tyler usually sits up the other end of the side room, but that night he made a point of sitting near the doorway, like he wanted to be seen. I'm telling you, it was proper suspicious.' He pushed himself up from the bench and stretched painfully before picking up his pint. 'You want to ask Hal where he was that Friday night,' he advised, then turned and shuffled back to the bar.

'That was interesting,' Lauren said. 'Hal. That's kind of an odd name, isn't it?'

'It's usually short for Henry,' Meg informed her, 'like Prince Hal in *Henry the Fourth, Part One*.'

'Isn't that a Shakespeare play?'

'Yes,' Meg smiled, the retired schoolteacher in her taking over. 'Falstaff refers to the young Prince Henry, later to become Henry the Fifth, as Prince Hal. It's often considered a derogatory nickname as Hal is portrayed as a bit of a wayward, rebellious young man who consorts with criminals.'

'Sounds appropriate for this mate of Tyler's then,' Lauren remarked.

Before Meg could reply, the landlord, Greg, arrived with their two ploughman's lunches. Lauren's eyes lit up at the plates packed full of chunks of cheddar and stilton, pickled onions, chutney, cherry tomatoes and sticks of celery with a huge hunk of crusty bread.

'Oh, my goodness, I'll never manage to eat all of that!' exclaimed Meg.

'It looks very good, though,' Lauren pointed out.

'Enjoy your meal,' said Greg, 'and if you can't eat it all, I can always pack up a doggy bag for you.' He hesitated. 'I hope old Jacob wasn't bothering you too much?' he asked.

'Not at all,' Meg reassured him, 'he was telling us about Tyler's friend Hal.' She repeated what they'd been told, and Greg confirmed that Hal hadn't been in that night. 'Now you come to mention it, that was a bit odd. Those two are always together.'

'Did you mention that to the police?' Meg asked.

'No, they weren't here that long. Came in, asked if Tyler was here that night, left again. Didn't even have the courtesy to buy a drink while they were here.' Greg shrugged his shoulders and walked away.

'That sounds more like a box-ticking exercise than a proper investigation,' grumbled Meg. 'Ideally, we need to talk to Hal next. I'm just not sure how we find him without a surname to help.'

✸

By the time she'd finished her ploughman's lunch, which was surprisingly fresh and tasty, Lauren had come up with an idea. First, she dropped Meg back at Britford Lodge, complete with doggy bag. Meg had been dropping heavy hints about needing an afternoon nap after such a big lunch, and that suited Lauren just fine.

Then she sent her friend Jed a text and arranged to meet him in the Starbucks on Southampton Road. Jed was a fitness trainer and vlogger who she'd known since they were at school together. He was one of the few who'd bothered to keep in touch after she dropped out just before her GCSE exams, when her father died.

Over coffee and cake, she swore him to secrecy and briefed him on the case. Together, they devised a plan for that evening. It would help that Jed was blond-haired and blue-eyed with a well-toned muscular body. He would have more luck infiltrating RAS successfully than she would, especially as Tyler had already met her in relation to the case. And she could hardly ask Meg or Albert or Viv, now, could she?

'Are you sure you don't mind me asking you?' Lauren asked, for the umpteenth time.

'Not at all. I told you, I'm happy to help. It sounds intriguing.'

'It could also be dangerous. These aren't nice people, Jed.'

'Yeah, so you told me. Listen, I can handle myself pretty well. I don't agree with their views, but I know the kind of people you're talking about, and I can put on a good act. It's like when I'm filming a vlog; it's all about being *that* person.'

'Drama GCSE?' asked Lauren with a grin, remembering one of the joint school productions they'd both had parts in.

'One of my two grade As,' smirked Jed. 'That and Sports Science. Old Hargreaves said on my final school report that I'd never amount to much, having such poor grades in all the academic subjects. How wrong was he?'

They both laughed. Jed was making a very good income, driving a top-end sporty Mazda and renting a luxury flat near the town centre.

Once Jed was fully briefed, and they'd caught up on some gossip, he took his leave and Lauren reluctantly drove home. She wished she could go with him to The Hanging Man, but it was too risky. If Tyler saw Jed with her, it would blow his cover. She just had to trust that he could pull this off on his own.

And, of course, it could all be a wasted effort as there was no guarantee that Tyler and Hal would even be at the pub that evening.

Chapter Twenty-one

When Lauren arrived home later that afternoon, she was surprised to find Viv there once again. 'I thought we were going to meet at the cinema later?' she commented after a lingering kiss in the living room whilst her mum was in the kitchen putting the kettle on.

'I thought it might be easier to talk here, before we go out,' he replied, looking serious. Lauren's heart sank to her stomach. Was Viv about to interfere in their case? The one he'd told her he couldn't be involved in?

'Okay,' she said, flopping onto the settee and patting the seat beside her for him to sit down. Bekka returned with their coffees and settled herself into the armchair opposite with her cup of tea.

'What have you been up to today?' Bekka asked, looking at her daughter.

'I'll tell you in a minute,' Lauren replied, 'but Viv says he wants to talk to me, and I'm curious to know what he's looking so serious about.'

'Oh, would you like me to make myself scarce?' Bekka looked at Viv enquiringly.

Viv hesitated. 'It's about the case,' he said awkwardly.

'Well, that's okay, you can talk in front of my mum,' Lauren said firmly.

'Look, I know that you don't understand this but, as policemen, it's drummed into us during training not to discuss cases with anyone outside the force. Even more so once you're in CID. I feel uncomfortable enough as it is sharing information with you, without involving your mum as well.'

'I'll go upstairs and read my book, don't worry about me,' Bekka said cheerfully, rising from her chair.

'No, Mum, sit down,' Lauren insisted. She turned to look

her boyfriend in the eyes. 'Listen, Viv. Mum and I are close, and we share everything. She's just asked me about my day, and everything I've done today relates to the case. And I'm going to share that with her whether you like it or not. You told me you couldn't be involved in this investigation, and I get that. I really do. But now you're saying you've got stuff to tell me about the case? I don't understand. Are you now getting involved?'

Viv looked taken aback at her outburst. 'Whoa, hold your horses a minute! Calm down, let's talk about this like two sensible adults.'

'Are you implying that I'm not?' snapped Lauren.

'Lauren, darling, take a deep breath,' advised Bekka, moving to sit next to her daughter and giving her shoulders a squeeze. 'I think Viv's trying really hard to compromise here, and you're making it a whole lot more difficult, going off the deep end at him.'

Lauren swallowed. The worst of it was, she knew her mum was right. She was jumping to conclusions without giving Viv a chance to speak.

'I'm sorry,' she muttered, looking at her feet.

'Hey, love, this is something you and Viv need to sort out between the two of you, and I think it's better if I don't get involved. You can tell me a bit about your day later, and I really don't need all the details. But, for now, I'm going to go upstairs with my cup of tea, and I'm going to start reading the new LJ Ross I've just bought.' She gave Lauren another hug and left the room.

There was a moment's silence and then Lauren spoke in a softer voice. 'If this relationship is going to work, we need to be able to tell each other everything. No secrets.' She looked up at Viv. 'I know the police keep some of the details of cases from the public, for lots of good reasons. But you can trust me not to blab. And Dan has already given Meg and me indirect permission to be involved in this case, in a roundabout sort of way. And you did say that you couldn't be involved because the case belongs to another team.'

Viv nodded thoughtfully. 'Yes, I did. But this case is exceptional, because of who the SIO is, and the fact that a child is missing, and because Dan has given you and Meg the green light, so to speak.'

'And just last night, we were sitting here chatting about the case with my mum,' Lauren pointed out.

'Yes, you're right. Perhaps I was being a bit oversensitive about her being here this afternoon. It's just … I'm not used to discussing cases outside of work. It feels wrong.'

'But you have something you want to tell me, and I have something I want to tell you. So, let's talk about the case, just the two of us. And when I talk to Mum later, if there are any specific details you really don't want me to tell her, I won't. But just don't ask me not to talk to her about it at all.'

'Fair enough.' Viv took a deep breath. 'You know that Dan and I are working on a complicated fraud case that's taken us weeks to unravel. We've got DC Moira Gordon working with us, plus two officers from the Regional Fraud Squad. All other personnel are currently working with DI Barnes on Noah's abduction. And that includes DC Aaron Johnson, who I play squash with.'

'I didn't know that,' interrupted Lauren.

'You know I play squash.' Viv looked puzzled.

'Yeah, but I didn't know that you played with DC Johnson.'

'Oh, right. Well, I do. And we were playing this morning before work, so I asked him how the search for baby Noah was going and how he thought the case was being handled. He told me that, initially, the search was well organised and in line with the correct protocols. Alerts in all the media, door-to-door enquiries, following up possible suspects, like Mia's ex-boyfriend, extensive searches of gardens, alleyways, wasteland, public spaces, etcetera. And there was nothing, no sign of Noah at all. But once the results started to come back from forensics, showing that there was no evidence of a break-in, and no unaccounted-for fingerprints, DI Barnes was convinced that either Mia or Vikram, or the two of them together, had to be involved. That's not an unreasonable line of enquiry,' he added hastily, seeing the look on Lauren's face, 'but Aaron said Barnes became focused on those two, to the exclusion of all other possibilities. Aaron was particularly concerned that some witness statements weren't being followed up on as thoroughly as they should have been.'

'Like the neighbour's, Harold Norman?' Lauren suggested.

'You know about him?' Viv sounded surprised. 'Well, yes, I think that was one of the witnesses Aaron mentioned.'

'Was the landlord of The Hanging Man another?'

'Yes, how the hell did you know that?'

'You forget, Meg and I have been investigating.'

'And I should know better than to underestimate the two of you!' Viv grinned ruefully. 'Go on, then, tell me what you know about those two witnesses.'

Lauren told them how they'd found out that nosy Norman was the witness who'd supposedly seen Vikram walking down the road with a black sports bag on the night of the abduction, and all about their visit to him. Viv agreed; as a witness statement, it was full of holes and inaccuracies.

Then Lauren told him about her and Meg's visit to The Hanging Man and their conversations with the landlord, Greg, and the customer, old Jacob. Viv shook his head in disbelief. 'To be honest, I thought Aaron was being a bit harsh on Billy Barnes, but it's even worse than I thought! I need to report this back to Aaron right away so that the team can follow up on this friend of Tyler's. What did you say his name was?'

'Hal.'

'Yes, Hal. And it sounds as though Tyler might have been deliberately setting himself up with an alibi for that night, which begs the question, why? That needs following up on too.'

Chapter Twenty-two

Lauren agreed, happy that they were on the same page now. She eagerly told Viv about her idea to get her friend Jed to infiltrate RAS to find out more about Tyler and Hal.

'You did what?' Viv exploded, looking at her incredulously.

'Well, I can't do it, seeing as I've already talked to Tyler ...'

'When? You never told me that!' Viv interrupted crossly.

Lauren remembered that she'd deliberately not mentioned Tyler to Viv before, so she sheepishly filled him in about their conversation at B&Q.

'And having seen what a nasty piece of work this Tyler is, you thought it would be a good idea to put yet another civilian in harm's way?'

'What's that supposed to mean?'

'Lauren, it's bad enough you and Meg taking risks. Dan only agreed to let you continue investigating discreetly on the condition that you report anything you find out back to the police and let them follow it up. This is exactly the kind of thing you should be letting the police handle.'

'And what if DI Barnes doesn't handle it?' argued Lauren. 'What if he ignores this in the same way he's ignoring the holes in nosy Norman's statement?'

'Lauren, it's one thing to put yourself in danger, not that I like that one little bit, but it's another thing altogether to get someone else involved! What if this RAS group suspects Jed of being a mole? Are you willing to be responsible if he comes to any harm?'

Lauren looked indignant. 'Hang on a minute, I think you're overreacting. Jed's well aware of what Tyler and his buddies are like. And he was more than happy to go undercover to see if he can find anything out for us. All he's going to do is ask a few questions and listen to what's being said among the group.'

'I can't believe you're being this irresponsible!' Viv looked at her thunderously.

'And I can't believe you're telling me what I can and can't do,' Lauren snapped back, 'again!'

'Please, just think about this,' Viv said, trying to reason with her. 'You're getting involved in a police case that's really none of your business ...'

'Oh, so now you're going to order me to stop investigating, I suppose!'

'No ... well, yes ... but only because I don't want to see you or your friends get hurt.'

'Well, I can't stop. I made a promise to Mia. And I told you; this relationship isn't going to work if you can't trust me.' She was fighting to hold back the tears.

'It's not a matter of trust ...'

'Isn't it?' Lauren stared at Viv. She couldn't believe that he was being like this. Try as she might, she failed to stop a few tears trickling down her cheeks.

'Lauren, I want you to phone Jed, right away,' Viv ordered, not heeding the warning signs. 'Tell him to leave this to the police.'

'And how are you going to do that? You've already told me that *you* can't get involved in another team's case. So, what happens? You tell Aaron? And he tells his DI, who's probably just going to ignore him anyway?'

'Now you're just being silly!'

'What the ...! You think I'm silly and childish and irresponsible, do you?'

'That's not what I said!' snapped Viv.

'Actually, yes, it is.' Lauren looked at him disbelievingly.

Viv looked fit to explode. 'I can't talk to you when you're being like this,' he said, shaking his head in frustration. He stood up.

'That's right; just walk out again,' challenged Lauren, wanting him to do anything other than that. Why couldn't he understand that she'd made a promise to Mia and would do everything in her power to find out what had happened to baby Noah?

'If that's what you want!' Viv choked out angrily. He glared at her for a moment then turned round and walked out of the house.

Lauren stared after him in horror, and then the dam burst.

✿

Meg had faced a similar, if less acrimonious, grilling from Albert when she'd returned to Britford Lodge earlier that afternoon. In his case, it wasn't that he disapproved of what Meg and Lauren were doing; it was that he felt left out.

'I don't know that I like the idea of you going into pubs on your own,' he insisted. 'It would have been much better if I could have been there to protect you.'

'I wasn't on my own,' Meg protested mildly. 'I was with Lauren.'

'All the same, it's not done for a couple of women to be in a pub without a man.'

'I think you're a bit behind the times, Albert. This is the twenty-first century. Women go to pubs on their own all the time.'

'Supposing this Tyler character had been there?' Albert challenged.

'Then we wouldn't have stayed,' said Meg, quite reasonably, 'but he wasn't, which means that we were able to confirm his alibi for the night Noah was taken.'

'That means he didn't do it, then?'

'Unfortunately, he couldn't have. But it did sound as though he was purposefully setting himself up with an alibi,' Meg said thoughtfully.

'What? What? Why would he do that?'

'He would have known he'd be the prime suspect, given that he's Noah's father and he failed to get custody. I think it's possible that he made sure he had a watertight alibi and arranged for one of his friends to abduct Noah for him.'

'Aha! This Hal person you mentioned?' put in Albert.

'Yes. Apparently, they're best friends and are nearly

always in the pub together. In which case, it seems odd that Hal wasn't there on the Friday night in question.'

'If this Hal kidnapped the baby for Tyler,' pondered Albert, 'then what has happened to the baby?'

'That's a good question. I can't believe that Tyler would hurt his own child. That means Noah must have been taken alive. But why didn't he cry? And where is he now?'

'Did the police go to Tyler's house?'

'Another good question. It's quite possible that once the police had confirmed his alibi at the pub, they didn't see any need to go to his home. But would Tyler really risk keeping his child at his own house? One of his neighbours might have reported it.'

'Does he live alone?'

'I have no idea.'

'Do you know where he lives?'

'No, I don't,' Meg said ruefully, beginning to realise just how little they knew. 'But maybe Lauren does.'

'Do you think it might be a good idea if we went to talk to his neighbours?' suggested Albert, keen to be involved.

'Perhaps,' said Meg, not wanting to commit herself.

'Or maybe you think Hal is keeping the baby?'

'That's another possibility,' agreed Meg. 'We need to find out where Tyler and Hal live and whether they live alone or not. I'll send Lauren a text message and ask her if she can find that out this evening, if she hasn't already thought of it herself. She was going to do some research this afternoon into RAS and Tyler and Hal, on the internet.'

'What's this RAS?' demanded Albert.

'Radical Action Salisbury,' explained Meg. 'It's an anti-immigrant racist group.'

'Why didn't they call it Racist Action Salisbury?' grumbled Albert. 'Tells you exactly what it's about, then.'

'Another good question,' sighed Meg, not bothering to explain to him that they wouldn't get away with using the word 'racist' in their title.

She began to wonder if they were really cut out to investigate a case outside of their own little care home bubble. It was all very well and good talking to people she knew and saw on a daily basis. But finding out about things the way Lauren did, on the internet … that was beyond her. As was all this gadding around, which had left her feeling quite tired. And how could she and Albert talk to people like Tyler and Hal? It just wouldn't be possible, would it?

'You're not thinking of giving up, are you, old gal?' asked Albert, reading her mind.

'No, of course not,' Meg replied, with a hint of doubt in her voice.

'I'm sure Sanjeev would understand if you couldn't do anything,' he offered helpfully. That reminded her why she and Lauren had agreed to do this in the first place. They had promised Sanjeev and Mia that they would investigate this case. And that's just what they were going to do!

Chapter Twenty-three

With fresh determination, Meg went to her room for her afternoon nap, as planned, but instead spent most of her time writing out a list of questions to which they needed answers. She also sent a text message to Lauren but was disappointed not to get a reply straight away.

When Meg still hadn't heard back from Lauren by the time she'd finished dinner, she decided to phone her friend.

'Hello, Meg,' Lauren said flatly.

'Whatever's the matter with you?' asked Meg, instantly worried.

Lauren told her about the argument she'd had with Viv, and Meg's heart went out to her.

'I'm so sorry to hear the two of you have fallen out,' she said gently. 'I understand why you're so keen to investigate, but I can also understand Viv's point of view. He's just trying to protect you.'

'Yes, I get that,' Lauren said, 'but I wish he would trust my judgement a bit more.'

'I can sympathise. But you have only been dating for a few months; it takes time to build trust in a relationship. Particularly when you consider that, to Viv, this is a job he's trained for. And he's not used to sharing work matters outside of the workplace.'

'Your second husband was a DCI, wasn't he?' Lauren enquired. 'Did you have the same problem with him? If you don't mind me asking.'

'I don't mind, and you're right, he was a DCI by the time he died from cancer. But when we first met, he was a DS – just like you and Viv – and he never talked about his work to me while we were dating. Of course, I was totally occupied with my teaching, and I wasn't trying to investigate anything myself, in the way that you are. But it wasn't until we were married that he began sharing things with me, and then that developed little by little, starting with things he thought I might be able to help with. In the end, I knew the details of most of his cases. But that's my point; it took years to build up that level of trust.'

Lauren conceded that Meg had a point.

'There was a reason for me calling you,' Meg reminded her. She explained what she wanted Lauren to research, and they arranged to meet the following morning, before her late shift.

Jed had just arrived at The Hanging Man and was pushing his way through to the bar. The place was rammed! There were two barmaids serving, but no sign of the barman Lauren had described. He had to shout to make his order heard over the noise of the karaoke and the babble of chatter. He took his pint and loitered near the bar, trying to suss out the people in the room to see if he could spot Tyler and his mates.

Someone was belting out a painful rendition of *I'm Holding Out for a Hero* when a barman pushed his way through a group of noisy thirty-somethings carrying a heavily laden crate of dirty glasses.

'Can I help you, mate?' Jed leapt forward and lifted the bar hatch at the man's nod.

'Thanks!' the man grunted, as he lugged the crate through to the kitchen behind the bar. Jed waited until he returned.

'Are you Greg?' The man nodded. 'I'm a friend of Lauren's. She was here earlier, asking about Tyler Ford.'

'Yeah, I remember her.'

'I was hoping to speak to either Tyler or Hal this evening. Are they in?'

'Not yet, mate,' Greg said, shaking his head. 'And if you know what's good for you, don't bother!' He moved away to serve another of his clamouring customers.

Jed shrugged his shoulders and ignored the barman's

advice. He worked his way slowly around the pub, sussing out the people there. They were an eclectic mix. The karaoke continued relentlessly in the side room, which was now incorporated into the bar thanks to one of those zig-zag walls you can open. Having established that none of the groups in the pub looked like potential neo-Nazi thugs, he found himself a spot from where he could watch both front and rear entrances.

Just after nine, a group of five lads came in from the car park side, and Jed's interest immediately went on high alert. They were all wearing jeans and Doc Martens, and some were skinheads. He watched as they approached the bar, happy to shove people out of their way if they didn't move quickly enough. They loudly ordered their drinks and as Greg was serving them, he looked across to Jed and gave a slight nod. This was Tyler and his gang!

Having got their drinks, they made their way back to the corner furthest from the karaoke. The couple sitting there took one look and hastily moved, freeing up a curved corner bench. With a bit more intimidation, a couple of chairs were added to the other side of the circular table and the group settled down.

Jed gradually worked his way across the pub, careful not to draw attention to himself. There was a partial screen giving this corner a little privacy, so Jed stood the other side of it and tried to listen in. He caught snatches of conversation between the karaoke acts, but it was impossible to hear anything when people were singing. Frustratingly, he could hear nothing of any use to Lauren's case.

Until a couple came in through the rear door on the other side of the corner table from Jed. The woman was pretty, with bouncy curls and a smattering of freckles across her pale cheeks. Her partner was of Afro-Caribbean descent. The atmosphere changed in a blink. The bloke Jed had decided was probably Tyler saw the couple first. He frowned and gave the others a nudge. They all stared and started muttering among themselves. Then one of them stood up and shouted out, 'We don't need scum like you in here,' and the others joined in with a chorus of racist slurs.

For a minute, Jed thought it was all going to kick off, but Greg rushed across and told the group to shut it or he'd ban them. The couple quickly moved away into the side room, and Tyler and his mates reluctantly sat down.

Jed tried in vain to listen to their animated conversation; the snippets he could catch now a completely different tone to before. Eventually, one of them stood up and made his way to the gents' and Jed saw an opportunity.

He sauntered across to the group and asked if the empty chair was free. Their responses were downright rude and mostly unrepeatable, but Jed persisted. 'Look, I was over the other side just enjoying a pint or three, but this couple came in and it quite spoiled the view, if you understand what I mean.'

Tyler looked at him suspiciously before nodding to the three on the bench seat. 'The chair's taken, mate,' he explained, 'but you can squeeze in there if you want.'

The three reluctantly slid across, and Jed set his pint on the table and joined them.

From then on, it was just a case of listening in, saying as little as possible and trying to blend in when he did speak.

Chapter Twenty-four

Meg and Albert ate a light breakfast that Sunday morning before strolling down to the farm shop café. The weather was a little cooler, with high clouds obscuring the sun periodically but, when they parted, the sun was pleasantly warm. When they arrived in the farmyard, they were disappointed not to see Lauren's car among the few already parked. But Meg looked suspiciously at a sporty red Mazda, thinking that she'd seen it before.

When they entered the café, Lauren was sitting at their favourite table with a young man of similar age. He was quite tall with neatly cut blond hair and well-developed muscles visible beneath his tight-fitting T-shirt.

Lauren beckoned them over, saying, 'Meg, Albert, this is my friend Jed.'

'Ah, you're the one with the bright red sports car, aren't you?' replied Meg, remembering him dropping Lauren off on a previous occasion. He nodded. 'It's good to see that you're still in one piece,' she smiled.

'Pardon?' Jed looked baffled.

'Lauren told me that you were going to The Hanging Man last night,' Meg explained. 'Although, perhaps Tyler and Hal weren't there?'

'Oh, they were there,' Jed informed her. 'I'll tell you about it in a minute. Why don't you two sit down and get comfortable, and I'll go and order for us all.'

'That's jolly decent of you,' said Albert, shaking hands with Jed before sitting down. 'I'll have a milky coffee with two sugars, please.'

'A pot of tea for me, please,' added Meg, sitting between Albert and Lauren. Jed moved away, presumably already knowing Lauren's order.

'Is this a new boyfriend?' Albert demanded, eyeing Lauren suspiciously.

'No, he's just a friend.' She explained how she'd met Jed and what a good friend he'd been over the years they'd known each other.

'Jolly good show,' said Albert. 'I take it you're still dating that detective sergeant, then?'

'Umm, well ...' began Lauren awkwardly.

'Have you been able to do that research I suggested?' Meg hastily interrupted, saving her from having to answer.

'Yes, I've got most of what you asked for,' Lauren replied gratefully, 'but let's wait for Jed to get back first.' She got her notebook out of her bag and opened it up ready while Meg slipped off her cardigan and draped it over the back of her chair.

'Right, I've ordered our drinks and some of their homemade cookies,' Jed said as he hurriedly slipped into the remaining empty seat. 'What have I missed?'

'Nothing,' replied Lauren. 'We didn't want to start without you.'

'Great. Shall I go first?'

Meg and Albert agreed, and Lauren signalled for him to carry on.

'Right. Well, I went to The Hanging Man last night, got there about half eight-ish. It was certainly a lot busier than when you went, Lauren.'

Jed described the scene in great detail, and Meg was beginning to wonder if he was ever going to get to the point. But she let him continue without interruption as she didn't want to undermine his confidence. When he finally revealed that Tyler and his mates weren't in the pub, Albert couldn't hold back.

'You didn't see them, then?' he asked irritably.

'Yeah, but not until a bit later,' replied Jed.

'Well, stop waffling and get on with it,' grumbled Albert. Meg cast him a warning glance, but Jed didn't seem at all perturbed as he carried on with his account.

'So, who was with Tyler?' interrupted Albert again, when Jed had described joining them at their table.

Before Jed could reply, the waitress arrived with their drinks and a stack of four plates with cookies on top.

'Okay, I got four different cookies, not knowing what you all like,' Jed said, pointing to each of them. 'There's chocolate chip; white chocolate and macadamia; raisin and almond, and Smarties. Ladies first, Meg?'

Meg took the raisin and almond cookie and thanked Jed. Albert took the chocolate chip and Lauren the Smarties cookie. Jed grinned. 'I knew you'd go for that one.'

'And I knew you wanted the macadamia one,' retorted Lauren.

There was a short silence as they each took a bite of their cookie, and Meg poured her tea before it got too strong.

'Back to your question,' said Jed, setting his cookie down so that he could continue his tale. 'The other men with Tyler were his mates Hal, Mark, Gary and Liam. They're all members of RAS.'

'That's great!' exclaimed Lauren. 'Tell us about Hal.'

'He's tall and kind of lanky with short blond hair. Arms covered in tattoos, including a swastika on his left forearm. Nasty piece of work, if you ask me.'

'Did you get a full name?' Lauren asked hopefully.

'Hal Winters.'

'Good, now I should be able to get some background on him,' she declared, immediately tapping away on her notebook.

Jed continued with his story. 'We chatted on and off for about an hour; sometimes, the music was too loud to talk over. Then I said that I had to go – I didn't want to stay too long and push my luck – but I told them I was interested in joining their group. Hal invited me along to their meeting next Friday, and then Tyler said he had some pamphlets at home if I wanted to call round sometime in the week.'

'That's great news,' said Meg.

'But what about the case?' grumbled Albert. 'Did you find out if any of these louts was responsible for kidnapping the baby or not?'

'One thing at a time,' cautioned Meg.

'He could hardly dive straight in with questions, now, could he?' added Lauren.

'No, I suppose not,' Albert said sulkily before taking a sip of his coffee.

'I did what Lauren suggested I do; try and get to know these guys a bit and work my way into their group,' Jed explained to Albert. 'She said not to ask any questions on my first time meeting them, as it would've looked too suspicious.'

'Do you think Tyler could've put one of these others up to taking Noah?' Meg asked.

'I don't know,' Jed said slowly. 'Liam asked if he'd heard any more about his son, and Tyler seemed really cut up. Either he's a very good actor or he's genuinely upset. But something was slightly off about their conversation.'

'Sounds like a complete waste of time to me. You've got nothing,' Albert muttered darkly.

'Not at all,' Meg rebuked him. 'This is a case of softly, softly, catchee monkey. I'm afraid it's going to take time.'

'Harrumph!' snorted Albert. 'Go on then, what are we going to do next?'

'We are going to listen to anything else Jed has to say,' replied Meg firmly. 'Then we'll hear about the research that Lauren has done, and then we'll formulate a plan. But that won't include you, if you're going to keep interrupting and being so negative.'

Albert looked a bit sheepish as he mimed zipping his mouth shut. Lauren suppressed a giggle as she caught Jed's raised eyebrow.

'Was there anything else?' Meg asked Jed.

'Actually, yeah. While Liam and Tyler were talking about Noah, I noticed the oddest of expressions on Hal's face. I can't really explain it …It was just… like… he knew something that they didn't.'

'Do you think Hal could have abducted Noah?' asked Meg curiously.

Jed shrugged. 'I don't know; it was just an impression I got. I could've been wrong.'

'I think that leads us nicely into asking Lauren what she's found out about Tyler and this group of his,' suggested Meg.

Chapter Twenty-five

Lauren started off in her usual businesslike way, referring to the notes she'd made on her notebook. 'Right. Tyler Ford is twenty-nine years old and lives in a flat off Westwood Road, up on Bemerton Heath.'

'That tallies with the address he gave me,' added Jed.

'He's been there for nearly six years, and has lived alone since Mia left, so far as I can make out,' Lauren continued. 'Before that, he lived with his parents and one brother in Amesbury, which is where he went to school. As you know, he works full time at the B&Q on Southampton Road, where he's been for six years, so that was probably the reason for him moving to Salisbury. Now, here's where it gets interesting. According to his social media, he became a member of National Action, a far-right extremist group, in 2014, after becoming online friends with one of its co-founders, a Ben Rogers of Swindon. From what I could find out online, National Action is a "self-proclaimed unapologetically racist organisation" founded in 2013 that promotes ethnic cleansing, as well as attacks on LGBTQ people and liberals. The government used terror legislation to ban it in 2016, but members continued to meet in secret and on online forums.'

'Couldn't the police do something about them, if they're members of a banned organisation?' grumbled Albert.

'Yeah, I'm sure they would if they could prove anything against them. In fact, Ben Rogers was convicted of terror charges in 2021, and he wasn't the only one. A police raid discovered a cache of weapons including rifles, a machete, a crossbow and CS gas.'

'Really not a group you want to mess with, then,' said Meg sombrely, wondering if perhaps they were making a mistake in asking Jed to get involved.

'No,' agreed Lauren, 'but I did warn Jed what he was getting into, in case you're wondering.' Meg smiled ruefully, thinking that Lauren could read her mind.

'Anyway, after Rogers was arrested, it appears that Tyler stepped back from NA and founded his own group, Radical Action Salisbury. Because it has a different name, and it's not affiliated with National Action, it's not specifically banned – yet – although I suspect that's a bit of a legal grey area.'

'Yes, I'm sure it is,' Meg said, nodding. 'But it seems that Tyler is quite clever. In distancing himself from the national group, he's making it harder for the police to prove that he has any involvement in their activities.'

'Exactly. Anyway, it seems RAS is more anti-immigration than anything else, whereas Rogers was an avid fan of Hitler: against blacks, Jews, gays; in fact, anyone who wasn't straight, white and Aryan.'

'Bloomin' hell!' exploded Albert, the reference to Hitler like a red rag to a bull. 'Didn't the Second World War teach anybody anything?'

'I'm sure it did,' Meg replied mildly, 'but unfortunately, there will always be extremists.'

'If I may continue?' asked Lauren, looking at Albert. 'So far as I could see, in the two years since RAS was formed, it's grown to about twenty members. They join in protests, distribute leaflets, and several of its members have been prosecuted for attacking people from ethnic minorities. But it seems Tyler is too wily to ever get caught.'

'And Mia actually dated this man?' Meg shook her head in wonder.

'Yeah, for about eighteen months. For twelve of those, she lived with him in his flat, but she went back to her parents' about a year ago, according to what she told us.'

'Good thing too,' remarked Albert, getting an approving nod from Meg.

'Too true,' agreed Lauren. 'And, unfortunately, he is Noah's biological father. But we know that Mia was granted sole custody after they split, due to his violent tendencies.'

'What about Hal?' Meg asked. 'I don't suppose you've got anything on him?'

'Yes, Hal,' said Lauren, checking her hastily compiled notes, mostly gleaned from his Facebook profile. 'Henry Winters is twenty-eight years old, born in Salisbury, lives with his parents on Devizes Road. He works at that tyre and exhaust place on the Churchfields estate. He went to Salisbury High School, as it was when he started there. He was also a member of National Action and moved to RAS when it was formed, and he appears to be second-in-command. Tyler and Hal have been friends on Facebook since 2015 although neither of them posts much on that platform these days. But there's a lot on Instagram and they appear to be best mates.'

'Thank you, Lauren,' Meg said appreciatively. 'Jed, you said that Tyler invited you to go to his flat. Did you arrange when?'

'Yes. Tyler's working today but he's got a day off tomorrow, so I said I'd pop round during my lunch break,' Jed replied earnestly.

'Good, try to find out a bit more about the group, but don't push the questions about Noah unless he brings the subject up first. We don't want to make him suspicious.'

'Understood. And I'll have as much of a look round as I can, in case there's any sign of Noah there. But I don't think he'd be stupid enough to try to hide a baby in a block of flats. It's not as though you can keep a baby quiet, is it?'

'No, I agree. If someone took Noah on Tyler's behalf, they could be hiding him somewhere else. By all means, have a look for clues, but don't put yourself in danger.'

'Got it.'

'What can I do?' asked Lauren, a little put out that all the attention was on Jed.

'I have an idea for you,' said Meg, 'which will involve a little role play, if you're up for it?'

Lauren eagerly agreed and Meg explained what she had in mind.

'Don't suppose you need my help, old gal?' Albert put in hopefully.

'I'm sorry,' Meg put a conciliatory hand on Albert's arm, 'I rather think this is a case for the younger ones, for the time being. Neither you nor I can go gadding about all over Salisbury, and we're hardly likely to blend in with the kind of people involved in this. But we will keep in close touch with Lauren and Jed, so that we can put our brains to good use. We have a lot more time for thinking things through.'

'Ah, good idea, m'dear. Lauren and Jed can gather the intel. We'll analyse it and develop the strategy moving forwards.'

'Something like that,' agreed Meg.

The conversation then turned to other things, with Jed trying to explain to Meg and Albert exactly what a vlogger was. When they'd finished their drinks and cookies, Meg and Albert excused themselves and wandered slowly back up the hill to Britford Lodge.

Chapter Twenty-six

Monday 26th June 2023

Lauren was working an early shift that Monday and time seemed to drag. Bossy Barclay was in charge, so she and Stef kept out of her way as much as possible. Twenty-six-year-old Stefania Popescu was a Romanian carer who had recently got engaged to her twenty-five-year-old compatriot and co-worker Florin. Whilst the two women worked, stripping and making beds on the first floor, Stef talked non-stop about wedding plans back home in Romania, but Lauren only listened with half an ear. She was more concerned with how despondent Mia had been the previous evening when they'd spoken on the phone.

It was now twenty-three days since baby Noah had been taken in the middle of the night, and Mia had heard nothing from the police in over a week. 'It's like they've given up on him,' she had sobbed. Lauren felt helpless. It was going to take time to get Jed into RAS and, even then, there were no guarantees that he'd be able to find out anything useful. They were pinning all their hopes on that one line of enquiry: what if they were wrong, and neither Tyler nor Hal had anything to do with Noah's abduction?

She was on edge all morning, knowing that Jed was planning to call on Tyler during his lunch break.

❁

Jed parked his mum's old Fiat close to the block of flats where Tyler Ford lived. He hadn't wanted to risk taking his expensive Mazda there. Although, to be fair, the area didn't look quite as rough as he was expecting. The block was one of three overlooking a wide expanse of grass, and there were several mature horse chestnut trees around.

He found the flat and knocked on Tyler's door. A very sleepy-looking Tyler eased it open, still dressed in shorts and T-shirt-style pyjamas.

'Ah, come in, mate,' he muttered, rubbing his eyes.

Jed apologised for getting him out of bed before following him down a narrow corridor to a living room at the far end of the flat.

'You want a coffee?' Tyler offered. Jed accepted and Tyler disappeared into the kitchen next door. There were sounds of a kettle being filled, and then Tyler reappeared briefly before disappearing into a bedroom back down the corridor. 'Make yourself comfortable,' he called out, 'I'll just grab some clothes.'

Jed took the opportunity to have a thorough look around. The living room was L-shaped, with a huge corner sofa completely filling one end of the room, a large modern desk under the window at the opposite end and an old pine dining-room table and chairs in the smaller side of the L. There were piles of paper and pamphlets everywhere and a huge printer on top of the desk, which was probably where Tyler printed them. He could still see a feminine influence in the decor – no doubt Mia's – from the chintz curtains to the scatter cushions on the sofa and a couple of cute prints of cats hanging on the walls. But the only sign of Noah was a large framed photo of a newborn baby on one wall and a couple of photos in frames on the bookcase. Just Noah on his own; none of his mother. There was nothing else; no baby clothes, toys, bottles or anything like that.

Jed heard Tyler returning from the bedroom to the kitchen and the chink of mugs. He positioned himself so that he was standing in front of the large portrait of Noah when Tyler returned, now wearing jeans and a white T-shirt.

Tyler handed Jed his coffee. 'That's my son,' he said, seeing Jed's questioning look.

'Didn't know you were married, mate!' Jed feigned ignorance of the situation.

'I'm not!' grimaced Tyler. He indicated for Jed to sit down and settled himself on the opposite end of the sofa before telling him a little about Mia and Noah – or, at least, his version of it. This was liberally laced with Tyler's opinions about Mia leaving and taking his child with her. But when Tyler spoke about his son, his voice became choked with emotion, and it was clear to Jed that this guy was genuinely cut up about his abduction.

'That's bad,' Jed sympathised, 'and you've no idea where he is?'

Tyler appeared to be telling the truth when he said no.

'And what about your ex?' Jed asked, keeping an eye on Tyler's face. His reply was a lengthy tirade about how Mia had shacked up with an immigrant, the racist slurs and bad language making Jed feel distinctly uncomfortable. But he couldn't help thinking that Tyler was not telling the truth when he said that Vikram had taken his son. And, interestingly, he'd said *taken* and not *murdered*. Did that mean that Tyler knew that his son was still alive? What's more, Tyler's emotions were all over the place. One minute he was effing and blinding about Mia and Vikram, the next he was choking back tears as he wailed that he didn't know if he'd ever see his son again. Jed was confused; it didn't make sense.

After a couple of moments' silence, Tyler pulled himself together and went to get some pamphlets, which he handed to Jed before starting to talk about RAS. Jed put up with the recruitment spiel, nodding and muttering his agreement at all the appropriate places, but he couldn't wait to get away from the repugnant views Tyler was propounding. It made Jed feel sick to his stomach.

❖

It was well after lunch before Lauren finally felt a ping in her pocket. She surreptitiously glanced at her phone and was relieved to see that it was from Jed.

Been to Tyler's – call me when u can

Hastily, she excused herself and went to the staff toilets. After checking that no one was in any of the cubicles, she pulled out her phone and called him.

'Hiya, mate,' Jed answered.

'How did it go?' she demanded.

'Well, I got to Tyler's flat just after one o'clock to find Tyler still in his pyjamas! I'd say he only got out of bed to answer my knock.'

'It is his day off,' Lauren pointed out.

'Yeah, anyway, it meant that I had a chance to have a good look around while he was getting dressed.'

Jed told her everything that he'd seen and heard, glossing over the foul language and sick ideology. When he mentioned Tyler's raw emotion concerning his son's abduction, Lauren gasped. 'That kind of contradicts everything we thought we knew,' she said.

'I'm telling you, either that guy is an Oscar-winning actor, or he genuinely didn't know where his son is,' Jed replied. Lauren asked Jed some more questions, but neither of them could work out what on earth was going on.

'Listen, Jed, I can't tell you how grateful I am to you for doing this. You've given us a lot to work with, so if you feel you want to call it a day, that's fine.'

'Lauren, have I ever broken a promise to you?'

'Never.'

'Exactly! And I'm not going to start now. I promised to infiltrate RAS for you to find out whatever I can, and I'm well up for it. I'm going to their meeting on Friday, and I'll be keeping my eyes and ears wide open. It looks like Tyler doesn't have Noah, but I've got a hunch that one of the others might know something. Either Hal, or Liam, is my bet.'

'That's great news. Thank you so much. Jed. You really are a star!'

'I know! And best of all? You're going to owe me one now!'

Lauren could hear the grin in his voice, and chuckled.

Chapter Twenty-seven

After she'd said goodbye and ended the call, Lauren went in search of Meg. She found her sitting in the conservatory near the open patio doors, playing rummy with Albert.

'What? What?' spluttered Albert, on seeing her approach.

'You've got news?' guessed Meg, looking at the expression on Lauren's face.

Lauren sat down and quickly told them everything that Jed had said. 'You see, it's got me really puzzled. We know that Tyler had a very strong motive to take his son, and he was as fishy as anything talking to me. And Mia, her parents and her boss all thought he was the prime suspect. Except … he has a watertight alibi, so he can't have done it. We then suspected that Tyler must have set up his alibi while Hal did the deed for him. But now, according to Jed, Tyler seems to be quite genuinely afraid that he'll never see Noah again. It doesn't make any sense.'

'Then we'll just have to unpick all those threads,' replied Meg.

'What d'you mean, old gal?' asked Albert.

'Well, let's consider the options. A: Tyler took Noah from Mia's house and someone else is looking after him until the heat dies down. In which case, how did Tyler fake his alibi so convincingly? And where is Noah now? Maybe Hal is in on this or one of his other cronies.

'Option B: Tyler set up his alibi so that someone else could abduct Noah for him, and either Tyler or that person has him hidden away somewhere. Was that Hal or one of the others? And again, where is Noah? And is there a reason why Tyler thinks he might not see his son again? Perhaps something unforeseen happened during the abduction and Noah died.'

'I hope you're wrong about that,' Lauren said with feeling.

'Me too! I'm just going through the options, my dear, as logically as I can. Now, where was I? Yes, option C: Vikram abducted Noah …'

'No!' cried out Lauren indignantly.

'We have to consider the option,' Meg said firmly, 'until we have proof to the contrary. If Vikram took Noah, did he kill him or take him somewhere? That, of course, begs the question, why?'

'Exactly! Vikram doesn't have a motive,' said Lauren.

'That we know of,' replied Meg. 'There is also an option D, I'm afraid. Someone else altogether took Noah and we have no idea who, or why, and whether Noah is dead or alive.'

'It doesn't look like you've got very far with this investigation, does it?' chipped in Albert unhelpfully.

'On the contrary,' replied Meg, 'we're making progress. It's a case of gathering all the information at this stage and, given the circumstances, that could take time.' She sighed. 'Time that Noah might not have. Hopefully, Lauren will be able to tell us more tomorrow, after her undercover work this afternoon.'

'Oh, what's that?' asked Albert.

Meg had just started filling him in when Lauren exclaimed, 'Uh-oh!' and ducked down. 'Bossy Barclay's heading this way, and I think she's on the warpath,' she whispered. She slipped out of her seat, snuck around the back of Albert's chair and dashed out through the patio doors. By the time Sue Barclay reached Meg and Albert, Lauren was nowhere to be seen, and they, of course, said that they hadn't seen her.

🌣

Time seemed to crawl slowly during the rest of the afternoon, but eventually three-thirty arrived and Sue Barclay indicated that Lauren could go home. She all but raced to the staff changing room. Instead of her usual jeans or cropped leggings and a T-shirt, she donned a pretty summer dress in kingfisher blue, which she'd borrowed from her mum. To that she added strappy white sandals, again borrowed, before applying a little make-up. On her way to the car park, she passed Stef, who did a double take.

'Is that you, Lauren? I hardly recognised you!'

Lauren was chuffed, because that was the whole point, but she simply explained it away to Stef by saying that she was going on a special date.

Once in her car, she pulled on a long bottle-blonde wig, which her mother had bought for a friend's hen weekend a few years ago. She checked herself in her rear mirror – the transformation was complete. Not even Viv would recognise her now! With that thought, her spirits fell. She had no idea how things stood between them, but she hoped she hadn't completely blown her chance with him. Perhaps she'd phone him later.

She drove across Salisbury to Bemerton Heath and pulled up outside the block of flats where Tyler lived. Although this part of her task seemed slightly redundant after Jed's revelations, she was determined to be thorough. She transferred her purse and phone into a small cross-body shoulder bag, picked up her clipboard and set off.

She went straight to Tyler's block and knocked or rang the bell for all the other flats. At each, she posed as an employee of the council's housing department, saying that they had received complaints of a recent daytime noise nuisance and were asking residents for their comments, in complete confidence. Not everyone was in, but of those who did answer their doors, not one mentioned hearing a baby crying. In fact, most people were surprised to learn there had been a complaint, saying that the flats were normally quite quiet during the day.

'It's the evenings we get problems, love,' said one woman. 'Come round here about bedtime and you'd understand there being a noise complaint. But these flats are as quiet as a church in the daytime.'

Returning to her car, Lauren felt satisfied that Tyler could not have brought a baby to his flat, although that didn't mean he couldn't have taken Noah somewhere else. She wondered if perhaps they should consider Tyler's parents and made a mental note to suggest that to Meg.

Next, she drove to Devizes Road, parking slightly downhill from Hal's family home. Because these were sizable semi-detached houses, she used a different ruse this time, posing as an employee from the planning department. At each house, she conducted a short survey she'd prepared in advance about which local services were used by each of the occupants. In this case, it was only Hal's house that she was interested in, but she started with his immediate neighbours, to maintain her cover.

At Hal's house, she held her breath. Would someone be in?

The door was answered by a woman in her early fifties wearing smart cropped white trousers with a peach-coloured T-shirt that shouted M&S at you. She had brown hair in a short bob tucked behind her ears and wore glasses.

'Yes?' She looked at Lauren with a puzzled expression. 'If you're selling something, we're not interested.'

Lauren explained the purpose of her visit and the woman agreed to participate, saying, 'It's about time the council did something to improve services in this area.'

She introduced herself as Audrey Winters and confirmed that three adults lived at the property: herself (female, 50–60), her husband, Gerald (male, 50–60) and their son, Henry (male, 20–30). She mentioned that she also had a daughter, Amelia, who didn't live at home, and a grandson, which was news to Lauren.

'That's lovely,' she enthused, 'your first grandchild. How old is he?'

'He must be about fourteen or fifteen months old by now,' Audrey replied wistfully.

'Do they visit you regularly?' Lauren asked.

'Sadly, no, we haven't seen our grandson in nearly a year.' Her lips pursed tightly shut, and an air of sadness passed across her face.

Lauren quickly moved on to the next question, ticking boxes about which members of the household used various services such as local buses, the leisure centre and childcare facilities. She finished the survey and thanked Audrey before turning to descend the short flight of stone steps to the pavement. She was just about to let herself out through the low cast iron gate, when a beanpole of a young man with bleached-blond hair turned to enter it. Lauren felt her breath catch in her throat, realising that this was probably Hal. He was wearing steel toe-capped work boots and dirty blue overalls with the sleeves pushed up, revealing heavily tattooed arms. She noticed the swastika that Jed had mentioned and felt a slight shiver run down her spine.

Chapter Twenty-eight

Hal looked Lauren lasciviously up and down. 'Who are you?' he challenged.

'I'm from the council.' She explained about the survey that his mother had just finished helping her with.

'Oh yeah, where's your ID, then?' He looked at his mother, who was still standing on the doorstep. 'I hope you checked her ID before answering any questions?'

Audrey's demeanour suddenly changed. No longer the confident woman who'd answered Lauren's questions in such a polite and friendly way, she crumpled into a nervous wreck.

'Umm, well … actually, I-I never asked about ID,' she stuttered. 'She said she's from the council's planning department—'

'Oh God, you're flippin' useless, as always,' Hal spat out angrily. 'She could be anyone, for all you'd know. I hope you didn't give her any personal information.'

Before his mother could reply, he rounded on Lauren, who was trying to sneak out of the gate as unobtrusively as possible.

'ID, now,' he snapped at her.

'My lanyard broke earlier, so I left it in the car.' Lauren tried her best to sound cool, calm and collected, although she felt none of those things, and her heart was thumping in her chest.

'Get it,' he snarled.

Lauren was beginning to fear that he would follow her to the car and was trying to work out what she'd do then, when a dark blue BMW X3 pulled up at the kerb, and an absolute giant of a man got out. He was almost as broad as he was tall, dressed in dark grey chinos and a white short-sleeved shirt, open at the neck.

'Hal, what are you doing home already?' he demanded in a no-nonsense voice. 'And you can stop gawking like a fishwife. Get back inside the house!' he barked on seeing his wife.

Lauren took the opportunity to slip out through the gate, praying it wouldn't creak, and headed for her car as quickly as she could while Hal was distracted answering his father. Only once she had pulled away did she dare breathe a sigh of relief. Phew, that was a narrow escape!

She drove to her third destination for the day, Birch Close, where Mia lived in Laverstock. She drove past nosy Norman's house, deliberately turning her head away in case he was curtain-twitching as usual, and parked just out of sight around the corner, near Mia's. Hoping that no one here would ask for her ID, she started ringing on doorbells. This time, she posed as a civilian investigator, working with the police. She explained that she was just revisiting everyone who had given a statement regarding the child abduction at number twenty-five, on the off-chance that they had thought of something else since being interviewed. To her amazement, not one person questioned her credentials, and she discovered two houses where the residents had never given a statement to the police in the first place. Talk about sloppy police work! Even she knew enough to know that someone from uniform should have gone back to anyone not at home on the first canvas.

At thirty-one Birch Close, three doors down from Mia, a young woman in her thirties opened the door. She looked a bit frazzled, with two young boys hanging around her legs and a baby crying in the background. In answer to Lauren's question, she said that they'd been away the weekend Noah had been abducted.

'My husband had a couple of days off work tagged either side of the weekend, so we went down to Devon to visit my parents. I couldn't believe it when we got back, and I heard about that poor little lad being taken. I can tell you; we've been so careful about locking up at night, and we've not left the kids in the garden without one of us being with them, since then. I dread to think what that poor woman is going through, not that I know her 'cos they haven't lived here for long, but even so.'

'May I come in, to ask you a few questions?' Lauren managed to say when the woman paused to take a breath.

'Yes, of course, but you'll have to excuse the mess. Kyle's working extra hours and I just can't seem to keep on top of everything, what with three kids under five to look after.'

Lauren followed her through a relatively tidy hallway, apart from a muddle of shoes piled on the carpet beneath some overladen coat hooks, into a lounge that resembled a war zone. Toys, books, heaps of laundry waiting to be washed or ironed, dirty crockery and opened letters seemed to cover every available surface. The woman picked up a pile of letters, paperwork and kids' storybooks from a mustard-coloured armchair and moved it onto a similar stack already on the dining-room table. She indicated for Lauren to sit down.

'I know you said you weren't here the weekend that the incident occurred,' Lauren began gently. The woman picked up the still-whimpering baby, a girl if its pink babygro was any indicator, and bounced her up and down over her shoulder. 'But can you tell me if you noticed anyone suspicious hanging around in the days before the third of June?'

'It's funny you should ask that,' the woman said, her baby now snuggled quietly into her shoulder. 'I said to Kyle, we ought to tell the police about that strange couple I saw. But he said they were probably just visiting one of our other neighbours, and we shouldn't get involved.'

'When was this?' Lauren asked.

'It was the Friday morning, as we were loading up the car and getting ready to go away.'

'The second of June?' Lauren clarified.

'Yeah, that's right. The bloke was probably about my age, late twenties, and he was tall and skinny with bleached hair.'

Lauren's ears pricked up; that sounded an awful lot like Hal Winters.

'The woman was younger, maybe early twenties, with long blonde hair. She looked kind of down and out, if you know what I mean, and tired, like she'd been ill or something. Anyway, they were just walking along the pavement, kind of slow, and they were looking at every house, but they stopped outside number twenty-five for ages. He lit up a cigarette and just stared at the house and she kept looking around, as though trying to see if anyone was watching them. I don't think she saw me 'cos I was sorting out the kids' car seats through the door on the opposite side of the car from them. I particularly noticed them because they looked so secretive. Of course, Kyle just says I'm imagining it after the event, once I knew that baby had been kidnapped. But honestly, I know what I saw.'

'Is there anything else you can add to their descriptions?' Lauren asked hopefully.

'He had tattoos covering both arms, I remember that. And she was wearing baggy clothes, like she'd lost a lot of weight. And their faces were kind of similar, like they might have been brother and sister.'

Lauren pricked up her ears; could Hal have been working with his sister? She took some further details and reassured her that she'd been very helpful. Now, she felt like she was making progress.

'Will the police come back and want a formal statement?' the young woman, who'd given her name as Molly, asked a little nervously.

'Possibly,' Lauren said cautiously, 'but only if they're likely to need it properly recorded for a court case, so they might not come back if it turns out not to be relevant.' She sensed that Molly was wary of making a formal statement and, in any case, she couldn't guarantee that DI Barnes would take any notice of her research.

Chapter Twenty-nine

At twenty-six Birch Close, a house on the inside curve of the road almost opposite Molly's, a young man answered the door in shorts and bare feet. Lauren explained who she was, and he looked taken aback. 'Crikey, I thought you lot weren't going to bother,' he said.

Lauren asked what he meant.

'I work shifts, and I was asleep the first time someone called. My girlfriend answered the door and spoke to a couple of coppers, not that she could tell them anything. But she told them I might have seen something, as I was on earlies that week. You see, my early shift starts at 2am at Southampton Docks. Anyway, the coppers that spoke to her said they'd be back to take my statement, but they haven't been yet.'

'Do you mind if I come in and ask you some informal questions?' Lauren asked, trying not to sound too eager.

'Knock yourself out.' He turned and led the way into a small but relatively tidy living room. Lauren took a seat on a black leather two-seater sofa.

'Can I get you a coffee or a glass of Coke or something?' he asked.

'I'd love a Coke, please.' Lauren looked around the room with interest whilst she waited for him to return from the small kitchen off to one side of the living room. This house was smaller than Mia's and furnished almost entirely with modern black furniture against stark white walls, with some abstract prints adding splashes of bold colour.

'Here you go.' He passed a glass to her and sat himself in the single black leather armchair.

'And you are?' Lauren asked, after she'd taken a long drink and set her glass down on the small black coffee table.

'Sam,' he said. 'Sam Wallace. I live with my girlfriend, Jenny Harris. Like I said, she's already given a statement, but she didn't know then that I'd seen anything.'

'And what did you see?'

'I was getting dressed for work, just after one o'clock in the morning, I guess. I heard a car pull up outside, which is unusual in this neighbourhood at that time of night, so I looked out of the window. I saw a bloke get out of the passenger seat and then the car moved on round the road. This road loops back on itself so most people drive round to get out again rather than trying to turn. Anyway, this bloke or, at least, I assume it was a bloke from his height, walked back up the road to number twenty-five and let himself in the front door with a key. I thought it was a bit odd that the car didn't drop him right outside his door, instead of three doors along. But it could just be that the driver didn't know exactly where the bloke lived and overshot the house.'

'But you definitely saw him go to number twenty-five?' Lauren checked.

'Yes, definitely. Look, you can come upstairs and see for yourself, if you want to.' He got up and Lauren followed him as he sprinted up a narrow staircase and into the one and only bedroom at the front of the house. Sure enough, you could see Mia's house quite clearly from his window.

'But wouldn't it have been dark at that time of the night?' she asked.

'Not that night, it wasn't,' Sam replied. 'It was a full moon and the footpath up to the front door of number twenty-five was lit up as good as if the streetlights were on.'

Lauren mentally kicked herself. She and Meg had considered whether the streetlights would have been on or off but hadn't once thought about the moon. If it had been a clear night with a full moon, perhaps that lent more credence to nosy Norman's statement? Then again, maybe not!

'Did you see his face at all?' she asked hopefully.

'No, sorry, he was wearing a black hoodie with the hood up, so I can't tell you much about him, except that he was quite tall.'

'What about the car, did you see what kind of car it was?'

'It was a dark grey SUV, possibly a Hyundai. I'm not totally sure.'

'And did you see the driver?'

'I caught a glimpse, and I think it was a woman, but I couldn't swear to it. Could've been a bloke with long hair? Or even just a trick of the light. Like I said, I only caught a glimpse.'

'That's really helpful,' Lauren said as they moved back towards the staircase. She was thinking rapidly; could the driver have been Hal's sister? It sounded as though she had dropped him off up the road from Mia's house to reduce the risk of waking them. But if she drove off, how did Hal – assuming it was Hal – get away with baby Noah?

Once she was seated in the living room again and had taken another long drink of her Coke, she asked if there was anything else he could add.

'Yes, but this is going to sound weird,' Sam said.

'Don't worry about that,' Lauren reassured him. 'Any little detail could be important.'

'Well, I usually aim to leave here about one-fifteen when I'm on that shift, but it was perhaps a bit later that morning, say, one-twenty, maybe even one-twenty-five? I know I was about five minutes late getting into work. Anyway, as I drove down the road, I passed a car parked up on the left just before the junction, and I could've sworn it was the same car. But that doesn't make any sense, does it?'

Oh yes, it does, thought Lauren to herself. 'How certain are you that it was the same car?' she asked, sounding a lot calmer than she felt.

'This one was a dark grey Hyundai Tucson, with a registration starting SW. I remember those two letters 'cos they're my initials, see. And it looked very similar to the one I'd seen earlier.'

Lauren felt like punching the air, but she restrained herself and thanked him politely, saying the same thing she'd said to Megan at number thirty-one, that a police officer might return to take a formal statement if it was needed.

As soon as Lauren returned to her car, she pulled off the wig, which was making her head hot and itchy, and ran her fingers through her hair to try to fluff it up a bit whilst she considered what to do next.

She'd discovered two important witnesses the police had missed, and she knew that she needed to report this immediately. It sounded as though Hal and his sister had scouted the area in advance and then returned that night to abduct Noah. Presumably, the man nosy Norman saw – if indeed he saw anything – was Hal and not Vikram. According to Sam, he was wearing a black hoodie with the hood pulled up. If Sam couldn't see the man's face from his bedroom window, then, sure as hell, neither could nosy Norman!

The question was, should she contact Viv? Or maybe Dan? But neither of them was on the investigating team, and she wasn't sure whether Viv would even want to talk to her, the way they'd left things. Particularly when he found out that she'd been investigating again.

That meant she had to try to talk to someone on DI Barnes' team. If only she had a phone number for Viv's friend Aaron! But she didn't, so there was no choice: she'd just have to go to the police station.

She was aware of a sinking feeling in her stomach as she put the car into gear and pulled away.

Chapter Thirty

A little while later, Lauren pulled into a visitors' parking spot outside Bourne House, the headquarters of Salisbury Police. Just as she was pushing through the front doors, with butterflies in her stomach, she ran directly into Dan and Viv, who were on their way out. Her heart immediately started pounding.

'Lauren, whatever are you doing here?' exclaimed Viv tensely.

'I have something I need to report regarding Noah's abduction,' she said stiffly.

'You're still investigating? After everything I said?' Viv looked and sounded furious.

Dan held a hand up to silence him. 'Hold on a minute, Viv. Lauren, why don't we take you to an interview room.'

His tone brooked no argument, so Lauren followed Dan into the inner regions of the police station whilst Viv, looking disgruntled, followed her.

Dan took her into an informal interview room, the one they used for talking to minors, vulnerable people and bereaved relatives. This room was furnished with two comfortable sofas and a coffee table. Video cameras and microphones, used to record interviews, were discreetly hidden so as not to intimidate nervous witnesses.

Dan left Viv and Lauren together whilst he went off to find someone on DI Barnes' team. There was a moment of awkward silence whilst Lauren fidgeted with her dress and Viv appeared to be searching for something to say.

'What's with the dress?' he eventually asked.

'It's Mum's,' Lauren explained sheepishly. 'I was doing some undercover investigating today.'

'And you thought a dress would be a good disguise?' He spoke sarcastically.

'You should've seen me earlier, with a wig on as well,' Lauren replied. 'You wouldn't have recognised me then.'

'You, in a dress and a wig? Well, under any other circumstances, I'd have given anything to see that. But I can't believe you're still digging into this case. Tell me, why did you need a disguise, eh? Because someone might have recognised you, I suppose. Which means you were putting yourself into danger … again. Why can't you just leave this alone?' He sounded as much frustrated as angry.

'I was never in any real danger,' Lauren crossed her fingers behind her back, 'and I have found out something important. Or two somethings, I suppose. Except they're probably linked.'

'You're not making a lot of sense,' Viv said, shaking his head. 'I just hope you can explain it a bit more coherently than that.'

'Of course I can,' Lauren snapped, cross with herself for feeling so nervous.

'And dare I ask about your friend? Jed, wasn't it?'

'What about him?'

'Is he still going ahead with this hare-brained scheme of yours?'

'Yes, he is, and he's already making progress.'

Viv shook his head again and pursed his lips disapprovingly, but the pair were saved from further argument by the arrival of Dan with DC Aaron Johnson.

'Dan says you've got some information on the Noah Jenkins case?' Aaron asked. 'Shall we all take a seat?'

'Actually,' Dan intervened, 'Viv and I were just on our way out to interview a witness when we ran into Lauren, so I think it might be best if we leave you to get on with it.'

Viv seemed about to protest, but Dan steered him out through the doorway and quietly shut the door behind them. Lauren wasn't sure if Dan was being tactful or if he really did have a witness to talk to, but either way she was grateful not to have to explain what she'd been up to in front of Viv.

'Take a seat.' DC Johnson smiled at her, trying to put her at ease. 'Would you like a coffee or tea before we start?'

'I'd love a coffee, please. Black, no sugar.'

'I won't be long.' He disappeared and returned moments later with two plastic cups of steaming coffee. 'It's from the machine, I'm afraid,' he grimaced. 'Hot and drinkable but that's about all.'

'Thanks.' Lauren took her cup and set it down on the coffee table.

'Now, this is an informal interview,' he explained. 'That means I'm not recording it and no one's watching. It's just you and me. I know Viv's angry about you investigating, but I'm not going to comment on that, and I'm not going to tell him whatever you tell me now. Your relationship is between the two of you. All I'm interested in is what you can tell me about the case.'

Lauren nodded gratefully. 'Thank you, DC Johnson.'

'Please, call me Aaron. Now, tell me what you've been up to, from the beginning.'

Feeling more at ease, Lauren explained everything about their investigation from the moment Sanjeev had approached her to her final visit of that day to Sam Wallace. After she'd begun, he interrupted to ask if she minded if he took notes as they were talking, and she indicated that was fine. For nearly half an hour, she talked, and he listened and scribbled in his notebook, his admiration for her resourcefulness growing. By the time she'd finished, he was impressed that she'd made more progress on the case in less than a week than their entire team had in more than three. Although that was largely down to Billy Barnes' reluctance to look further than Vikram Chopra.

'Thank you very much for all of that,' he said warmly. 'You've certainly given us some further leads to follow, and we will be visiting Hal Winters, Molly Read and Sam Wallace to take their statements. I can promise you that.'

'What about Vikram?' asked Lauren. 'Do you have enough to release him, now?'

'Uh … I can't promise that,' Aaron began regretfully.

'But, surely, you can see that he can't have let himself into his house with a key when he was already asleep in bed with Mia?' she cried. 'And I've shown you just how ridiculous nosy Norman's statement is, so you've no evidence that it was Vikram carrying that sports bag down the road.'

'I'm sorry, I have a lot of sympathy for Vikram, really, I do. But just as a lot of the evidence against him is circumstantial, so is your evidence, until proven one way or the other. I will speak to DI Barnes, but I can't promise that Vikram will be released.'

'Isn't there a maximum length of time you can hold him for?'

Aaron sighed frustratedly. Privately, he was in complete agreement with Lauren but, unfortunately, it wasn't up to him. Barnes was playing the system; not that he was doing anything illegal, but …

'It's complicated,' he replied carefully.

'Go on, then, explain it to me,' Lauren challenged.

'When we arrest someone on suspicion of a crime, we have an initial period of up to twenty-four hours to question them, then we need to either charge or release them. We can apply for an extension of that period in certain cases. Once a suspect has been charged, we can either release him on police bail or remand him in custody, pending an initial hearing before a magistrate. Vikram Chopra was arrested and charged with child abduction within the statutory twenty-four hours and held in our cells overnight before appearing before the magistrate the next morning. He was refused bail on the grounds that he was a flight risk.'

Lauren opened her mouth to protest, but Aaron raised a hand to stop her. 'Barnes asked for more time to investigate, so that he could possibly add a charge of murder before the plea hearing, which he's allowed to do. Effectively, Vikram is being held on suspicion of murdering Noah.'

'But, surely, you can't hold him on that charge for more than twenty-four hours?' Lauren asked, puzzled.

'Exactly, but it's more complicated than that. Officially, Vikram was remanded in custody on the initial charge of abduction.'

'That's bullshit!' Lauren protested.

'Unfortunately, it is what it is,' Aaron replied diplomatically.

'How long until the next hearing?' she demanded.

'Umm … I'm not sure that a date has been set yet.' Aaron prevaricated, knowing that Barnes was trying to stall the plea hearing for as long as possible.

'But once it goes before a magistrate, he'll be released?'

'It depends on how he pleads, and on the charges brought against him. He could be granted bail pending a trial at either the magistrates' court or Crown Court or remanded in custody until trial. That's up to the magistrate.'

'But does it have to go to trial? Can't the charges be dropped before then?'

'That depends on the Crown Prosecution Service.'

'And how can they be persuaded to drop the charges?' Lauren demanded.

'Usually, charges are dropped either due to lack of evidence or because a prosecution is not in the public interest.'

'And would you say there's sufficient evidence in Vikram's case?'

'That's a very good question.' A moment of silent understanding passed between them.

'I promise, I will follow up on what you've given us,' Aaron reassured her.

Lauren realised that she would just have to accept that, for now.

Chapter Thirty-one

Meg had spent an anxious few hours the previous evening wondering how Lauren was getting on. It hadn't felt right leaving the investigation up to the young pair, and she had been restless and irritable, wanting to be able to do something herself. Unfortunately, Albert hadn't exactly helped, asking her repeatedly if she'd heard anything, until she felt like screaming at him.

It had been a huge relief when Lauren had finally phoned at about half past nine – just after Albert had gone off to bed in a huff – to tell her everything. And this morning she had relayed Lauren's news to Albert over breakfast.

'Jolly good show,' he commented, spreading butter on his toast. 'Those two youngsters seem to have taken to this investigating malarkey like ducks to water, what?'

Meg agreed but still felt frustrated that she wasn't involved. What could she usefully contribute to this investigation?

She was still turning it over in her mind whilst working on her jigsaw puzzle, when Lauren came round with the morning drinks trolley.

'What's up?' Lauren enquired when she saw Meg's low mood written across her face.

'Oh, nothing much.'

'I disagree. What's that expression my mum told me her grandma used to use? You look like you've lost a shilling and found a sixpence?'

That made Meg smile, as she hadn't heard that saying in years.

'That's a bit better,' Lauren grinned cheekily. 'Look, I'm due my break as soon as I've finished this, so how about we meet up in your room where no one can see us talking? Then, you can tell me what's wrong.'

Meg agreed, hoping that Lauren could suggest something for her to do.

Ten minutes later, Lauren reappeared with a mug of coffee in her hands and beckoned to Meg from the day-room door. She held the lift until Meg arrived, and they went up to Meg's room together.

Meg sat in her armchair whilst Lauren perched on the edge of her bed.

'What's up?' Lauren asked.

'I just wish I could do something to help you with the investigation,' replied Meg. 'I know it's silly, but I feel like a spare part at the moment.'

'No, of course it's not silly. And I'm sure there's plenty you can do.'

'For example?' Meg raised a hopeful eyebrow.

'Well, I was thinking through everything I found out yesterday, and there are quite a few questions to be answered. I know Aaron promised that his team would follow up on the leads I gave him, but I just don't trust Barnes to get on with the job.'

Meg nodded her agreement.

'Thanks to Sam's statement, it looks likely that whoever took Noah had a key, which is why they didn't need to break in,' Lauren continued. 'So the first question is, how did they get hold of the key?'

'Yes, that's a good question.'

'Did they steal the key that's missing from Mia's parents? Or could they have made a copy?'

'How is that even possible?' Meg asked.

'Basically, you borrow a genuine key and make an impression in clay or plasticine or something similar. Then you pour molten metal into the mould to make a copy. I watched a YouTube video that shows you how to do it.'

'Goodness gracious, the things you can find out about on the internet!' exclaimed Meg.

Lauren grinned. 'Absolutely anything you want, if you know where to look. The point is, yes, someone *could* have stolen the key from Mia's parents, but they'd have had to have known that her parents had a key to Mia's house, *and* where they kept it. Is that likely?'

'Fair point.'

'But if whoever was planning to abduct Noah could *borrow* a key from either Mia or Vikram, they could quickly make the impressions and return the key without anyone even knowing.'

Meg looked puzzled. 'But how would they do that?'

'Whenever you go out, you take your front-door key with you, so just think of all the places you go to where you leave your key unattended or out of sight. For example, I keep my key in my handbag. But when I'm at work, my handbag is in one of the staff lockers. They're an absolute doddle to break into.'

'Yes, I think I see what you're getting at. But I still don't understand how I can help?'

'I was going round to Mia's after I've finished work to make a list of where and when either her key or Vikram's could have been borrowed. But if you want to come with me, maybe you could sit with Mia and do that while I get on with some other things.'

'I could definitely do that,' said Meg, brightening up, 'but what are you going to do?'

'I want to go back to speak to Molly again at number thirty-one with some photos I found online of Hal and his sister, Amelia. Wouldn't it be great if she could positively identify them as the people she saw that Friday morning?'

'But weren't you wearing a disguise when you went there yesterday?'

'Already thought of that. I have the same wig and a different dress to wear today.'

'Well done.'

'I also want to show the photos to Sam at number twenty-six, just in case. And I thought I could go round all the other houses within sight of Mia's and see if anyone else saw those two hanging around in the days before Noah was taken.'

'Very well. I'll be ready to go out just after three-thirty then,' promised Meg.

When Meg popped into the office to say that she was going out, Sue Barclay was chatting to Petra, who was taking over from her on the late shift.

'Can I help you, Meg?' asked Petra politely.

'I just wanted to let you know I'm going out for a couple of hours. I'll be back in time for dinner this evening.'

'Thank you, I'll make a note in the daybook,' Petra replied, reaching for a pen.

'And where are you off to this time?' Sue demanded, in her usual officious voice.

'A friend has kindly offered to take me out shopping,' Meg replied diplomatically.

'Hmm, and I suppose that friend wouldn't be Lauren Peachy, by any chance?'

'Yes, it is.' Meg chose to tell the truth, knowing that the care manager, Maureen Wilkinson, was quite happy with the situation.

Sue sniffed disapprovingly, but Petra smiled and told Meg to have a good time.

On her way out of the office, she saw Lauren hurrying along the corridor and did a double take. The pretty floral dress in pastel shades of pink and peach was so unlike anything that Lauren usually wore. And the touch of make-up, whilst not overdone, made her look about ten years older.

'You look very elegant,' Meg commented with a smile.

'As you very well know, I'm in disguise,' Lauren quipped back. She looped her arm through Meg's, and they made their way out to the car park. Once in the car, Lauren again pulled on the long blonde wig. Meg was impressed; it was nigh on impossible to recognise her now.

'What ploy are you going to use today?' she enquired.

'Same as yesterday, that I'm a civilian doing some follow-up work on behalf of the police. No one batted an eyelid yesterday.'

'Are you sure you can't be accused of impersonating a police officer?' Meg cautioned.

'I'm very careful to say I'm a civilian,' Lauren insisted, 'and that I'm working *with* the police, not *for* the police. It's kind of true, isn't it?'

Meg nodded with a smile as Lauren fastened her seat belt and started the engine.

Chapter Thirty-two

Lauren parked directly outside Mia's this time. They walked up the short path together and Mia opened the door almost as soon as Lauren had pressed the bell.

'My goodness, I nearly didn't recognise you!' Mia exclaimed, looking at Lauren incredulously.

'I'm going undercover,' she explained, 'but Meg will sit down with you and do that thing we talked about on the phone, if that's all right with you?'

Mia agreed, so Lauren said she'd catch up with them later and left them to it. Mia led Meg into the living room, which was spotlessly clean and tidy today. 'Please, have a seat. I'm sorry, I still don't have any tea, but perhaps you'd like a glass of lemonade?'

Meg accepted gratefully and settled herself into an armchair, taking her notebook and pen out of her handbag.

Mia returned swiftly with two glasses of cloudy lemonade and settled herself on the sofa, taking a nervous sip of her drink before looking at Meg expectantly.

'Did Lauren explain what we need to ask you?' Meg began.

'Yes, she wants to know about any time that one of us could've left our front door keys unattended during the week leading up to … that night.' She swallowed, unable even to say what had happened for fear of becoming emotional.

'That's right,' Meg smiled, trying to put her at her ease. 'We're just wondering if someone could have borrowed one of your keys without you knowing, in order to make an impression of it.'

'That's what Lauren said on the phone. Okay, I've been going through it in my mind. When I go out, I always put my front door key inside the front zipped pocket of my handbag. You probably know that I don't drive, so I don't have a whole bunch of keys, not like Vik.'

Meg nodded her encouragement.

'When I'm on the bus, I keep my bag across my shoulder with my hand on it, so it's secure. When I get to work, I hang my bag on a peg inside the little cloakroom out to the back of the kitchen. The only person who would have access to it is Linda, and I can't believe she's involved. And I really don't think anyone could sneak past us from the shop into the kitchen, as there's usually one of us serving and one in the kitchen, unless it gets stupidly busy.'

'What about the back door?' Meg asked.

Mia shook her head. 'Linda insists we keep it locked at all times.'

'Okay, where else did you go during that week?'

'I took Noah to my mum's every day and collected him again. But you surely can't suspect my parents?'

'Not at all,' Meg reassured her. 'In any case, they already had a key to your house. Or they did, before it was mislaid.'

'Yes, of course, how stupid am I?' Mia laughed nervously.

'It's okay, you're doing fine,' Meg soothed.

'Apart from doing a bit of shopping on my way home from work a couple of times, in which case my handbag was always with me, I didn't go anywhere else that week. I'm sorry, but I don't think anyone could've taken my key and returned it without me knowing.'

'Where do you leave your key when you're at home?'

'We have a set of key hooks just inside the front door, I hang it on there.'

'And was there ever a time when someone called at the door and you left them there to go and do something?'

'No, I never leave the front door open because of Noah. And I don't remember anyone calling that week anyway. Apart from our shopping delivery.'

'What happens when that comes?'

'We always choose an evening delivery slot, 'cos it's easier if we're both here. Vik stays with Noah in the living room while I take all the shopping through to the kitchen and put it away.'

Meg wondered if the delivery driver could have done it. 'Do you always have the same delivery driver?'

'Yes, he's a lovely man.'

'What does he look like?'

'Probably in his late fifties, older than my dad for certain. He's kind of bald on top with bushy grey hair around the edges.'

It certainly didn't sound like any of the members of RAS they'd come across so far.

'Fair enough,' Meg said, after making a brief note. 'Now, what about Vikram? I appreciate it's harder for you to answer for him, but tell me whatever you can.'

'That's okay. We were able to speak on the phone this morning. His front door key is on the keyring with his car keys. When he gets to work, he puts his keys into his jacket pocket, and he usually leaves his jacket hanging over the back of his chair all day. So, it's unattended whenever he's in meetings or with clients, but his desk and chair are visible to several other people in the office.'

'Okay. Where else did Vik go that week?'

'He goes to the gym twice a week before work; he went on Tuesday and Friday that week. When I asked him about it, he said he hadn't thought anything of it at the time, but on the Friday morning, the day before … well, when he came back to his locker after his workout, he found the door open. There was nothing missing, so he didn't worry about it.'

'Did he tell the police?' Meg asked eagerly.

'No, he said he'd forgotten all about it until I asked him about his keys this morning.'

Meg scribbled a few notes. 'What gym does he go to?' she asked, looking up.

'The one on Castle Street. It's between Linda's Lunches and his office.'

'That's great, thank you. Was there anything else he did that week?'

'No, that's it, so far as we can both remember.'

'Then that's everything, I think. How are you holding up?'

Meg and Mia chatted until Lauren eventually returned.

'I'm guessing you've had some success?' Meg asked when Mia came back to the living room with Lauren, who was grinning like a Cheshire cat.

'You can say that again!' Lauren flopped onto the other end of the sofa to Mia. 'I've got a positive ID on Hal and Amelia!'

'Really?' Meg was amazed.

'Yeah. Molly at number thirty-one was certain that the two people she saw on the Friday morning were Hal and his sister. And Terry at number thirty-three said he was sure he saw Hal on the Wednesday evening of that week. He was shoving advertising leaflets through letterboxes and spending a lot of time looking closely at the locks. Terry was worried that he was checking out houses to burgle, which is why he kept an eye on him. I asked if he mentioned this to the police and he said no, he hadn't thought it was connected.'

'Good work. What about the other witness you mentioned?'

'Sam at number twenty-six? He said he thought the man he saw could've been Hal, but he wasn't sure.'

'You know my neighbours better than I do!' exclaimed Mia.

'You're lucky, they all seem like decent people,' Lauren replied. 'Nicer than some of the ones around where I live.'

'Would you like a drink?' Mia offered.

Lauren checked her watch. 'Thanks, but no. Meg needs to be back at Britford Lodge for dinner, so we'd better get going.'

They said their goodbyes and returned to Lauren's car.

On the way home, Meg asked if Lauren knew whether the police had done anything to follow up on what she'd told them.

'Yes, I meant to tell you. Both Molly and Sam said that a plain clothes officer called yesterday evening to take official statements from them. It sounded like Aaron, from Molly's description. Luckily, they both thought I was following up on that visit.'

'That is good news.' Meg was relieved that the police had taken Lauren seriously.

Chapter Thirty-three

Meg shared what Mia had told her about Vikram's gym locker, after which Lauren declared her intention of going to the gym with Hal's photo.

'If we can get a positive ID on Hal at the gym, that will be another piece of evidence against him!' she said excitedly.

Meg felt a slight flutter of concern, wondering if perhaps the police should be doing that.

'And don't forget that Jed's going to the RAS meeting on Friday,' Lauren continued. 'He might pick up something else against Hal.'

'Do you think that's wise? Now that Hal is our number one suspect, we don't want to risk tipping him off until the police are ready to arrest him,' Meg cautioned.

'I'll warn him to be careful, don't you worry.'

'Perhaps we should hand this over to the police now?' Meg suggested tentatively.

'No way!' Lauren sounded horrified.

Meg didn't push the point; she understood Lauren's keenness to pursue the case themselves. 'It would be helpful to find out whether Tyler put Hal up to this, or if Hal acted alone,' she said, changing the subject.

'Tyler has the motive, but I don't believe that Noah was ever at his flat. It did occur to me that Tyler's parents might be looking after their grandson, but Jed was convinced that Tyler genuinely didn't know where his son was. If Hal acted on Tyler's behalf, surely Tyler would know where Noah is? It just doesn't make any sense! But why would Hal take Noah if he wasn't put up to it by Tyler?' Lauren asked, as she navigated the heavy traffic on Salisbury's ring road.

'There's still the racist angle,' Meg suggested. 'Perhaps he did it to frame Vikram?'

'If that's true, where on earth is Noah?'

Meg didn't answer. In this scenario, things didn't bode well for the child.

'We know that Hal's sister, Amelia, is likely involved in this. What if she's looking after Noah?' Lauren suggested.

Meg's heart lifted a little. Could that be possible? She turned the idea over in her mind and thought that it was a lead well worth following up on.

Just as Lauren was turning into the car park at Britford Lodge, her phone rang. She quickly swung into a parking space, pulled her handbrake on and switched the engine off before answering it.

'Hello? … Oh, hi, Aaron. Just a moment, I'm sitting in my car with Meg. I'll put you on speaker so we can both hear you.'

'Okay, Lauren,' Meg could now hear Aaron, 'and hello to you, Meg.'

'Hello, Aaron,' Meg called out.

'I was just phoning to update you on where we are with the case. After you left me yesterday, Lauren, I went straight round to talk to the two neighbours that you told me about, and they gave statements that tally with what you told me. I also checked out the statement that Harold Norman gave, and you were spot on; he couldn't possibly have seen anyone coming from number twenty-five. This morning, I took everything to DI Barnes. I must admit, he wasn't very happy to hear that you've been, as he put it, interfering in his investigation. But he did reluctantly admit that Hal could be a viable alternative suspect to Vikram, and he's instructed me to check him out.'

Lauren and Meg exchanged a silent fist bump.

Aaron continued. 'Strictly between you and me, I went round to Hal's place of work this morning. I asked him to account for his whereabouts on the morning of Friday the second of June and the early hours of Saturday the third. His alibi for the morning is weak – his parents couldn't verify it – and he said that he was in The Hanging Man at the RAS meeting all evening.'

'That's a lie!' protested Lauren.

'Yes, it is,' agreed Aaron. 'I went to the pub and took statements from the landlord and the customer you spoke to, who both confirmed what they told you. That's given us sufficient grounds to bring Hal into the station for formal questioning under caution.'

'That's great news!' exclaimed Lauren, beaming from ear to ear.

'Ah well, don't get your hopes up too much,' Aaron warned. 'Hal immediately demanded his solicitor and, when she arrived, he vehemently denied being in the vicinity of Noah Jenkins's home at the times in question. He then answered everything else we asked with "No comment". We can hold him overnight, but we'll need more evidence before we can charge him. I'm just about to revisit your two witnesses to see if they can pick Hal out from a photo line-up.'

'There's no need.' Lauren excitedly informed him that she'd just returned from taking photos of Hal and his sister, Amelia, around Mia's neighbours.

'You did what?' Aaron asked incredulously.

Lauren glanced at Meg, a little worried that Aaron didn't sound too pleased. She slowly reiterated what she'd just said.

'That's what I was afraid you said.' Aaron sounded cross. 'I really wish you hadn't done that.'

'But why?' Lauren demanded defensively. 'Haven't I just saved you some time?'

'No. You've just invalidated any ID I now get.'

'What?' Lauren was taken aback.

'If Hal's solicitor finds out that you showed the witnesses a photo of Hal before they saw the official police photo line-up, she can claim that they only picked out Hal because of the photo you showed them. That's enough to throw the ID evidence out.'

'Shit!' Lauren exclaimed, then turned crimson when she remembered that Meg was still sitting next to her. 'Sorry,' she mouthed to her. 'Oh, Aaron, I'm so sorry, I honestly didn't think about that.'

'No, I understand why you wouldn't,' Aaron said tersely, 'but it's not going to go down at all well with DI Barnes.'

'I don't suppose Viv will be too pleased, either,' Lauren muttered glumly. 'It kind of proves that he was right, doesn't it?'

'I'm not going to take sides between you and Viv,' Aaron said firmly, 'but don't feel too bad. If it hadn't been for you, Hal Winters wouldn't even be on our radar. At least now we have a valid line of enquiry besides Vikram Chopra.'

'Thanks, but I've still made a real mess of things, haven't I?' Lauren sounded forlorn.

'Let's just hope we can find some other evidence against Hal,' replied Aaron diplomatically.

Seeing that Lauren had fallen silent, Meg told Aaron their theory about the front door key. 'It's possible that Vikram's gym locker was broken into on the Friday morning,' she explained. 'I'm sure you can ask him for the details. Assuming his front door key was in his locker, someone could have taken it to make an impression then put it back. I'm told by a reliable source that it's possible to duplicate a key from such an impression.'

'It would be useful if we could prove that,' Aaron replied thoughtfully. 'The absence of signs of a break-in is one of the main reasons for suspecting Vikram. If we can prove how someone else could've gained entry, it would undermine the case against Vikram.'

Lauren brightened up a little. 'I'm planning to go to the gym—' she began saying when Aaron cut her off mid-sentence.

'No, you're not going to any gym,' he warned. 'Please leave that to us.'

'Oh.' Lauren sounded crestfallen.

'Look, all the information you've passed to me has been very helpful,' Aaron assured her, 'but you need to let us handle it from here on, so that we can gather watertight evidence that will stand up in court. If I can get a positive ID from someone at the gym who saw Hal there that day, it will help.'

'Yeah, I get it.'

'If your hypothesis about Hal abducting Noah is right, then proving a motive will also help the case against him. Do you think that he was acting on Tyler's orders?'

'We're not sure.' Lauren relayed their earlier conversation on that subject, but Aaron didn't sound convinced.

'Listen, I've told you far more than I should have. My instructions from DI Barnes were to inform you that we have Hal in custody and to tell you in no uncertain terms that you are not to interfere in this investigation any further. I'm trusting you not to breathe a word of anything I've said to anyone.'

'Thank you,' replied Meg. 'I most certainly won't say a word to anyone.'

'Me neither,' said Lauren. 'But can I just ask you about Jed? He's planning on going to the RAS meeting in the pub on Friday evening.'

'No, call him off,' Aaron replied firmly. 'That group is far too dangerous to put a civilian in undercover. And, in any case, we have Hal in custody now.'

'Okay,' Lauren conceded, sounding disappointed.

Chapter Thirty-four

Wednesday 28th June 2023

Lauren was on another early shift the following morning, and she was feeling tired from three early starts in a row and dejected about the case. Luckily, Maureen Wilkinson was back on duty after a long weekend off, so at least she didn't have bossy Barclay on her back.

Meg was having a relaxing morning, grateful for not having to rush to get ready to go out, but her brain was still working overtime on the case. Although her friend Jeannie was doing their jigsaw puzzle as usual, Meg had decided to sit quietly and read her book instead to try to stop her thoughts going round and round in circles.

Neither Meg nor Lauren noticed when a car pulled into the car park and two detectives got out.

DI Barnes and DC Johnson made their way to the office, introduced themselves, showed their badges and asked Maureen if they could speak to Meg Thornton and Lauren Peachy somewhere in private.

'Goodness me,' exclaimed Maureen. 'Whatever have those two been up to?'

'I'm sorry, we can't divulge that,' spoke DI Barnes, in a slightly pompous manner.

Maureen glared at him before going to look for Lauren, whom she found in the treatment room preparing to change a dressing. She asked her to find Meg and bring her to the office.

'Whatever for?' Lauren gasped.

'There are two detectives here to see you,' Maureen informed her.

'Dan and Viv?'

'No, not the two who usually visit you,' Maureen said. 'I

150

didn't recognise these two. They did show me their ID. I think they were called Barnes and Johnson – does that mean anything to you?'

Lauren nodded; unfortunately, it did.

She found Meg reading in the conservatory and explained the situation. Gravely, they made their way to the office and knocked on the door. The butterflies in Lauren's stomach were doing little backflips, and her pulse was hammering in her head.

'Come in,' ordered Maureen, standing as they entered. 'I'm going to take my coffee break now and then check around the other members of staff, so you've got about half an hour,' she said in a no-nonsense voice to the two detectives. 'After that, I will require the use of my office again.'

'Not a problem,' said the short balding man, who Meg assumed was DI Barnes. 'We're grateful to you for allowing us to use your office. This won't take long.' Maureen left, closing the door as she went.

Aaron spoke for the first time. 'Shall we all sit down?'

Meg studied DI Barnes as he took Maureen's chair behind the desk. He was barely five foot six, probably in his late fifties or early sixties, and he had a comb-over in a vain attempt to disguise the fact that he was clearly quite bald. His face was well lined with wrinkles, and he wore a shabby tweed suit with an old-fashioned checked shirt. He looked a complete anachronism beside the smartly dressed junior officer. Aaron sported a dark grey suit, and his thick black hair was neatly trimmed. Meg had met DC Johnson on several occasions when he had worked with Dan and Viv on their cases. He looked as though he'd rather be anywhere else than here.

'I've come to tell you that, thanks to your unwanted intervention, we've been left with no choice but to release Henry Winters without charge.' Barnes spoke deliberately and disdainfully. Meg and Lauren looked at each other, concern in their eyes.

'You need to understand that just because DI Bywater has allowed your amateur sleuthing to go unchallenged, that does not give you the right to go poking your noses into police business just because you want to be Miss Marple.' He glared at Meg before turning his withering gaze on Lauren. 'Or her sidekick,' he added.

Lauren bit her bottom lip, wanting to protest but realising that it was unlikely to help.

'I've a good mind to charge you both with obstructing a police investigation.'

Lauren gulped uncomfortably.

'I'm very sorry you feel that way—' Meg began.

'As indeed you should,' Barnes interrupted. 'You've caused me a considerable headache. The CPS is questioning the strength of our case against Vikram Chopra, given that we've been questioning another suspect. And I understand that it's thanks to you that one of our key witness statements has been cast into doubt.'

'That's hardly our fault,' Lauren burst out. 'If you're referring to Harold Norman at number eleven, then all we did was to point out the blindingly obvious holes in his statement.'

Meg laid a cautionary hand on Lauren's arm and cast her a warning look.

'Really?' Barnes retorted condescendingly. 'And you would know better than a trained police detective, I suppose?'

Lauren somehow managed to stop herself from responding to that.

'Will you be releasing Vikram Chopra?' Meg enquired with frosty politeness.

'Not at all,' Barnes declared. 'Given the weight of the remaining evidence, it is still my belief that he is the likely culprit. As soon as we find the child's body, we can charge him with murder.'

'You're assuming that Noah Jenkins is dead?' Meg raised an eyebrow.

'That is, unfortunately, the most likely outcome,' Barnes said, his voice softening a little. 'You must realise that the odds of finding him alive now are miniscule.'

'And the fact that Henry Winters could have been acting on the orders of Tyler Ford, who has a very strong motive—'

Meg was interrupted again by Barnes, who spluttered, 'Complete nonsense!'

'And yet you brought him in for questioning?' she pointed out.

'Only in the interests of being thorough.'

'You didn't really think him a viable suspect then?' Meg persisted.

'Not for one moment,' snapped Barnes.

'Then I fail to see why you are so upset at having to release him without charge.' Meg delivered her coup de grace.

Billy Barnes sat gaping like a goldfish at Meg's argument. Aaron Johnson had to suppress a smile at her logic, and Lauren was itching to give her a round of applause.

'However, I think you are being extremely short-sighted,' Meg continued scathingly. 'Hal Winters was seen lurking outside Mia and Vikram's house on two separate occasions in the days before Noah's abduction, he has a very weak alibi for the Friday morning and he lied about where he was on Friday night. Not only is he best friends with Noah's biological father, Tyler Ford, he's also an out-and-out racist who would love to see Vikram Chopra go to prison for something he didn't do.'

'Even if that was true,' Barnes bravely countered, 'your interference has discredited any ID evidence. And as to your ridiculous theory about Winters breaking into Vikram's gym locker to make a copy of his front door key, well, that is pure fantasy.'

Meg looked across at Aaron.

'I'm afraid we were unable to find anyone who could remember seeing Hal at the gym,' he confirmed ruefully.

'Exactly, for the very simple reason that he wasn't there,' Barnes said smugly.

'But you are going to continue to investigate him?' Meg demanded.

'It would be a complete waste of police resources,' Barnes replied airily. 'And now, if you don't mind, we've wasted quite enough time talking to you. We have work to do, collating all the evidence against Vikram Chopra.' He stood up to underline the fact that the conversation was over.

Meg and Lauren both rose to their feet, Meg being considerably taller than Barnes. 'If you won't investigate Hal Winters, then you leave us no choice,' she said firmly.

'And if you continue to interfere in a police investigation, then I will have no choice but to charge you both,' Barnes retorted as he walked out, his chest puffed out and his head held high.

'I'm sorry,' whispered Aaron, as he dawdled behind Barnes.

'What a twat!' Lauren exclaimed after they'd gone.

'A very apt description,' agreed Meg.

'Are we going to continue investigating?' Lauren asked hopefully.

'Unless we want to see a grave miscarriage of justice, then I don't think we have any choice,' Meg replied solemnly.

Chapter Thirty-five

Lauren found it hard to concentrate on her work for the rest of the morning, alternating between indignant fury at DI Barnes, concern for Mia and Vikram, and despair for baby Noah. She wasn't in the best of moods by the time Sue Barclay arrived to take charge of the late shift that day.

'What are you doing?' Sue demanded, coming out of the office after handover to see Lauren walking across the entrance hall.

'I've just finished in the dining room,' Lauren answered defensively, 'and I'm going to check on the residents in the day room.'

'No doubt so that you can chat to your friend Meg,' Sue declared scathingly. 'You need to stop showing such blatant favouritism to one resident; it's not fair on the others. I want you to spend the afternoon tidying the sluice.'

'But I wasn't—' Lauren began indignantly.

'And don't answer back, girl,' snapped Sue.

Lauren stormed off to the sluice room, barely holding back hot tears.

※

Meg returned to the day room after her lunch and sat with Jeannie to work on the now nearly finished jigsaw puzzle. Jeannie noticed that Meg was unusually distracted; she hadn't slotted a piece into place for at least five minutes.

'Penny for them, my dear?' she asked gently

'What? Oh, sorry, I was miles away,' Meg replied.

'Yes, so I noticed. Is there something I can help with?'

'Probably not, although it's kind of you to offer.' Meg thought for a minute and then told her friend about the visit she'd had that morning, without mentioning any specific details of the case.

'Barnes does sound like a pompous twit,' Jeannie sympathised.

'That's an understatement,' Meg replied dryly. 'The problem is, we're caught in a catch-22 situation now. If we carry on investigating, Barnes will be furious and might even try to charge us with something. But if we don't investigate, not only might an innocent man stay in prison but a guilty one could get off scot-free.'

'Quite the conundrum,' agreed Jeannie. 'Is there any aspect of the case that you can be reasonably sure this detective inspector is not investigating, which could provide some evidence against the person you believe to be guilty?'

Meg paused and then a flash of inspiration hit her. 'Amelia Winters!' she exclaimed.

'It looks like you've got your answer.'

Meg pushed herself up and leant across their puzzle to place her hands lightly on Jeannie's cheeks. 'Thank you so much, my dear friend.'

She left Jeannie beaming with pleasure as she hurried off to find Lauren.

When Meg eventually found her banging bedpans around in the sluice, she almost burst out laughing. 'Why on earth are you in such a bad mood?' she asked.

'That bloody bossy Barclay,' Lauren muttered sulkily, before telling Meg what had happened.

'In that case, my dear, I won't stop. I'll be waiting outside for you in the car park when you finish your shift later and we can chat in your car, out of sight.' With that, Meg turned around and walked thoughtfully back to the day room.

⚙

Aaron Johnson was torn in two. On the one hand, he agreed with Barnes that civilians had no business sticking their noses into a police investigation. But, on the other hand, Meg and Lauren had brought valuable intel to the case, and he was convinced that Barnes was fixated on the wrong suspect. Moreover, Barnes was trying to fit the evidence to the suspect and ignoring any pieces that suggested a different scenario, and that was bordering on incompetence.

It was frustrating that they'd had to release Henry Winters, but Aaron believed they should still be investigating him. Two witnesses had placed Winters in the vicinity of the Jenkins' house in the days before the abduction, even if their ID evidence wouldn't stand up in court. Winters had lied about being in the pub on the Friday night. Then, when they'd confronted him about it, Winters had changed his story to say he'd been visiting his sister in Ludgershall that evening. Why hadn't he said that the first time around? Worse still, Barnes had simply accepted Winters' story without even checking it out!

Aaron decided he'd have to track Amelia Winters down, as soon as he could get a moment without Barnes looking over his shoulder.

Another thought occurred to Aaron. Vikram Chopra had used the gym early in the morning, before starting work, whereas it had been evening when he went there asking questions. It might be worth going back in the morning and showing Hal's photo again, just in case there were different staff on duty at that time of day.

❖

When Lauren finished work, she found Meg strolling pensively around the car park. She beckoned her over and held the passenger door open until Meg was comfortably seated, before climbing into the driver's side.

'What a day!' she sighed.

'Yes, it has been,' agreed Meg sympathetically. 'I think we shall have to be very careful from now on to keep our chats outside of your work hours.'

'That's so unfair! Other carers clearly have favourite residents, but they don't get picked on.'

'I doubt any of the other staff are investigating a serious crime with one of the residents,' Meg remarked mildly, getting a twitch of a smile from Lauren. 'We work very well together, my dear, but it won't do for you to forget which job is paying your salary.'

Lauren knew that Meg was right, but it still didn't feel fair. 'You were looking for me earlier,' she said. 'Was it about the case?'

'Yes, it was. I believe that we need to look further into Amelia Winters. It's clear that Barnes won't be investigating her, so he can hardly claim that we're stepping on his toes if *we* do. And it does look as though she was probably working with her brother.'

'She might even be looking after Noah,' Lauren added.

'We can only hope.' Meg wanted that to be true but had a feeling it wasn't going to be that straightforward. 'Do you have an address or phone number for her?'

'Not yet but …'Lauren grinned and snatched up her phone from the console where she'd dropped it when she got into the car. Meg watched as her thumbs flew back and forth over the screen, pausing occasionally as she read something. Seconds turned into minutes, and the expression on Lauren's face became progressively more puzzled. Eventually, she heaved a sigh and looked up at Meg.

'I can't find any record of an Amelia Winters in Salisbury, other than when she was at school and living with her parents. And we know she's no longer living at their address.'

'Perhaps she's married and changed her name?'Meg suggested. 'Or maybe she no longer lives in Salisbury? Why don't you go home and spend this evening doing some research on her?'

'Looks like I'll have to. I was hoping we could have gone to talk to her now, though.'

'Not to worry, it's not as though there's a lot of time to do much this evening anyway. When are your next days off? We could go and visit her then.'

'I'm off tomorrow and Friday.'

'That's perfect, Why don't we aim to go out for the day tomorrow? Assuming you can find an address for Amelia, of course, and that it's not too far away.'

'Okay. Shall I pick you up at half past nine?'

'I'll be ready and waiting,' Meg promised.

Chapter Thirty-six

That evening, something happened that threw all their plans out of the window.

Whilst Meg was reading her book in bed, having decided on an early night to prepare for the adventures of the following day; whilst Lauren was watching a film with her mum and trying to decide whether or not to risk phoning Viv; whilst Aaron was trying to track Amelia Winters down, having stayed late after Barnes had left the office; whilst Viv was at home worrying about the apparent stalemate in his relationship with Lauren, and whilst Dan was relaxing with his heavily pregnant wife, a storm was brewing at The Hanging Man that was about to change everything.

Had anyone been watching, they would have seen two men talking behind the cars at the far end of the car park where it bordered a patch of wasteland. Their body language revealed increasing anger in one, defensiveness in the other. Talking gave way to arguing and then shouting. Finally, the defensive one said something that tipped the aggressive one over the edge. A knife appeared. A struggle ensued. The knife flashed repeatedly as it was wielded with terrible precision. One body slumped to the ground and the other man looked around, frantically checking that no one had seen the encounter. He saw that the coast was clear.

With a grunting effort, he manoeuvred the inert body into the back seat of the victim's car, flinging a dirty old blanket from the boot over the corpse to hide it. He found a broken branch from a nearby tree and used it like a broom to sweep the ground where the body had fallen, covering up all traces of footprints and, more importantly, blood. Flinging the branch aside, he jumped into the driver's seat and quietly shut the door. Then he drove away from The Hanging Man, no one any the wiser as to what had just happened.

Chapter Thirty-seven

Meg was eating her breakfast and thinking about the day ahead. Albert was sulking, having learnt that she was going out investigating with Lauren and, once again, he wasn't invited. Jeannie and Betty were trying to engage their friends in a normal conversation and failing miserably. So, when Maureen Wilkinson came to ask Meg if she could come to the office, she was glad of the interruption.

'You've got visitors,' was all that Maureen would say.

Meg checked her watch, but it was only five to nine so it couldn't possibly be Lauren this early. And, in any case, her friend would've phoned or sent a text message, not come in and spoken to the care manager. She followed Maureen to the office, wondering what this could be about and hoping that it wasn't DI Barnes again.

Dan and Viv were waiting in the office, their faces serious.

'What is it?' gasped Meg, immediately concerned that something bad had happened to Lauren.

'Meg, come and sit down,' directed Dan.

'No, please tell me, it's not Lauren, is it?'

'Whyever should it be Lauren?' exclaimed Viv. 'What have you two been up to?'

'Nothing, I just thought … you looked so serious … and Lauren is coming to pick me up in about half an hour. I was worried in case there had been an accident.'

'No, it's not that at all,' Dan reassured her.

Meg sank onto a chair. 'Okay, what is it, then?'

'This is strictly confidential, of course, but I have a reason for telling you. The police were called out to a report of a car on fire on a rarely used track on farmland north of Salisbury last night,' Dan explained. 'It's the sort of thing that usually happens when joyriders want to dispose of a car they've stolen; they torch it to get rid of any evidence. Normally, it's something for uniform to follow up on, but we were called out shortly after midnight when the fire crew discovered the charred remains of a body on the back seat.'

Meg gasped.

'At first, we wondered if it could have been an accident, but once the pathologist arrived, he quickly dispelled that theory; the victim had been stabbed repeatedly in the chest and abdomen.'

'Making it murder,' Meg said, looking at Dan's face in consternation. 'Which is terrible, obviously, but why are you telling me this?'

'Because the vehicle identification number identified the car as belonging to Henry Winters.'

'The same …'

'Yes, the same Henry Winters that DI Barnes had in custody following the evidence that you and Lauren uncovered. And then chose to release.'

'Oh, my goodness me,' Meg gasped, blanching. 'Do you think the victim is Hal?'

'We need to wait for official confirmation, but yes, we think so.'

'Is this connected to Noah's abduction?'

'For the moment, the superintendent wants to keep the two cases separate until we can prove otherwise. DI Barnes is continuing with Noah's case, and we've been allocated the murder enquiry, which takes priority over our fraud case. But, obviously, one of our lines of enquiry has to be, was the victim murdered because of his possible involvement in the abduction?'

'How can I help?' Meg asked.

'We'd like you and Lauren to talk us through everything you've uncovered about Henry, or Hal, as I understand he was known. I gather Lauren's not on duty today, so we were intending to speak to you first then drive to her house to interview her there. But you said she's on her way here?'

'Yes.' Meg told them that Lauren was due to pick her up

at nine-thirty. Dan glanced at his watch; it was already ten past nine.

'I doubt Mrs Wilkinson is going to be very happy if we occupy her office for too long,' he said. 'Is there somewhere better we could go? It would be nice to have a coffee while we're waiting for Lauren.'

Meg told them about the farm shop café.

'Isn't that a bit too public?' he asked.

Meg reassured them that she and Lauren often discussed cases there, before sending a text to Lauren informing her of the change of plan. Dan and Viv returned to their car and waited for Meg whilst she went back to her room to get ready. Then Dan drove the three of them to the café, despite Meg protesting that it was close enough to walk.

❁

Lauren heard the ping of an incoming text, but she was already driving so she couldn't look at her phone until she pulled into the car park at Britford Lodge. She was surprised to see it was from Meg.

Don't come to BL, meet at farm cafe instead

This was all very mysterious. She refastened her seat belt and drove the short distance down Lower Road to park in the farm car park, pulling in beside a silver Nissan Juke that she thought she recognised. What was DI Dan doing there?

When she entered the café, it was empty apart from their usual table in the corner, where Meg, Dan and Viv sat quietly chatting. Lauren hesitated, not sure if she could face talking to Viv. Then she pulled herself together and marched up to them.

'Hello, what are you two doing here?' she said in a slightly over-bright voice.

Dan looked up at her with a smile. 'Lauren, it's good to see you. Come and sit down.'

Meg chipped in, 'We've only just arrived ourselves. I took the liberty of ordering you a black coffee. I hope that's okay?'

'Yes, of course it is,' Lauren said, as she took the remaining empty chair between Meg and Viv.

'Lauren, how are you?' Viv sounded as tense as she felt.

'I'm fine, thanks. And you?'

'Yes, fine.'

'Right, now we've got that out of the way,' Dan smiled wryly, wishing these two would just kiss and make up, 'we need to turn to the reason why we're here.'

He quickly brought Lauren up to date with what he'd already told Meg. Lauren was equally horrified by the news that Hal Winters was probably dead.

'That's terrible!' she exclaimed. 'If only I hadn't screwed up the ID evidence, he might still have been in custody!' She looked shell-shocked.

There was an awkward silence.

'You can't blame yourself,' Meg said gently, 'you weren't to know. If anything, I should have realised that what you were planning to do with the photos of Hal and Amelia might be problematic. Grant drummed the importance of following procedure into me often enough. I'm absolutely kicking myself that I didn't stop you.'

'Before anyone starts apportioning blame, can you bring Viv and me up to speed on what you've uncovered about Hal Winters, please?' Dan requested calmly. 'Go through everything, from the start, in as much detail as you can.'

Meg and Lauren took turns in speaking, with Dan chipping in with questions from time to time to clarify something they'd said. They were interrupted once by the arrival of their drinks, and again when another couple entered the café and passed close by their table. All the while, Dan listened impassively, and Viv made notes, keeping his eyes studiously on his notepad and not once looking at Lauren.

'Thank you,' Dan said quietly when they'd finished. 'The first thing I'm going to say is, don't play the "what if" game, Lauren. We don't know yet whether Hal's murder is connected to the abduction or not. He could've been killed for a completely unrelated reason. And even if it is connected, it wasn't your decision to release Hal on bail. That's on DI Barnes.'

'But I screwed up,' Lauren whispered.

'I'm not going to deny it. Yes, you messed up by showing Hal's photo to several witnesses and, yes, it's possible that Hal might still be in custody if you hadn't. But there was other evidence, and other ways of dealing with that issue than the route Barnes took. He chose not to follow up on the case against Hal because he's convinced that Vikram is guilty. As a police officer, you just can't let yourself become that blinkered in a case.'

'Lauren.'

She startled at the sound of Viv's voice next to her. 'I know I was against you investigating, but I've been talking with Aaron, and he says you've uncovered more leads in a week than Barnes has in three. And, thanks to you, a key witness statement against Vikram has had to be excluded on the grounds it's unreliable. The CPS is now re-examining the evidence against Vikram and, I'm telling you, it's looking very flimsy indeed.'

'Do you think Vikram might be released soon?' Lauren asked.

'I don't want to get your hopes up too much, but I'd be very surprised if the case makes it past the magistrate's hearing, which has been set for Monday morning.'

'That is good news,' Meg smiled at Lauren, 'and isn't that the very reason we agreed to investigate in the first place? Because we didn't want to see an innocent man stuck in prison?'

Lauren nodded.

Chapter Thirty-eight

Dan stretched. 'I don't know about the rest of you, but I could do with another coffee and something to eat. I had very little sleep last night, thanks to being called out to a crime scene, and I haven't had breakfast yet. Do they do bacon butties here?'

'They do,' grinned Lauren, 'and they're very good. I'll have one too, seeing as I also skipped breakfast.'

Viv grabbed a menu and studied it, looking for a healthier vegetarian option. 'My treat,' he said, standing up. 'Meg, what can I get you?'

'I'll have another pot of tea, please. And a toasted teacake would be nice.'

'No problem.' He went to the counter to order.

When he returned, Dan lowered his voice and spoke to them confidentially.

'We went to break the news to Hal's parents first thing this morning, before we came here, and they were able to give us a few basic details but, as you can imagine, they were very distraught. We'll interview them again later today when they've had time to assimilate the news. I understand that Hal has a sister but that she's estranged from her parents. When I pushed her, Mrs Winters admitted that she had no contact details for her daughter, Amelia. Do you know anything about her?'

'We've got no details for her, either,' Meg replied, 'unless you had any luck last night, Lauren?'

'No, I'm sorry. I couldn't find anything at all.'

'We were planning on going to visit her this morning,' Meg informed Dan, 'but that's obviously not possible. We wanted to confirm whether it was her with Hal on the morning before the abduction and whether she was driving that night. On the grounds that DI Barnes had dismissed

Hal as a suspect, we thought that he could hardly accuse us of stepping on his toes if we went to talk to her.'

'No, but you could be stepping on our toes now,' Dan pointed out.

'Oh yes, of course.' Meg sounded disappointed.

Dan hesitated. 'Under normal circumstances, I'd assume that her parents would tell her about her brother's death. But, as they are estranged, perhaps we should go and break the news ourselves. We should be able to get an address for her through official channels, and we'll need to talk to her at some point anyway. I wonder ...'He paused and then looked at Lauren thoughtfully. 'When do you next have some time off work?'

'I'm off today and tomorrow,' Lauren said.

'Okay, I'll get someone at the office to trace Amelia Winters' current address. Viv and I are going to Hal's workplace next to talk to his boss and workmates. We also need to speak to Hal's parents again, but then we could go to see Amelia later today. I could ask her if she'd mind having some more visitors tomorrow, if you'd like to go and see her then.'

'That would be very helpful, thank you,' said Meg.

'You're going to let us continue investigating?' asked Lauren, surprised.

'You absolutely can't investigate the murder,' Dan warned, 'but, unofficially, I think it wouldn't do any harm for you to continue looking into the abduction. DI Barnes is going to be up to his eyes today, going through the evidence against Chopra with the CPS, so he certainly won't be following any other lines of enquiry. And I have a feeling that, when and if we can establish that the two cases are linked, the super might well give us the abduction case too. I know she's regretting letting Barnes run the investigation. The point is, we can't investigate that until it's officially handed over to us, so anything you can find out will help us to hit the ground running, so to speak. Just be careful when it comes to collecting potential evidence.'

'And what do you think, Viv?' Lauren asked nervously.

'I'll go along with Dan,' he said reluctantly. He looked Lauren straight in the eye. 'But please don't go putting yourselves into any danger.'

'That's fair enough,' she replied. She saw the longing in his eyes and knew that he was only concerned for her safety. She was about to say something to him when the waitress arrived with their drinks and food.

Dan's bacon butty was on thickly sliced white bread, loaded with bacon and dripping with melted butter. 'Are you really going to eat that?' Viv asked in mock horror.

'What's wrong with this?' Dan asked defensively, picking his butty up.

'Oh, just a heart attack waiting to happen,' Viv replied, tongue in cheek. 'Highly processed bread, saturated fats, enough salt to send your blood pressure rocketing.'

'And I suppose you want me eating rabbit food, like you've got?' Dan scoffed.

'Nothing wrong with a nice bowl of granola with mixed berries. Lots of antioxidants, low in fat …'

'I think I'll take the heart attack,' Dan retorted with a grin, before taking a huge bite out of his butty. 'Mmm, so good,' he muttered with his mouth full.

Lauren smiled. She knew that Viv was very conscious of his diet and often took the mickey out of Dan for his love of red meat. She tucked into her bacon butty, which was marginally healthier than Dan's in that she'd opted for granary bread.

Silence reigned as they all ate.

Dan was the first to finish, licking his lips and wiping his fingers on a paper serviette. 'Come on then, back to work,' he said.

Meg nodded for him to continue.

'Another line of enquiry in the murder is Hal's involvement with Radical Action Salisbury. We can get a full rundown on them from our colleagues in counter-terrorism,' Dan said, 'but anything you can tell us now will be useful.'

Lauren filled them in on what she knew. 'Obviously, you'll need to talk to Tyler Ford, because he was Hal's best mate,' she added, 'but there are several others who seemed close, according to Jed. Mark, Gary and Liam are the three names I know, but I'm afraid I don't know their surnames.'

'Thank you, that's helpful,' Dan acknowledged. 'Now, about your friend Jed.'

'I know, I know, I shouldn't have involved another civilian,' Lauren declared, raising her hands in surrender. 'And Aaron has already ordered me to call him off.'

'And have you done that yet?' asked Dan.

'Well, no, not yet. I was going to get around to it later today.'

'Well, don't. You said he's already made contact with RAS, and Tyler in particular?'

'Yes, that's right.'

'And he's planning to go to their next meeting?'

'Yes, tomorrow evening at The Hanging Man.'

'Good. I don't like involving civilians, but the police find it very hard to infiltrate groups like that. Given Hal's connection with them, they've got to be suspects in his murder, but we're very unlikely to get anything out of them in a routine interview. People like that just don't talk to the police. I'd like to meet Jed, if that's possible, so that I can brief him properly. I don't want him asking questions that could put him in danger. But it would be very valuable to have someone inside the group, watching and listening.'

'I can phone Jed now, if you like,' Lauren offered.

'Yes, please. I think we're going to have a pretty full day, so could we arrange to meet him sometime this evening? Perhaps somewhere neutral, like a pub?'

Lauren grabbed her phone and left the table, going out into the bright sunshine in the farmyard. She spoke with Jed before returning to the others.

'That's all okay. He said he'll meet you at The Cathedral Inn at seven this evening.'

'Thank you, Lauren, we should make it by seven. Could you possibly give us a phone number for him, just in case we're delayed?'

'No problem, but would you mind very much if I come too?' Lauren asked hopefully. 'After all, Jed is my friend, and you don't know what he looks like.'

'Okay,' Dan nodded. 'That will help us to find him, and I already have your number.'

He checked his watch. 'Right, we need to get cracking with some work. Come on, Viv.'

'Yes, guv,' Viv replied, drinking the last mouthful of his coffee before standing up.

Lauren watched as they moved away.

'That wasn't too painful, was it?' asked Meg, who'd been watching Lauren's interactions with Viv.

'No,' she admitted. 'I know he's only concerned for my safety, and that's quite touching, really.'

Chapter Thirty-nine

Lauren arrived at The Cathedral Inn just after seven that evening, to find Jed loitering in the entrance way, waiting for her.

'Hi there, been waiting long?' she asked, giving him a friendly hug.

'Nah, you're all right,' he grinned. 'Shall we find a private corner away from other people? I'm guessing your boyfriend and his boss won't want to be overheard.'

Lauren agreed and they scouted the interior of the pub for somewhere suitable. Luckily, it was still early and not too busy, so they quickly found the perfect spot. Jed went to the bar to order drinks whilst Lauren settled herself into a semi-circular padded bench wrapped halfway around a circular dark oak table. She looked around at the smart interior, with its striped wallpaper and velvet curtains. It wasn't the kind of pub they would normally come to, and she wondered why Jed had chosen it.

When he returned with two pints of Coke – they were both driving – he slid in beside her, leaving the two wooden chairs on the outside of the table for Dan and Viv. He checked his watch. 'They should be here by now.'

'Oops, sorry,' Lauren pulled a face, 'I should've mentioned, they're running a bit late.'

'Do you know how late they're going to be?' Jed demanded.

'Viv texted me about ten minutes ago to say they'd be another half an hour, at least. Is that going to be a problem for you?'

'I could do with being away by nine,' Jed replied.

'You should be okay,' Lauren said, keeping her fingers crossed.

They chatted and sipped their drinks slowly. 'Why this pub?' she asked.

'Because I can't imagine Tyler or any of his mates coming somewhere like this,' Jed replied. She nodded; that was good thinking. 'And I wasn't sure I wanted any of my friends seeing me hanging out with two detectives, either,' he added.

'Why? You're not a criminal!'

'Of course not, but I do want to keep my street cred intact.'

They laughed.

By the time Dan and Viv hurried in, nearly forty minutes later, they were cosied up close together watching crazy cat videos on Lauren's phone and giggling like two schoolgirls.

Viv felt a twinge of jealousy, wishing it could be him so close to Lauren and not this blond-haired Adonis.

It was Dan who spoke to them first. 'I'm sorry we're so late. Can I get you both another drink?'

'I'll get them,' Lauren insisted, easing her way out of the curved seat. 'You two sit down and meet Jed. Jed, this is Daniel Bywater.' She indicated Dan, who leant over and shook hands with Jed. 'And this is Viv Williams.' Viv nodded politely before sitting down. 'What will you have?' She looked at Dan.

'I'll have a bottle of non-alcoholic lager, please,' he said, taking the seat next to Viv.

'Viv?' Lauren raised an eyebrow at him.

He bounced out of his seat. 'I'll come with you. You can't manage to carry four drinks on your own,' he said eagerly.

They went up to the bar together and Viv caught Lauren's hand. 'Can we talk later?' he asked nervously. Lauren nodded, not able to speak as her throat was suddenly choked with emotion.

Dan spent the time they were away taking down Jed's details. 'I have to risk assess this,' Dan explained. 'Bloody paperwork!' He'd just finished taking down Jed's details when the others returned.

Dan took a long swig of his lager. It was a pity it wasn't the real thing, but at least it was refreshing after a long hot day. 'Right,' he said, setting his bottle down on the table, 'Jed, I want you to talk me through your previous encounters with RAS and Tyler Ford. Lauren has briefed me already, but I need to hear it directly from you, please. You don't mind if Viv records this, do you?'

Jed said he didn't mind, so Viv set his phone to record and placed it on the table between Jed and Dan.

Jed spoke fluently and added a few details that Lauren hadn't mentioned.

'That's great, thank you,' Dan said appreciatively when Jed had finished. 'Now, there's a development you need to be aware of.' Dan leant forward and lowered his voice before telling Jed about Hal's murder.

'Bloody hell!' exclaimed Jed.

'You're going to have to be careful with this information. Although we've issued a press release this afternoon about the discovery of the body and the cause of death, we haven't named the victim publicly yet. I'm hoping to get clearance to release that sometime tomorrow, so that it's in the public domain before your meeting.'

'I understand,' said Jed. 'I'll check online before I go out.'

'I'll text you that and anything else I think you need to know,' Dan reassured him. 'But this does increase the risk to you,' he warned. 'Not only are RAS a vicious group of racist terrorists, but it's possible that one or more of them is responsible for Hal's murder. So, I need to ask, are you sure you're happy to go to this meeting tomorrow?'

'Absolutely,' Jed replied.

'Okay then, we need to run through a few sensible safety precautions,' Dan said.

'I can handle myself pretty well,' objected Jed.

'I'm sure you can, but you're one person against a group. I'm only giving you the same advice I'd give to an officer going undercover.'

Jed nodded his understanding and listened. It was mostly common-sense advice about not asking questions, not challenging any of the RAS members and keeping a low profile. Dan also advised him not to give out personal details if he could avoid it, and to keep his phone in a pocket where he could always reach it easily.

'Can you add my number to your speed dial?' he asked. Jed immediately did that.

'Can you dial it without taking your phone out of your pocket, if you need to?'

'Easy,' replied Jed. 'When I was at school, I could send whole texts with my phone in my pocket.'

'Well, if you start feeling uneasy, the best course of action is to make an excuse and leave as soon as you can. I suggest you park your car in the road outside the front of the pub, so that you don't have to walk through the car park, particularly after dark. If it's turning ugly and you can't get away without incriminating yourself, speed-dial me from your pocket. I'll keep my phone close all evening and pick up immediately. If you can't talk, I'll assume there's a problem and send backup.'

'Got it.'

'And text me when you get home safely, please. I don't want to be sitting by my phone all night unnecessarily.' He smiled to take the sting out of his words.

'I will,' Jed promised. 'Is that everything?' he asked, looking from Dan to Viv and back. 'Only I have someplace else to be this evening, if that's okay with you?'

'Yes, of course,' replied Dan. He glanced at his watch. 'I should be getting home too. Katie's going to be wondering where on earth I've got to.'

'How's she doing?' asked Lauren.

'Oh, well enough. Feeling permanently tired and craving bananas this week! Oh, and complaining that she feels like a beached whale.'

'Dan's wife is pregnant,' Lauren explained to a puzzled-looking Jed.

'When's she due?' Jed enquired politely.

'In about three weeks,' Dan replied.

'Any day now, then,' Lauren joked.

'Don't! I'd like to get this investigation out of the way first, please,' Dan said with feeling.

Dan and Jed both said their goodbyes and left.

'Would you like another drink?' Viv asked Lauren hopefully.

'Only if you buy me dinner as well, I'm starving,' she replied.

'Done,' he said with relief.

He went to find a couple of menus whilst Lauren sent a text to her mum to say she was eating out and might be late home.

With Jed or with Viv? her mum replied.

Lauren replied *Viv* and was rewarded with a huge smiley face emoji. It almost matched the smile on her own face.

Chapter Forty

Once Viv had bought more drinks and ordered their food at the bar, he returned and gestured to the spot recently vacated by Jed. 'Do you mind?' he asked.

'Don't be silly, you don't have to ask,' Lauren chided him.

He manoeuvred his six-foot muscular frame into the curved bench seat beside her. 'I didn't like to presume; things haven't exactly been great between us this week.'

'I know, and I'm sorry ...'

'No, I'm sorry,' he said. 'I just can't help worrying about you.'

'And why's that then?' she teased, trying to keep it light-hearted.

'Because I care,' he replied seriously. 'I care a lot about you, Lauren.'

Her heart did that little flip thing it had done the first time he'd asked her out, and her pulse quickened. 'I hate the fact that we argued,' she began nervously.

'Me too, so can we put all of that behind us?' he suggested, taking her hand in his.

'I'd love to,' said Lauren, 'but I need to know where I stand on this investigation.'

'How do you mean?'

'Well, Meg and I are still working on Noah's disappearance. And, just this morning, Dan gave us the go-ahead to visit Amelia Winters tomorrow, if you can give us her address.'

'Ah, about that.' Viv's tone sounded ominous.

'Don't tell me you're going to stop us from going?' she asked with a sinking feeling, withdrawing her hand from his.

'No, it's not that!' he hastened to reassure her. 'Aaron did some research last night and tracked her down from Salisbury to Andover and finally to an address in Ludgershall.

But when Dan and I went there this afternoon, she wasn't in. We asked around several of the neighbours and no one has seen her recently. One neighbour said she thought she must have moved away, because a man came with a box van three or four weeks ago, and they were loading furniture and bags on board.'

'Bugger!'

'Yes, that's pretty much what Dan and I said,' agreed Viv. 'No one seems to know where she's gone to, either.'

'Did you find out anything more from Hal's parents?' Lauren asked.

'Mrs Winters was still very tearful, which is only to be expected, but Mr Winters seemed to have recovered from the worst of the shock. He confirmed that the last address they had for their daughter was in Fugglestone Red.' He referred to an estate on the northern edge of Salisbury, not far from where the Winters lived.

'He told us she was no longer there and, I must say, he appeared to genuinely not have a clue as to where she'd gone.'

'What happened to cause that, I wonder?' Lauren mused. 'Why would a daughter not even tell her parents where she was moving to?'

'It's more common than you think,' Viv said. 'We see it all too often in the police, families estranged like that. I think it's why some of these young people go off the rails, to be honest. They no longer have the advice and support of their parents.'

'It depends how much help the parents were to begin with, I guess.'

'That's true, not all parents are as supportive as yours or mine.'

'Did they say very much about Hal?' Lauren asked.

'All the sorts of things parents usually say when they lose a child. What a lovely boy he was. How well he did at school. How much everyone loved him. It's amazing how every child, grownup or not, suddenly becomes such an angel after they've died. And I know that Hal was no angel; I've seen his police record. And some of his workmates said

177

a few less than complimentary things about him too. He was quite capable of manipulating situations to his advantage, according to one.'

'Did his parents know about his police record?' Lauren wondered.

'We asked them about that, and they did. But they put the blame on the group he's been hanging around with. RAS were, quote, "leading him astray", they said. And they were concerned about his friendship with Tyler, describing him as a bad influence.'

'It's always someone else's fault, isn't it?' said Lauren.

'Oh yes. And I can tell you where Hal probably got his racist views from, and it wasn't his friends. His own father is as racist as they come!'

'Oh no, was it really bad?' she asked, looking at him with concern.

'I've faced worse,' Viv admitted. 'I've been refused entry to people's homes because of my colour, and called derogatory names, even spat on. The Winters didn't go that far, but Mr Winters made a point of addressing all his answers to Dan regardless of which of us asked them. And he kept making sly references against immigrants every time he got the chance.'

'But you were born here!' she protested.

'You know that, but to some people, if I'm black, I must be an immigrant. I've lost count of all the times people have told me to go home.'

'What do you say to them?'

'A lot of the time, I ignore them as I know they're only trying to provoke a reaction. But I have been known to say, okay, I'll go back to my parents' in Southampton, if you like.'

Lauren chuckled. 'Good for you.'

'Enough of me; tell me what you've been up to today,' Viv said.

Lauren was about to tell him when her phone started to ring.

'Hi, Mia,' she answered. 'Yeah, I was told that too … Yes, I'll keep my fingers crossed for you and Vikram on Monday. What time is the hearing? … Oh, that's great. Listen, can I

call you back tomorrow and we'll chat properly then? …
Thanks. By-ee.'

'I'm guessing Mia's just been informed that Vikram's hearing is on Monday?' Viv said.

'Yes, she says she's allowed to be present in the magistrates' court, which is good news, I guess. So long as the outcome goes their way. But it's going to be tough on her if he gets remanded in custody again.'

'Between you and me, it's looking very likely that the case against Vikram will be dropped due to lack of evidence. But don't breathe a word of that to anyone, please.'

'I won't,' Lauren promised.

Just then, their food arrived, so they ate their meal and chatted about other things for a while.

'Coming back to the subject of Hal's murder,' Lauren said, as she dipped her last chip in the traces of ketchup on her plate.

'Hmm,' replied Viv, his mouth full.

'Do you know if he was killed in the car where he was found, or somewhere else?'

'And why do you want to know that?' asked Viv, wiping the last of the curry sauce from his plate with a piece of naan bread.

'Just curious, that's all.'

'Dan said you were absolutely not to investigate the murder,' Viv reminded her.

'It was worth a try,' she sighed, 'but can I just ask one last question? What colour and make was the car?'

'Please don't keep pushing me for information,' Viv begged her. 'I really don't want to fall out with you all over again. There are some things I just can't tell you.'

'I get that. It's like Meg said, it takes time to build trust in a relationship.'

'A very wise woman,' smiled Viv.

'Definitely. Did you know, she helped her late husband with a lot of his cases when they were married?'

'Did she really? And he was a DCI, wasn't he? But isn't that just the point? They were married, and he obviously had complete trust in her.'

179

'Do you think you'll ever have that much trust in me?' she asked timidly.

'Let's just keep working on our relationship,' he said with a twinkle in his eye, 'and we'll see how it goes.' He leant across and planted a kiss on her lips, and Lauren felt a flutter of excitement.

'It also helps when you're the boss,' he added, tongue in cheek. 'It's more than my life's worth to disclose information to you that Dan hasn't sanctioned.'

'Really? You're more afraid of your boss than you are of me?' she demanded.

'I'm not afraid. I just don't want to lose my job. I kind of like it. Now, how about a dessert?'

'Yes, please.'

Chapter Forty-one

Whilst Viv and Lauren were enjoying their meal out at The Cathedral Inn, DI Barnes, Aaron and several other members of the team were working late in the office. The CPS was not happy with the evidence against Vikram now that Barnes had been forced to throw out the statement made by Harold Norman. Extensive forensic tests on the black sports bag taken from Vikram's car had shown absolutely no trace of Noah Jenkins, or any foreign fibres at all. And, like Meg and Lauren, the CPS wanted to know why there were no prints on the baby monitor, as there would've been no need for Vikram to wipe it clean. They felt that the case against Vikram was too weak to go to court as it stood.

They had given DI Barnes an ultimatum: find some more conclusive evidence before ten tomorrow morning or they would be dropping the charges.

Barnes was desperate, so he had his team going over every witness statement and every piece of forensic evidence again, hoping to find something they'd missed.

'Guv,' Aaron eventually said, 'don't you think it would be a good idea if we agreed to drop the charges? There's absolutely nothing new here, and everything we've got is circumstantial at best.'

'No, no,' snapped Barnes, looking almost wild-eyed. 'I just know Vikram Chopra did this, and we've got to find the evidence to prove it.'

'But there isn't any new evidence. The more I look at everything, the more I think that Hal Winters is a far better suspect.'

'No, no! That would be a disaster,' Barnes declared. 'I promised the super I could get this case to court quickly, and now she's on my back demanding to know why I haven't delivered. If I fail to get the case against Chopra to stand …' he groaned. 'I just don't know what to do!'

He had an air of desperation about him, and Aaron almost expected to see him wringing his hands at any moment. 'Why don't you just take a look at the case against Hal Winters, guv?' he suggested gently.

'Definitely not!' Barnes snapped. 'I told the super that Chopra was guilty. How would it look if I changed my mind now? No. No, I can't do that. In any case, Winters was murdered the very day we released him from our custody. Can you imagine what the press would make of that, if they found out?'

Aaron bit back the retort on the tip of his tongue. 'Wouldn't it be better to make a watertight case against Hal Winters, instead of hopelessly pursuing Chopra?' he persisted.

'What's the point?' moaned Barnes. 'It's not like we can prosecute him now.'

'It would show the super that you've cracked the case, even if it can't go to court.'

'But our evidence against Winters is tainted by that bloody interfering girlfriend of DS Williams. Why did she have to go sticking her oar into my case?' he whined.

'Lauren meant well,' Aaron said, 'even though her actions were misguided. But we've got several lines of enquiry we could pursue against Winters, if you'll just consider it. Wouldn't it look better to the super to have a viable alternative suspect in place, if the charges against Chopra are dropped?'

'Oh, very well. I'll give you permission to follow up on Winters, see what you can find, but I want the rest of the team with me, working on the case against Chopra,' Barnes conceded. 'But you've only got until nine-thirty tomorrow morning. I'm going to have to call it one way or the other before the meeting with the CPS.'

Aaron found it hard to celebrate his small victory, given that he now had a very long night ahead of him.

✿

Viv and Lauren were having an after-dinner stroll through the Cathedral Close. The streetlamps cast a warm glow over everything, and it was so peaceful. Even the looming presence of the city's prestigious cathedral was somehow reassuring. They paused outside the grandiose house of former prime minister Edward Heath.

'Can you imagine living somewhere like this?' Lauren whispered.

'No,' replied Viv. 'Can you imagine the electricity bill?'

Lauren giggled. 'Not to mention all the housework and gardening it would require.'

'Far too much,' agreed Viv, slipping an arm around Lauren's shoulder.

She turned to face him. 'One day, a long time in the future, I dream of living in a lovely little country cottage with the man I love. I can imagine him doing the gardening while I'm cooking dinner and looking after our child.'

'Just the one child?' Viv teased.

'That all depends,' she said, blushing.

'Well, my dream is a big townhouse, filled with children and laughter,' he replied, studying her face quizzically.

'I guess that might work too,' Lauren conceded.

'It's called compromise,' he murmured into her ear. 'I think it's something that we both need to work on.'

Lauren was about to agree when his lips closed over hers and she lost herself in the moment.

✿

Meg was tucked up in bed, but she was finding it hard to concentrate on her book. Hal's murder had to be connected to their case; she felt sure of it. But how?

She ran through what they thought they know. Hal was Tyler's best friend, so it was entirely plausible that Hal could have taken baby Noah for him whilst he set himself up with an alibi. They had evidence that Hal and his sister, Amelia, had been working together, so it was also plausible that she might be looking after the child for Tyler. She wondered if Dan or Viv had been able to track down an address for her.

If Tyler and Hal had conspired over the abduction, could the two have fallen out and Tyler murdered Hal? Perhaps Tyler was concerned that Hal would talk to the police?

Or had one of their other friends found out and argued with Hal over it? Could Tyler have been paying Hal, and one of the others wanted paying off to keep quiet?

Or maybe Amelia had become too attached to Noah and had refused to give him to Tyler, and she and her brother had fallen out over that? Could a woman have murdered her brother like that? Meg shuddered at the thought.

Then she remembered that Amelia already had a child. A boy, if she correctly remembered what Mrs Winters had told Lauren. Would a mother be willing to keep another mother's child, knowing how much she must miss him? And surely her neighbours would get suspicious when one child suddenly became two. After all, the appeal for Noah had been widely publicised.

And then there was the evidence from Jed that Tyler had seemed genuine when he said he didn't know where his son was. Why would Hal agree to take the child for Tyler and then not tell him where he was?

None of it made any sense.

Chapter Forty-two

Lauren was awake but hadn't yet summoned up the energy to get out of bed. She was feeling all warm and fuzzy inside after making up with Viv last night, and her thoughts, for once, were not on the case.

The ping of a message cut through her daydreaming, and she rolled over to see who it was from. It was from Viv. She smiled and was about to reply when her phone rang. She answered it without looking at the caller ID.

'Too impatient to wait for my reply?' she murmured sexily.

'Uh, no,' came a different voice.

'Oh, I'm sorry, I thought you were someone else,' she apologised.

'I gathered that,' replied Aaron.

'Do you have news?' she asked breathlessly.

'No news about Vikram,' he replied, correctly surmising that was what Lauren had meant. 'We're having a briefing at nine-thirty before meeting with the CPS at ten, and I hope to have news for you after that. But that wasn't why I was phoning you.'

'Okay, what do you want?'

'I persuaded Barnes to let me follow up on Hal, so I spent most of last night going through everything we know about him. Early this morning, I went to the gym that Vikram belongs to, in the hopes that going at the same time of day that Vikram went might yield better results. And it did.' He sounded smug.

'That's great,' Lauren squealed. 'You got a positive ID on Hal?'

'Yes, a member of staff picked out Hal from a photo line-up. They said he signed in as a guest for his first free trial

185

session. He went to the changing rooms but then reappeared about ten minutes later saying that he'd had an urgent phone call which had to be dealt with so he wouldn't be able to stay for his free session after all.'

'That is interesting.'

'There's more. I asked around some of the clients in the gym, in the hope that they might be regulars at that time. And I found a guy who was in the changing rooms and saw a man fiddling with one of the lockers on the day in question. I showed him the photo line-up, and he also picked out Hal. Better still, the witness knew that it was Vikram's locker, because he knows Vikram. He challenged Hal, who got aggressive. The witness was going to mention it to Vikram on his way out, but he couldn't find him, and he was in a hurry to get to work himself.'

'That's fantastic!' Lauren enthused. 'Barnes can't ignore the evidence against Hal now, can he?'

'No, he can't.'

'Thank you so much for calling to tell me that,' she said.

'Well, I felt you deserved to know that your theory was correct, so long as you keep it to yourself. But it wasn't the only reason for my call,' he replied.

'Go on.'

'I just wanted to check something you told me on Monday. When you spoke with Sam Wallace, he told you about the car he'd seen dropping Hal off and that he saw the same car later, parked up further down the road.'

'Yes, that's right.'

'Did he describe the car to you?'

'Yes. He said it was a dark grey SUV. On the second sighting, he identified the car as being a Hyundai Tucson with a registration starting SW.'

'That tallies with what I wrote down on Monday; I was hoping I'd written it down incorrectly. How sure was he?'

'He seemed pretty sure, why?'

'I wanted to interview him again this morning but he's at work. You see, Hal Winters did drive a dark grey Hyundai, but it was the Alcazar model, not the Tucson. I wondered if Sam could've mistaken the model.'

'Do they look alike?' she asked.

'From the front, no. But from the back, in the dark? It might be possible to mistake the two. It all depends on how certain he is about the model.'

'What about the registration letters?' Lauren asked.

'They tally with Hal's registration,' Aaron confirmed. 'It probably was his car that Sam saw that night, but I would've liked to have confirmation.'

'And it was Hal's car that was torched with his body inside, wasn't it?'

'Yes, unfortunately it was, so there's no hope of finding any evidence inside the car. But I can try tracking it using the ANPR cameras. They might give us an idea of what direction he headed in after leaving Laverstock.'

'That'll be helpful.'

'Okay, thanks for your help.'

Lauren had a sudden flash of inspiration. 'Wait a moment.'

'Yes?'

'If Hal broke into Vikram's locker to make an impression of the front door key, he would have seen Vik's black sports bag. Do you suppose he could have bought an identical one for the abduction, so that it would look like Vik's?'

'That's quite possible, but I won't have time to follow up on that before the briefing.' Aaron gave a frustrated sigh.

'Can I help?' Lauren offered.

'That depends on what you've got in mind,' he replied cautiously.

'Do you know what make and style Vikram's bag is?'

'I could give forensics a call and ask them, but that all depends on what you're planning.'

'I thought I could go online and try to find out where you can buy that kind of bag. I mean, it might be so common that you can buy it anywhere but if, on the other hand, it's exclusive to a particular shop ...'

'Are you sure you have time to do that?' he asked.

'I've got a day off today,' she explained. 'I am planning to pick up Meg at nine-thirty. But you need any information I can find before then, anyway, so that gives me ...' she checked her watch'… over an hour to do some research before I need to leave.'

'That would be a great help,' Aaron said eagerly.

'No problem.'

'Right, I'll get that info for you, ASAP, and we'll chat again later. Bye for now.'

Lauren ended the call and jumped out of bed. She was going to need coffee before she got stuck into her research.

❂

Lauren was washed and dressed by the time a photo and relevant details arrived from Aaron. The bag was made by a company called Tripp, which she'd never heard of, so hopefully that meant it wasn't too common. She opened her notebook and started a search for the brand.

Bingo! She found an exact match for the Tripp Ultra Lite Black Holdall. Better still, there were a limited number of places where you could buy it: the Tripp UK website, Amazon and Ebay online. And just one high street chain: Next.

It was unlikely that Hal could've ordered it online and had it delivered the same day, but he could easily have gone into Next in Salisbury. She checked the store's opening times. It didn't open for another five minutes but she decided to give them a call anyway, in the hope that the staff would be in already.

She was just about to give up when a female voice answered.

'Good morning, Next Salisbury, how may I help you?'

'Good morning, I wondered if you could tell me whether you stock the Tripp Ultra Lite Black holdall?' she asked.

'I'll just check for you.' There was a moment's silence. 'We normally do, but I'm sorry to tell you that it's currently unavailable. We're waiting on a delivery any day soon.'

'Oh, I wonder if you could tell me when you last sold one?'

'May I enquire why you're asking?' the assistant said, sounding suspicious.

'It's a research project I'm doing for college,' Lauren said, thinking on her feet. 'I'm, umm … I'm trying to compare how popular different brands of holdall are.' She cringed; did that even sound plausible?

'I'm sure I can get the information you need,' the assistant said, apparently accepting Lauren's explanation. 'Please hold a moment.' Vivaldi's *Four Seasons* started playing down the line.

Lauren waited impatiently.

'Hello again. I've accessed our sales records for the last three months and I can see that we had three in stock at the start of that period. We sold two in April and one in June.'

'I don't suppose you can tell me the date the one in June was sold, can you?'

'Yes, it was sold on Friday, the second of June.'

Lauren felt like punching the air. 'Thank you very much,' she said.

'You're welcome. Is there anything else I can help you with?' the assistant asked.

'Do you know how the customer paid?' Lauren asked, hoping for bank card confirmation that it was Hal who made the purchase.

'They paid cash,' the assistant replied. 'Anything else?' she asked.

'No, that's everything. Thank you.'

It might be circumstantial, but it seemed likely that Hal had purchased the black bag after seeing Vikram's at the gym. Lauren immediately called Aaron back with the good news.

Chapter Forty-three

Lauren picked Meg up outside Britford Lodge as arranged and eagerly told her everything that had happened last night and this morning.

'That's excellent progress,' Meg beamed, 'and I'm particularly happy to know that you and Viv have reconciled your differences. But if Amelia Winters doesn't live in Ludgershall after all, why didn't you just phone and cancel our outing today?'

'Because I thought we could try to trace her movements,' Lauren replied. 'Now that Hal is dead, it makes it even more important to speak to Amelia if we're to have any hope of finding Noah alive.'

'I agree that we need to find Amelia, but I don't want you to get your hopes up too much. It certainly looks as though Hal was the one to abduct Noah, and that Amelia assisted him, but there's no guarantee that Noah is still alive. We don't know for sure why Hal took him or where he's been all this time. I've been thinking about Hal's murder, and I'm concerned that whatever reason he was murdered for, it's not likely to be good news for Noah.'

'I know, but I have to do everything I can for Mia. Just because Barnes has all but given up searching doesn't mean that I will.'

'Well said,' Meg conceded. 'What are your plans?'

'Viv gave me Amelia's address in Ludgershall, so I thought we'd go there and question the neighbours and local businesses. It's possible that someone knows something but didn't want to tell the police. A lot of people won't give information to the police, on principle.'

'That's true.'

'I also assume she was renting, so I wondered if we could find out who her landlord was. It's just possible he might have a forwarding address.'

'That's a good idea. If the neighbours don't know, we could try the local letting agencies. We could always pretend to be interested in the property.'

'It sounds like we have a plan,' Lauren said with a satisfied smile on her face.

Meg fastened her seatbelt. 'Off to Ludgershall we go, then.'

Forty-five minutes later, Lauren pulled up in front of a ground-floor maisonette in Florence Court in Ludgershall. It was a modern-looking development with lawns and young trees in front of the maisonettes, tucked away behind what looked like an old pub that had been converted into flats.

'It's a more pleasant area than I was expecting,' Meg commented.

'Yeah, and it's nice and central too. Right, come on, let's try Amelia's flat first.'

They walked up the path and rang and then knocked on the door without success. Lauren stepped onto the lawn to have a peek through the windows and observed that there was no furniture, which bore out what they'd been told. Amelia had obviously moved on. Then they tried the door for the maisonette above her, also getting no response.

'Let's try the neighbours,' Lauren said, a little disappointed.

This time, they had more luck. A young woman opened the door of the adjoining ground-floor maisonette. 'Yeah?' she asked, eyeing them suspiciously.

'I'm sorry to bother you but I'm looking for an old school friend of mine, Amelia Winters. I've got her address as number five but there's no one in.'

'She's moved out.' The short overweight woman in her twenties spoke abruptly and was already moving to close her door.

'Wait a minute,' Lauren called out. 'Can you tell me where she moved to?'

'No idea, love.'

'Well, when did she move?'

'I don't know, about a month ago, I reckon.'

'But she hasn't been here that long! And I was so looking forward to seeing her new place.'

'Reckon she's done a flit,' the woman said, apparently now ready to gossip. 'Big white van appeared early in the morning, and a bloke helped her load all her stuff, like, and then they were off. Never said a word to me about where they were going. Next thing I know, I had the police round asking about her.'

'The police have been here?' Lauren feigned surprise.

'Yeah, they wouldn't tell me why, but they asked a whole load of questions. I couldn't tell them any more than I've told you, I'm afraid. Tell you what, why don't you speak to Rosie at number nine? It's the next block along.'

'Thanks. Was she friends with Amelia?'

'I don't know how close they were, but Rosie spends most of her day sitting looking out of her front window. There's not much that goes on around here without her knowing about it.' The woman closed her front door this time, and Meg and Lauren made their way to number nine. An elderly woman with wispy white hair and a deeply wrinkled face answered the door.

'Yes?' she asked, looking at Meg.

'I'm sorry to bother you but we're looking for Amelia Winters. She used to live at number five, but she seems to have moved out.'

'Are you anything to do with those two policemen that came calling yesterday?' Rosie asked suspiciously.

'No, nothing like that,' Lauren answered. 'She's an old school friend of mine, and she said to look her up next time I came this way. I can't believe she's moved on already as she's only been here a few months.'

'Listen, I can't stand around chatting on my doorstep for too long; it's my legs, you see. They're not what they used to be! You can come along in, if you want, just so long as you're not police.'

They assured her they weren't, so she beckoned them in, leaning heavily on a wheeled walking frame as she led them into a small living room. It was packed with mismatching furniture and almost every surface was covered in ornaments, with photos hanging on every available bit of wall space. Rosie moved slowly and was clearly in pain. She shuffled across the room to a well-worn beige easy-riser chair situated next to the window and sat down with some difficulty. She indicated an old-fashioned two-seater sofa upholstered in a floral print fabric opposite her. 'Sit yourselves down, don't stand on ceremony here.'

Lauren and Meg sat down facing her. 'Were you friends with Amelia?' Lauren enquired.

'Not really, m'dear. You see, I can't get out and about much with this old hip of mine.'

'Arthritis?' asked Meg sympathetically.

'Yes, and it's a bugger too. I'm on the waiting list, but they seem to be taking their time getting around to me.'

Meg felt for the woman, having been in a similar situation herself not all that long ago.

'I'd offer you a cup of tea,' Rosie said wistfully, 'but I don't think I've got it in me to stand up again.'

'Would you like me to go and make some tea for us all?' offered Lauren, feeling sorry for the old woman.

'Would you mind? That'd be lovely. There's tea and sugar with the mugs in the cupboard above the kettle, and you'll find the milk in the fridge. There's instant coffee too, if you prefer that.'

'No problem,' said Lauren. 'How do you like your tea?'

'Not too strong,' Rosie replied, 'with just a dash of milk. No sugar for me. When I say I like weak tea, some people make it strong and then add lots of milk to make it look weaker, and that's not the same at all.'

'Not at all,' agreed Meg. 'You like your tea exactly the same way I like mine!'

Lauren smiled as she left the two octogenarians comparing notes.

Chapter Forty-four

The kitchen was tiny but well organised, so Lauren quickly found everything she needed. Whilst she was waiting for the kettle to boil, her phone rang and, glancing at the caller ID as she took it out of her pocket, she saw that it was Aaron.

'Hi, Aaron, please say you've got some good news,' she demanded.

'Yes, Lauren, I have. The CPS has dropped the charges against Vikram – insufficient evidence – and he'll be released from prison this afternoon as soon as the paperwork has been done.'

Lauren punched the air with delight. 'That's fantastic. I can't wait to tell Mia!'

'She already knows; I phoned her before calling you.'

'I bet she's over the moon.'

'She certainly is. But she immediately asked if there was any news about Noah, and I had to disappoint her on that score.'

'You will keep looking for him, though, won't you?'

'Of course we will. The investigation is going to step up a gear or two, now that it's been handed over to DI Bywater.'

'Dan's taking charge? That is good news!'

'Yes. DI Barnes is not a happy bunny. I showed him the evidence I gathered against Hal Winters, a lot of it with your help, and he recognised straight away that Hal was a more viable suspect than Vikram ever was. The witnesses I found at the gym clinched it, I think. He and the rest of the team had made no progress at all overnight on Vikram's case, and I think he could see the writing on the wall. He cancelled the briefing and went to see the superintendent. Next thing we know, he's asking us to get everything ready to brief DI Bywater. Now that Dan's the SIO in charge of the joint investigation into Noah's abduction and Hal's murder, we've all been told to work together as one large team. This is the priority case now.'

'Well, about time too,' Lauren commented with feeling.

'I agree. I'd better go, as we've got a lot of work ahead of us today.'

'Thanks for taking the time to let me know about Vikram.' Lauren ended the call and finished making the hot drinks with a huge smile on her face. But then a little doubt began niggling at the back of her mind. If both police teams were now working together, that would include Viv. How would he react to her still investigating? She pushed that thought away, determined to carry on.

Meg could see that Lauren had news the moment she walked into the room with the hot drinks. 'Well?' she asked, raising an eyebrow expectantly.

'I've just had a phone call from Aaron, with the good news we were hoping for,' Lauren replied enigmatically.

Meg smiled. Hopefully, that meant the charges against Vikram had been dropped. 'That's great. Rosie and I have been chatting and it's amazing how much we have in common. In addition to the arthritis and how we drink our tea, we're the same age, we were both English teachers and we both lost our husbands to cancer.'

'That's kind of sad but also impressive,' Lauren said, carefully setting down the mugs on coasters.

'Thank you, m'dear,' Rosie smiled at Lauren. 'Now, settle yourself down next to your granny. While it's been lovely chatting to someone my own age, I know you came here to look for your friend. What do you want to know?'

Lauren suppressed a smile. Yet another person had mistaken Meg for her grandmother but, in this instance, she didn't want to disillusion her.

'Like I said, I'm looking for an old school friend of mine, Amelia Winters.'

'Let me stop you right there, dear. The young lady next door was called Amelia all right, but I'm sure she said her surname was Walters, not Winters. Although I am a little hard of hearing, so I could be wrong.'

'Amelia gave me the address herself, so I'm sure it's her,' Lauren persisted, wondering how she could confirm that they were talking about the same woman. 'She's petite with long blonde hair, and she's got a little boy, a toddler of about fifteen months.'

'Well, the description sounds like her, but she didn't have a child living with her, of that I'm certain.' Rosie looked at them with a puzzled expression on her face.

She wasn't nearly as baffled as both Lauren and Meg. Whatever had happened to Amelia's son?

Lauren had to think quickly to keep the conversation going. 'That's very odd, unless her ex-boyfriend has custody. But I can't imagine why she didn't tell me! Are you sure she didn't mention it to you?'

'No, dearie, I'm sorry.' Rosie looked thoughtful. 'But that would explain her sudden arrival and the fact she looked so miserable for weeks after she moved in,' Rosie said, nodding to herself. 'Poor little mite looked like she'd been through the wars the day she came here.'

'I've been working abroad on a short-term contract,' Lauren lied convincingly, 'so I've obviously missed out on all the news. Do you mind telling me a bit more about Amelia's arrival here?'

'Not at all, m'dear. Let me see now. It was between Christmas and New Year. I spent Christmas with one of my sons in Andover and he brought me home on the morning of the twenty-seventh. They wanted to go shopping in the sales, you see, so I told them they might as well take me home first. I can't walk round a load of shops, and what would I want to buy anyway? So, it wasn't that day that Amelia arrived, nor the next, because I was waiting in all that day for a delivery. But it was before New Year, because another of my sons insisted on me going there to see the New Year in with them, not that I like to stay up that late. It was probably the twenty-ninth or thirtieth of December that

196

Amelia arrived. It was most strange, because the couple that lived there before had only moved out just before Christmas. They were buying a new-build house, and it was ready, and they wanted to be in their new home for Christmas. But they told me they'd paid the rent up to the end of the month, so I wasn't expecting new neighbours until after the New Year.

Well, I remember I was sitting here with my morning cuppa when this big grey car pulls up outside. It wasn't one I recognised, so I watched. This tall, lanky fella gets out, like a beanpole he was, and he looks around like he owns the place. Then, the passenger door opens, and this poor wee mite gets out. She looked that unhappy, and she had bruises across her face, a big black eye, and her arm was in a sling. Like I say, it looked like she'd been through the wars.'

Meg and Lauren exchanged worried glances.

Meg's mind was in a whirl. Whatever had happened to Amelia? Had someone attacked her? An ex-boyfriend or her brother, Hal? Or maybe even her father? Was this why she was estranged from her parents?

Rosie was still speaking. 'Well, the fella gets some plastic bags out of the boot, and they take them into number five. Then he comes back out again and drives away, leaving her there on her own. A bit later in the day, he comes back and unloads a whole load of shopping bags from Tesco.'

'Is there a Tesco in Ludgershall? Lauren asked.

'Well, there's a small one that's useful for little bits and pieces, but I reckon he'd probably been to the big store in Andover. What do they call it? Tesco Extra. Well, he disappears inside and stays for a couple of hours, then he comes back out and drives off, leaving her there on her own. And not an item of furniture in the house, not that I saw go in anyway.'

'That is strange,' Meg said.

'Indeed, it was,' agreed Rosie. 'At first, I thought they were just dropping some belongings off ahead of moving in and that they'd both leave, so I was that surprised when she stayed behind. What did the poor woman sleep on? That's what I was worried about.'

Chapter Forty-five

Before Meg or Lauren could respond, the garrulous woman answered her own question. 'I must admit I had to ask her, although I didn't get the chance for several weeks. By which time, of course, that lanky fella had brought various bits of furniture in his car. It all looked like stuff he'd picked up second-hand, not new stuff. Anyway, where was I?

'Oh yes, I eventually asked her how on earth she'd managed with no furniture to begin with, and she said she had one of those blow-up mattress things. I wouldn't want to sleep on one of those, but then again, she's a lot younger than me.'

'It's strange that she moved in when she did, if the previous tenants had paid until the end of the month. Do you happen to know who the landlord is?' Meg enquired.

'I don't know the landlord,' Rosie replied, 'but I can tell you who the letting agent is. It's Castle Estate Agents, just across the main road from here. They'd only just put the sign up when Amelia moved in.'

'Thank you so much,' Lauren said with genuine warmth. 'We'll go and ask if they know where Amelia's moved to.'

'Aye, they might know. Mind you, her moving out was all very sudden too.'

'Oh?' prompted Meg.

'Well, I only spoke to her a few days before, and she didn't say a word to me about leaving. She used to pop in once a week to see if I needed any shopping, which was kind of her. My sons usually bring my shopping, not that I need a lot because I have all my meals delivered, apart from breakfast, and I can manage to get a bowl of cereal for myself. But sometimes I have a fancy for something extra or different, so Amelia used to get it for me. Like I said, when I saw her on the Tuesday of that week, she never mentioned that she was moving. And then, early on the Saturday, that big grey car turns up again. Come to think of it, perhaps he was the ex-boyfriend? I saw that he had a young toddler strapped into a car seat in the back of his car. A bonny wee lad with blond hair.'

'Which Saturday was this?' Meg asked quickly.

'Let me think, now. It was a few weeks ago. It can't have been the last weekend in May, because my eldest son and daughter-in-law took me to Bournemouth for a short break by the sea. Lovely it was, sunny every day and the sea air does you so much good, doesn't it? Anyway, I think it was the weekend after that one, so the first weekend in June. Or was it the one after that? No, I remember I was watching the women's final of the French Open on the second Saturday in June. I do love watching the tennis, you see. That nice Polish girl – can't pronounce her name – but she won for the second time in a row. Of course, it's Wimbledon on the telly now, and I shall be glued to my set again this afternoon. So, yes, Amelia must have moved out on the previous weekend, whatever date that would be.'

'Saturday the third of June?' suggested Lauren eagerly.

'That sounds about right, m'dear, yes.'

'After the tall skinny man in the grey car came with the toddler, what happened then?' Meg prompted.

'Oh yes, it was ever so odd. You see, Amelia was in the car with them, although I never saw her leave. Perhaps she'd been away overnight? Anyway, Amelia gets the little lad out, and he was crying, and she was doing her best to comfort him, and they all three went indoors. Then the lanky fella comes out again almost immediately and drives off. About an hour later, he was back again but this time in one of those big white vans you can hire and drive yourself.'

'Can you remember the company name on the van?' Meg asked.

'Ooh, now let me think. It was one of those boxy-looking vans, white, with green and black writing on it.'

'Enterprise?' suggested Lauren.

'That's the one!' exclaimed Rosie. 'Yes, it was an Enterprise van. Well, they loaded all her furniture and stuff into the van, then he drives off with it, leaving her and the toddler behind. Later in the afternoon, he comes back again in that big grey car of his, and he takes Amelia and the toddler, and off they drive. And that was it. She was gone, without so much as a goodbye.'

Meg and Lauren looked at each other, staggered at how much they'd learnt. 'You said you had the police here yesterday? Was that to do with Amelia too?' Lauren asked.

'Yes, it was two detectives, least ways, that's what they said they were. One was tall and black and easy on the eyes, and the other was shorter and white, and very average-looking.'

Meg smiled, recognising the descriptions of Viv and Dan. 'And what did they want?'

'They also asked if I knew where Amelia had gone to, and I told them, quite honestly, that I had no idea. Then they asked when she moved, and I said about a month ago. But that was it. I didn't tell them anything else.'

'You don't like the police?' Meg asked.

'No, I don't. I mean, I believe in them upholding the law, because where would this country be without the law? But my youngest, Derek, he had a bit of a run-in with the police when he was a teenager, and the detectives that dealt with it were none too gentle. And they kept on at him so much that he ended up confessing to something he didn't do.'

'I'm sorry to hear that,' Meg said seriously, 'but hopefully these two were nicer?'

'Oh, they seemed very nice, but I didn't want to invite them in, in case they pestered me into saying something that got that poor girl into trouble.'

Meg thanked Rosie for her valuable information whilst Lauren took the three mugs back to the kitchen and rinsed them. Then they said goodbye and let themselves out, to save Rosie from having to get up.

'Wow,' exclaimed Lauren as they walked away from Rosie's front door.

'Wow, indeed,' echoed Meg. 'We learnt so much more there than I had hoped for!'

As soon as they were on the pavement, Lauren turned to look at her. 'The lanky fellow in the grey car must have been Hal, don't you think?'

'Very likely,' Meg agreed.

'And the toddler Rosie saw on the third … that must have been Noah?'

'That was my first thought, although we still don't know what happened to Amelia's own son.'

'The timing all fits,' insisted Lauren. 'Amelia was away overnight and turns up here with Hal and Noah on the morning of the third. But why did they immediately do a flit?'

'That's a good question, and only one of many,' sighed Meg.

Chapter Forty-six

They walked in silence back to the car, overwhelmed by what they'd learnt.

'Where to next?' asked Lauren, unlocking her car.

They both got in before Meg replied. 'Well, the letting agent is just down the road, so let's go there first and see if he has a forwarding address.'

'I'm sure he must do,' Lauren started the engine, 'because he'll need to know where to send all the final bills. But whether he'll tell us is another question altogether.'

She drove about fifty metres down the road and then stopped again. 'Actually, it might be a good idea to leave the car here. I'm pretty sure the main road was all double yellow lines. Will you be okay to walk? I don't think it's very far.'

'A short walk will do me good,' insisted Meg, taking her seat belt off again.

They strolled to the end of the road and, sure enough, Castle Estate Agents was almost directly across the main road from the junction. Crossing the road took a bit of effort because of the traffic, but eventually they made it. They pushed open the door into a well-lit space with row upon row of photos of properties for sale or to rent.

When they asked to speak to someone about rental properties, the lettings agent turned out to be an attractive heavily made-up middle-aged woman with short magenta red hair and a Welsh accent. 'How can I be helping you?' she asked in a stereotypically sing-song voice.

Meg took the lead. 'We've been visiting my friend who lives across the road in Florence Court, and she told us that her neighbour has moved out. There's no board up yet, but she told us you were the letting agent previously. I'm looking for somewhere nice and manageable, not too far from my granddaughter.'

'Florence Court, you say?' The agent looked puzzled. 'We do have a couple of properties in that road, but both of them are occupied at present. Where to, exactly?'

'Number five,' Meg replied.

'Oh no, I'm sorry, there must have been some kind of mistake.'

'We've just walked round it, to have a little look,' Lauren protested. 'The property is quite definitely empty, and it would be perfect for my gran.'

'I'm only saying, it's occupied, so it can't be empty,' the woman insisted, getting a little annoyed. 'Listen, I'll go and get the file, just to double-check, like.' She spun round and disappeared into a back office and returned moments later with a buff-coloured folder open in her hands.

'Now, listen, I'm not being funny, but that property *is* currently occupied. Obviously, I can't give you the name of the tenant, but she's not given in her notice so I can't see as how it could be empty.'

'We were told, quite reliably, that the tenant moved out on the third of June,' Lauren insisted, 'and the rooms are all empty. I looked. No furniture, no belongings, nothing.'

'Well, that is odd.' The agent clicked her tongue in disapproval and moved to a desk. She laid the file in front of her and moved a mouse to wake her computer. She typed something, her bright purple acrylic nails tapping on the keys, then studied the screen before looking up at Meg and Lauren with a frown on her face.

'It says here that she usually pays her rent on the twenty-ninth of the month. She paid it in April, but May's payment is still outstanding, as is June's now, because it was due yesterday. This is most peculiar.'

'Don't you normally chase up overdue payments?' Lauren asked.

The agent visibly bristled. 'The accounts department deals with that, not me, although I should have been informed. Can you wait by here while I go and talk to someone upstairs in accounts?' She stood up and hurried towards a staircase.

As soon as she was out of sight, Lauren edged round the desk with her phone in her hand. She surreptitiously opened the folder and, checking the flash was switched off, she clicked a couple of photos, before closing the folder and returning to Meg's side. She winked at Meg and Meg smiled. Hopefully, they now had some other details for Amelia Winters, or Walters, whatever she was calling herself.

They waited several minutes, then the agent returned, looking flustered.

'Alison in accounts says she's been trying to get hold of the tenant, but her phone is disconnected, and she doesn't reply to her emails. And, because she didn't hand in her notice or fill out the proper paperwork, we've no forwarding address. It really is most annoying; it looks like she's done a flit on us! I don't imagine the landlord's going to be best pleased when I tell him.'

'Do you think the maisonette will be up for rent again soon?' Meg asked.

'I really have no idea. If you could leave your name and a phone number, I'll contact you as soon as we can clarify what the situation is.' She scribbled something onto a sheet of paper and passed it across to Meg to write her details on, then tucked it into the buff folder. 'Would you be interested in looking at some of our other rental properties?' she asked in a businesslike manner.

'I'm sorry, not today,' Meg said. 'We'll wait and see if that one becomes available; I'm not in a great hurry to move. Thank you so much for your help.'

The agent stood up and shook hands with them. 'Is there anything else I can be doing for you?' she asked politely.

'I don't suppose you could recommend a nice tearoom nearby, could you?' Meg enquired, her stomach reminding her that it was quite some time since breakfast.

'There's a nice one just around the corner, it's not far. Turn right out of the door and follow the road round into the high street. It's just past the post office on your right. As well as cream teas, they do a lovely selection of sandwiches and cakes there.'

Meg thanked her and they left the estate agency.

The tearoom was a little further round the corner than

they'd expected, but it was easy enough to find with its scarlet and white sign declaring it to be The Vintage Tea Rooms. Pretty lace nets adorned the windows, and inside it felt distinctly old-fashioned with its red and white gingham tablecloths each topped with a menu, a sugar bowl and a vase containing a single fresh carnation. Meg approved.

They found a seat by the window and had barely settled in when a cheerful waitress appeared wearing a vintage-style lace-edged apron. 'Good afternoon,' she said. 'Have you come in for lunch? Only I'm sorry to say that we only serve meals after midday.'

'No, that's okay, we're here for lunch, please,' Meg replied.

'That's fine, then. I'll give you a few minutes to look at the menu and I'll come back to take your order.'

Meg and Lauren studied the menu between them, Meg choosing a toasted ham and cheese sandwich whilst Lauren opted for a hot sausage butty. As soon as the waitress had taken their order, Lauren took out her phone and checked the photos she'd snapped at the estate agent's. Unfortunately, they didn't tell her a lot that they didn't already know, the only new thing of interest being Amelia's mobile phone number. She tried ringing it but got a message saying that the number was no longer in use. She supposed that was only to be expected, in the circumstances.

Chapter Forty-seven

Once the waitress had delivered their tea and coffee, Meg got her notebook and pen from her handbag so that she could jot down the things they'd learnt from Rosie and the letting agent that morning. 'You do realise, Rosie will probably have to give the police an official statement,' said Meg with a sigh. 'I just hope she doesn't refuse to confirm what she's told us.'

'I'm sure if Dan and Viv go, it'll be all right,' Lauren said. 'I mean, it must be a long time ago that her son was a teenager, and policing has changed a lot since then.'

'Yes, definitely,' Meg said with feeling.

'We're beginning to get a timeline for Amelia, I think,' suggested Lauren. 'Mrs Winters said that they became estranged from their daughter about a year ago, which is probably when she moved to Andover, although we don't know why that happened. Then Amelia moved to Ludgershall in December and, again, we don't know why. And how come she was all beaten up when she moved in? It can't have been her father, because they were already estranged by then, so I'm guessing it might have been an abusive boyfriend. What do you think?'

'That certainly makes sense,' Meg agreed.

'Maybe Hal helped his sister to escape, although she apparently had to leave her son behind. That must have been tough.'

'Unless the child was taken into care?' suggested Meg.

'Yes, that's another possibility. Either way, that explains her being so sad, and the fact that she had to change her surname.'

'Yes, it does.'

'And I think we can assume that the toddler Rosie saw on the third of June was Noah, and not her own son. It all ties in with the sightings of the dark grey SUV in Laverstock, Hal and Amelia being seen together on the morning before his abduction, and Amelia driving the car for the getaway.'

'We're making progress – we know the *who* and the *how*,' said Meg. 'Now we just have to find out where Amelia and Noah have gone to.'

'Which isn't going to be easy now that Hal is dead,' Lauren said dismally.

'And we still have the important questions: why did Hal abduct Noah? And who killed Hal and why?' Meg reminded her.

Before Lauren could reply, their food arrived so, by common consent, they dropped their discussion of the case and tucked in hungrily.

❁

When they finished eating, Meg remembered to ask Lauren about the phone call she'd had from Aaron whilst they were at Rosie's.

'Oh yes!' Lauren exclaimed. 'DI Barnes has admitted defeat and finally conceded that Hal is the more likely suspect in Noah's abduction. Aaron says that the superintendent has put Dan in charge of both the abduction and the murder cases now. And, best of all, the CPS has dropped the charges against Vikram for lack of evidence! He's going to be released from prison sometime this afternoon.'

'That is good news. I bet Mia's happy,' Meg beamed.

Lauren suddenly remembered something. 'After I spoke to Aaron, I put my phone on silent so that we could talk to Rosie uninterrupted. Then, when I looked at my phone just now, I saw that I had several notifications.'

She pulled her phone out of her pocket and checked it. 'Three messages and a missed call.' She tapped away at the screen. 'The missed call was from Viv, as was one of the messages, asking me to call him back. I'll do that in a minute. One of the other messages was from Mia.' She opened it and read it aloud to Meg.

Vikram is coming home and it's all thanks to u. I can't thank u enough xxx

She looked at the third message. 'This one's from Dan.'

I'm now SIO on both cases, please update me as soon as you get this

'It's a bit too public to make phone calls here,' Meg commented, looking around at the busy tables. 'Perhaps we should go back to the car, so we can talk without risk of being overheard.'

'That's a good idea,' Lauren agreed, 'but I'm going to grab a couple of those cakes to take with us for later! Which one do you want?'

'I'll have a chocolate eclair, please,' Meg replied. She couldn't remember the last time she'd had an eclair.

Lauren went up to the counter to pay, ordered two eclairs and watched as the assistant neatly boxed them up for her to take away.

✿

When they got back to her car, Lauren asked who she should phone first.

'Dan,' replied Meg firmly. 'He's the SIO now and needs to have our news right away. Then you can phone Viv and chat for as long as you like.'

Lauren grinned in appreciation as she found Dan's number and hit call, putting her phone on speaker so that Meg could join in too.

'DI Bywater speaking,' came Dan's voice.

'Hi, it's Lauren here and I've got Meg with me on speaker.'

'Great. Where are you?'

'We're in Ludgershall.' Lauren succinctly told Dan what they'd found out that morning.

'Good work, you two. We've also been following up on Amelia Winters, and everything you've just told me fits with the information we've got. We've established that she left home because she was pregnant, and she went to live with her boyfriend, Cody Johns, in Fugglestone Red. But three months after the baby was born, they moved to Andover, which is when Mr and Mrs Winters lost contact with their daughter. Johns was arrested on domestic abuse charges in Andover on the twenty-eighth of December last year and is currently out on bail awaiting trial. Amelia went into hiding, and the child, Freddie, was taken into care.'

'Poor Amelia,' Lauren gasped. 'Why couldn't she take her child with her?'

'Social services had their reasons,' was all that Dan would say on the matter.

'I believe Freddie was of a similar age to Noah?' Meg asked.

'Yes, that's right,' Dan confirmed.

'Is it possible that Hal took Noah to give to his sister? As a kind of replacement for her own child?' Meg suggested.

'We've thought of that possibility too. It's one of several lines of inquiry.'

'How about Hal's murder?' asked Lauren.

'What about it?' replied Dan cautiously.

'Oh, you know, just wondering …'

'Wonder away, but I'm not going to tell you anything,' Dan said firmly. 'In fact, as much as I appreciate your help to date, I really think it's time for the two of you to have a well-earned rest and let us take over.'

Lauren looked crestfallen. 'What about Jed going to the RAS meeting tonight? That's still on, isn't it?'

'Just leave that to me,' was all that Dan would say on the subject.

Frustrated, Lauren said goodbye and ended the call.

'Dan's shutting us out again, isn't he?' Lauren said with a pout.

'What do you expect? As SIO, he has a great deal of responsibility … and he's already told us more than he probably should have.'

'I know you're right,' Lauren sighed, 'but that doesn't mean I like it.'

'I want to send a text to Sanjeev to tell him about Vikram,' Meg said. 'I can do that while you phone Viv, if you like?'

'Yeah, I'll walk and talk and leave you to have a little peace,' Lauren said, getting out of the car again as she called Viv's number.

Meg sent Sanjeev a text and received an almost immediate response.

I knew you could do it! Thank you!

She felt guilty, getting congratulations from Mia and now Sanjeev. Yes, they'd helped to exonerate Vikram, which was what Sanjeev had originally asked them to do. But it was a long way from case closed, with Noah still missing and Hal's murderer on the loose.

She watched out of the window as Lauren walked up and down the pavement with her phone held close to her face. Lauren's smile gradually turned to a frown. The walking became brisker and more agitated, and her wild gesticulating suggested that the conversation wasn't going the way she wanted it to. Eventually, Lauren jabbed a finger at the screen and stormed back to the car. She slumped into the front seat with a loud sigh. 'That bloody man,' she exclaimed.

'Trouble in paradise?' Meg asked cautiously.

'I just wish he'd make up his mind,' fumed Lauren. 'How are we ever going to build a relationship based on trust if he doesn't trust me?'

Meg wisely refrained from answering.

Chapter Forty-eight

Meg discreetly looked away whilst Lauren used a tissue to wipe away the hot tears that were threatening to fall, and waited until her breathing had calmed down. When she judged that the moment was right, she gently asked, 'Do you want to talk about it?'

Lauren took a deep breath.

'Okay, perhaps I overreacted a little,' she said sheepishly, 'but I just find it so frustrating. One minute he's sharing things with me, and the next he clams up and goes all secretive. I mean, I understand that he can't tell me anything about Hal's murder. Dan's already made that clear to us, and Viv said that Dan had explicitly told him not to discuss the murder case with us. So, I get that he was only obeying orders.'

'I'm glad you understand,' Meg said reassuringly.

Lauren frowned. 'But then he gets all cross at me for coming to Ludgershall today, when we discussed that yesterday morning and Dan gave his approval, right in front of him! He even had the cheek to say that he doesn't come to the care home to do my job for me, so why was I constantly interfering in his job? He didn't seem to understand that Sanjeev asked *us* to look into Noah's abduction, and I made a promise to Mia that I'd do my best to help her get Noah back. I told him I don't break my promises. But then he said that I *had* broken a promise, because I promised him after the last case that I wouldn't put myself in danger again. But nothing we've done today has put us in any kind of danger! I just don't see why he's so mad at me.'

'Possibly because he loves you?' Meg suggested gently.

'Well, he's got a funny way of showing it,' Lauren replied sulkily.

Meg waited patiently to allow Lauren to pull herself together. 'I'm sorry, Meg,' she said finally. 'I shouldn't drag you into our arguments.'

'I'm always here if you need someone to talk to, or a shoulder to cry on,' Meg reassured her. 'Relationships can be difficult, particularly in the early stages when you're still getting to know each other.'

'I thought we had something special,' Lauren said glumly.

'Had – past tense?' asked Meg, raising an eyebrow.

'Well, no. Oh, I don't know. Part of me loves him to bits, but a bit of me is wondering if it's worth all the heartache.'

'Give it time,' Meg advised, 'but, in the meantime, I'm getting a little bit concerned about the state of our eclairs sitting in this hot car. What say we eat them before they melt?'

'Cake is always a good idea,' grinned Lauren, lowering the windows to allow some fresh air to circulate before reaching for the cake box.

After they'd eaten their cakes and licked their fingers, Lauren left Meg in the car whilst she went in search of cold drinks to wash the sticky sweetness away. She returned with a small pouch of orange juice for Meg and a bottle of soda for herself. After a long drink, she looked at Meg and asked, 'Right, where to next?'

'I think that, for once in our lives, we should do as we're told and have a well-earned rest. Would you like to drop me back at the care home and then you can be free to do whatever you want to do?'

❈

Lauren dropped Meg at Britford Lodge and drove home to Downton, feeling fed up after her argument with Viv. Her mother was still at work, so Lauren mooched around the empty house for a couple of hours, not really settling to anything. Part of her frustration also came from being shut out of the case. How was she supposed to know what was going on now that neither Dan nor Viv would talk to her about it?

There's got to be another way of keeping up to date, she thought.

Then she had a lightbulb moment: Jed!

She tried Jed's number, but it went straight to voicemail, so she left a message asking him to call her back ASAP. He called about ten minutes later.

'Sorry, mate,' he began, 'I was being briefed by DI Dan when you tried to call.'

'You're still on for tonight, then?' she asked eagerly.

'Yep, why? Was it ever in doubt?'

'Only something Dan said earlier, but it doesn't matter now. What did Dan say to you?'

'Okay. First, Vikram has been released from prison and is back at home with Mia now, so I need to be alert for anything RAS might be planning against him.'

'I knew the CPS had dropped the charges against Vik, but it's good to hear he's home already.'

'Second, Hal Winters has been named in the media as the fatal stabbing victim found in the burnt-out car on Wednesday night. The RAS members will likely know that, so I'm to keep my eyes open for anyone acting suspiciously when they're discussing it, which no doubt they will.'

'That makes sense,' Lauren agreed.

'Third, they've had Tyler Ford in for questioning about Hal's murder this afternoon. Apparently, he has an alibi, of sorts, for Wednesday night. He says he was in The Hanging Man with Mark, Gary and Liam until somewhere between ten-fifteen and ten-thirty and then he went straight home. As the pathologist has put the time of death between nine and eleven, it's possible for Tyler to have murdered Hal after he left the pub. But Tyler denied that, of course, and then he clammed up and wouldn't say another word.'

'Is Tyler still in custody?'

'No, Dan says they don't have any evidence against him and, although they could've held him for up to twenty-four hours, they decided to release him so that he can be at the meeting tonight. Dan wants me to listen out for anything that contradicts his statement or gives any indication that Tyler was involved.'

'Sounds like you're going to be busy tonight,' Lauren commented, feeling a tad envious.

'Sorry, mate, I wish you could come with me, but Tyler might recognise you.'

'Yeah, I know. And then I'd blow your cover. But I don't like the idea of sitting at home doing nothing while you're in danger.'

'Don't be silly, I won't be in any danger. I'm just going to watch and listen, so there's no reason for anyone to suspect me of being anything other than a slightly shy newbie.'

'Well, I wish you all the best of luck, and I expect a full debrief later.'

'What, later tonight?' Jed asked incredulously.

'Don't worry how late it is, I shall be waiting up to hear from you,' she insisted.

'Even DI Dan isn't that impatient,' Jed chuckled. 'He's going to debrief me at ten tomorrow morning.'

Lauren wondered for a moment if she was being a bit unfair, expecting Jed to phone her that night. 'I suppose I could settle for a text message to say you're okay,' she said reluctantly.

'I'll text both you and Dan when I get home,' Jed promised. 'By the way, Dan wanted to meet somewhere other than the police station tomorrow, so that no one spots me with them. I suggested the farm shop café at Britford, as I can hardly imagine any of Tyler's lot going there.'

'Ooh, great,' squealed Lauren. 'There's nothing to say that Meg and I can't just happen to be going for coffee there tomorrow morning, as well.'

'Don't you ever go to work?' he teased.

'Of course, duh! But I'm on a late shift tomorrow, so I don't start until one.'

'Okay, I'll accidentally bump into you tomorrow, then,' he said, before ending the call.

Feeling more energised, Lauren phoned Meg to make plans for the morning. Then she set about preparing dinner for her mum, who would be home from work soon.

Chapter Forty-nine

When Bekka came home, Lauren told her about their day and how much progress they'd made with the case.

'That poor girl!' Bekka declared, on hearing Amelia's history. She sympathised over Dan shutting them out of the case but pulled a long face when Lauren told her about the argument with Viv. She'd had high hopes for Viv, but now she wasn't quite so sure. Perhaps it might be better if they just decided to split up and call it a day?

Lauren could see that her mum was looking troubled, so she decided not to tell her about Jed being undercover, not wanting to worry her even more.

They had dinner and watched some TV together, whilst Lauren tried hard not to imagine the worst. When she made the excuse that she was feeling tired and wanted to go to bed early, Bekka wasn't at all surprised.

'Are you worrying about the row with Viv?' she asked.

Lauren shook her head; she was trying very hard not to dwell on that.

'Well, you've been out of sorts all evening. I hope you're not sickening for something?'

'No, Mum, I feel fine. It's just been a long day, that's all.'

'Well, if you will go off investigating all day with Meg, what do you expect? Most people like to have a rest on their days off work!'

'Yeah, only older people,' Lauren replied cheekily.

'Watch who you're calling older,' her mum retaliated as Lauren ducked out of the room, laughing.

Once in her bedroom, Lauren opened her notebook, knowing that she was unlikely to be able to sleep before hearing that Jed was safe. She put Cody Johns' name into a search engine to see what would come up. There were

215

lots of hits but, skimming through the list, she realised that there was more than one Cody Johns, so she refined her search to Cody+Johns+Andover. Among several hits, she found an article from the *Andover Advertiser* detailing Johns' appearance at Andover Magistrates' Court on the twenty-ninth of December on charges of grievous bodily harm, coercive control and actual bodily harm against a minor.

She read in horror the description of how he'd come home early from work on the twenty-seventh of December to discover his girlfriend in the act of leaving him and taking their child with her. He had snatched the nine-month-old from her arms and thrown him onto the settee, from where he'd fallen onto the floor, fortunately sustaining only minor injuries. Johns had then beaten his girlfriend, breaking both radius and ulna in her lower arm when he slammed it in a door. This followed what was described as months of physical and mental abuse.

No wonder Amelia had fled into hiding!

The article mentioned that the baby had been checked out at Andover Hospital before being taken into care, whilst the mother had stayed in hospital overnight before being discharged into the care of a family member. Neither Amelia nor Freddie was named, which probably explained why it hadn't come to the attention of Amelia's parents.

But Hal obviously knew, so why didn't he tell his parents? Surely, Amelia would've been better off going home after that ordeal?

She browsed through some more articles and found that Cody had previously been charged with being drunk and disorderly on two occasions, and with causing ABH in a brawl outside a pub in Andover on another occasion. It sounded like this man had some serious temper issues, particularly when drunk.

Lauren then tried Cody+Johns+Salisbury, in the hope that maybe he'd come from Salisbury originally. After all, he'd been living in Fugglestone Red when Amelia moved in with him. She discovered that Cody Johns was born in Salisbury in 1995 and went to Salisbury High School.

Hang on a minute; that sparked an idea!

She checked back in her notes and found that Cody was the same age as Hal and had gone to the same school. It was quite likely they would've known each other. Had Hal introduced his younger sister to Cody? Was that why Hal had done so much to help Amelia; perhaps he felt responsible?

But that didn't explain why she was still estranged from her parents even after leaving her abusive boyfriend.

Lauren dug around on the internet some more until she had a load of jumbled notes. She decided to organise them into a better timeline.

- Approx. June 2021 – Mia falls pregnant with Tyler's child
- Approx. July 2021 – Amelia falls pregnant with Cody's child
- Early 2022 – Amelia moves in with Cody in Fugglestone Red
- 29 March '22 – Noah born to Mia and Tyler
- 10 April '22 – Freddie born to Amelia and Cody
- Mid-May '22 – Mia leaves Tyler and goes home to her parents
- End June '22 – Mia starts work at Linda's Lunches – meets Vikram
- July '22 – Cody and Amelia move to Andover
- 27 Dec '22 – Cody abuses Amelia and Freddie. Freddie taken into care
- 28 Dec '22 – Cody arrested and charged
  – Hal takes Amelia from hospital to Ludgershall.
- 29 Dec '22 – Cody appears before magistrate and is granted bail
- 14 Feb '23 – Vikram and Mia have first date
- 13 May '23 – Mia and Noah move in with Vikram
- 30 May '23 – Hal checks out front door lock of Vikram's house
- 2 June '23 – Hal follows Vikram to the gym and makes impression of key
  – Hal and Amelia scout out the area
  – Hal and/or Amelia buy a duplicate sports bag from Next

- 3 June '23 – Amelia drops Hal near Vikram's house
  - Hal abducts Noah
  - Amelia is driving Hal's car when they leave
  - Mid-morning, Hal, Amelia and Noah arrive in Ludgershall
  - Hal hires a van and they move Amelia to WHERE?
- 16 June '23 – Vikram arrested and charged
- 17 June '23 – Vikram appears before magistrate and is remanded in custody

Looking at her timeline, Lauren could see so many questions: what caused Amelia to fall out with her parents? Why did Cody and Amelia move to Andover? Why didn't Amelia go home to her parents after the abuse? Why did Hal abduct Noah?

Where did Hal take Amelia and Noah?

Then there was the whole question of Hal's murder. Who had murdered Hal, and why?

She sighed in frustration; they had learnt a lot, but there was still so much they just didn't know.

Another thought occurred to her: where was Cody Johns now? And how come he was released on bail, but Vikram had been remanded in custody? Now, that didn't make sense. Cody was a repeat offender who'd committed a serious physical assault, whereas Vikram had no previous criminal record and was charged with child abduction. She hoped it wasn't just because of the colour of his skin.

Her thoughts were finally interrupted by the arrival of a text from Jed.

Home safely u can stop worrying!

She replied, *Thanks mate!*

Even though she was desperate to know what, if anything, he'd found out, she accepted that it was now nearly midnight, and she'd just have to wait until the morning like everyone else. She closed her notebook and went to bed, although the questions continued to swirl around in her head for quite some time before she finally fell asleep.

Chapter Fifty

Saturday 1st July 2023

It was the very early hours of the morning when a shadowy figure dressed all in black tiptoed silently towards Mia and Vikram's house. The streetlights were off, and the moon was hidden behind dark clouds that scurried across the sky, heralding the end of the spell of fine weather.

Surreptitiously, the figure posted a plain white envelope through the letterbox and winced as it plopped onto the hall floor. Hopefully, neither of the occupants of the house had heard it, but he slipped into the deepest shadows and scurried away speedily into the night, just in case.

❁

Vikram had been standing in Noah's bedroom staring mournfully at the empty cot, unable to sleep, when he heard the lightest of plops as something came through the letterbox. He stepped across to the window and thought he saw a shadow moving down the road. Who could be delivering post at this time of night?

He crept downstairs, not wanting to wake Mia. A white envelope lay on the hall floor, so he bent and picked it up and took it through to the living room. After closing the door, he turned on a lamp and sank into the armchair next to it. He turned the envelope over and over in his hands several times. It was an unremarkable white envelope. Blank on the sealed side and just the one word, his name, in bold capital letters – printed rather than handwritten – in the centre of the other.

He felt faintly queasy, knowing that this was unlikely to be good news.

Uncertain, he debated whether to open it or not. Should he wait and give it directly to the police, in case there was some evidence they could retrieve? But if it turned out not to be anything sinister, perhaps he would end up looking foolish.

In the end, he stood up and took the letter through to the kitchen, finding a sharp knife to slit open the top edge of the envelope. He peeked inside and ascertained that the envelope contained a single sheet of paper, printed on one side. Carefully, he tipped the page onto the kitchen worktop, so that he could read it without touching it. Just in case the police could recover some fingerprints, if that proved to be necessary.

Reading the message was like taking a punch to the stomach; he wanted to throw up. It was vitriolic. And wholly unjustified.

He returned to the living room and sank into the armchair, miserable and fearful, shaken to his very core. He'd wait until it was a more reasonable hour before phoning the police, but one thing was certain: he didn't want Mia to see that vile letter.

When his breathing had finally calmed down and the nausea abated, he returned to the kitchen. His eyes were drawn to the letter, as though to check he hadn't just imagined it. He tried hard not to look but some of the more hateful words leapt off the page and brought on another bout of trembling.

He reached for the phone and dialled 999. Then he went to wake Mia; he'd have to tell her before the police arrived.

❖

When morning came, it dawned dismal and grey. Leaden clouds cloaked the sun, and the temperature felt at least ten degrees cooler than on recent days. Intermittent drizzle was dampening the ground without providing the kind of soaking gardeners and farmers would have welcomed.

Meg opted to don trousers and a cardigan over a T-shirt rather than a summer dress, which had been her preferred choice over the last two weeks. She hurried down to breakfast, eager to be ready in time to meet up with Lauren so that she could hear what Jed had to say.

As she entered the dining room, Sue Barclay cast a disapproving eye in Meg's direction. 'Are you going out *again* today?' she enquired, raising one eyebrow.

'Yes, I am,' Meg replied unapologetically. 'Why? Is there something in the rules that says residents can't go out on consecutive days?'

'I'm just concerned for your health, Meg. At your age, it doesn't pay to overdo things.'

Meg bristled but refrained from replying. At your age – what a cheek!

Albert was waiting at their usual table. 'Morning, m'dear.'

'You're up bright and early today, Albert?' Meg queried, with a sinking feeling that she knew why.

'I thought that I could come with you and Lauren today, wherever it is you're off to? Give you a bit of moral support and all that.'

It was just as Meg had feared. Albert had been chuntering all yesterday evening about being left out. She understood that he wanted to be more involved, but this wasn't the sort of case she thought he should be involved in, given his own prejudiced views.

'We're only going down to the farm café for a catch-up,' she replied.

'Good-oh!' he replied cheerfully. 'My treat, old gal.'

Meg sighed. It was bad enough that she and Lauren were gatecrashing Jed's debriefing, but she couldn't imagine that Dan would be at all happy to see Albert there as well. 'I'm sorry, Albert,' she insisted, 'but I'd really rather go on my own.'

'Secretive stuff, what?' He scowled at her over his toast.

'Dan's going to be there,' she admitted.

'Ah, so you're discussing the case, eh? About time someone brought me up to speed, you've been keeping me in the dark.'

'Albert, this just isn't the right case for you,' Meg tried to say diplomatically.

'Harrumph!' he interjected indignantly.

At the sight of his crestfallen face, she felt guilty. After all, Albert had saved her life back in January. Twice. And he really did mean well; she knew that.

'Very well,' she relented, 'but only on the condition that you don't go leaping in with your own racist views,' she warned.

'Understood, old gal. Not the done thing to be racist in this day and age.'

'And no interrupting us with your constant questions.'

Albert put a dramatic finger to his lips. 'I promise to keep my lips sealed.'

Meg could only hope that he'd be able to keep his promise.

Chapter Fifty-one

When Meg and Albert strolled into the farmyard at nine forty-five, they could see Lauren's black Peugeot parked next to Jed's sporty red Mazda, but no other car that they recognised. Good, the plan was to be all sitting together when the detectives arrived. They went inside to see Lauren and Jed talking earnestly over mugs of coffee, seated not at their usual circular table for four but at a large rectangular table across the other side of the café.

'I'll go and order some drinks for us,' Albert said, after waving at Lauren. 'You go and sit down, m'dear.' Meg asked for her usual pot of tea and went to join the youngsters.

'Why have you brought Albert with you?' hissed Lauren, as soon as Meg was near enough.

'Because I couldn't stop him,' she replied through gritted teeth.

'You do know he's soft on you, don't you?' Lauren teased.

'Don't!' Meg groaned.

Lauren grinned. 'Never mind, he means well enough.'

'I know. And you should have seen his face when I tried to persuade him not to come. I had to give in, or I'd never have heard the last of it.'

'The more, the merrier,' Jed chipped in, gallantly rising from his seat to pull a chair out for Meg.

'I'm not sure Dan will see it like that,' grimaced Meg as she sat down. 'Thank you, Jed. Did you have a successful evening yesterday?'

'I did,' Jed confirmed as they were rejoined by Albert.

'What have I missed?' he demanded, after saying good morning to Lauren and Jed.

'Nothing yet, we'll wait for DI Dan to arrive before we start sharing updates,' Lauren informed him firmly.

Lauren had to admit that she was beginning to wonder if it was such a good idea for all of them to gatecrash Jed's debriefing; she had a feeling Dan wouldn't be too pleased. And her stomach lurched as she wondered if Viv would be coming with Dan. They hadn't spoken since their row on the phone yesterday afternoon, and she could just imagine what he'd have to say, seeing her here with Meg *and* Albert. The others chatted about the turn in the weather whilst Lauren's stomach tied itself into a knot.

At ten o'clock on the dot, a silver Nissan Juke pulled up outside the café and, from where she was sitting, Lauren could see that Dan was not alone. He got out and stretched, but she was more worried about the identity of his passenger. Her stomach settled a little at the sight of Aaron climbing out of the passenger seat, but then she worried that Viv was deliberately avoiding her, and she felt oddly disappointed that he hadn't come.

Dan stopped just inside the café door and looked around. The smile on his face abruptly turned into a frown when he saw the group with Jed. He marched up to them, looking thunderous.

'I might have known you'd be here, Lauren,' he ground out, trying to control his anger. 'But you too, Meg? And Albert as well? You do know this is a police matter, don't you?'

'I don't suppose you'd believe me if I said that Albert and I just fancied strolling down for a coffee this morning, would you?' asked Meg.

'Not in the slightest,' Dan replied. 'You know I don't believe in coincidences.' He pulled out the chair at the end of the table and sat down.

'Can I get you a coffee, guv?' asked Aaron.

'Yes, please,' Dan replied. 'A black Americano with an extra shot – I think I'm going to need the caffeine!'

Lauren was surprised; she'd only ever seen Dan drinking white coffee. It was unusual enough for him to take it black, let alone fortified! She concluded that perhaps he'd had a bad night and decided it might be best to tread warily.

'Anyone else need another drink?' Aaron offered. They all declined.

'Right.' Dan inhaled sharply as he looked at the faces around the table. 'I've half a mind to take Jed down to the station so we can do his debrief in private.'

He paused as three faces looked at him beseechingly.

'But as I'm pressed for time, I won't.' There was a collected sigh of relief. 'However, I want to lay down a few ground rules. One, not a word that you hear spoken at this table gets repeated to anyone else.' Meg nodded in agreement.

'Two, no one interrupts me, DC Johnson or Jed. This is our meeting, not yours. If you have anything to add, you can do that after we've finished our debriefing.' Meg glared at Albert, and he mimed zipping his mouth shut.

'Three, don't you ever do anything like this ever again. If the super hears about this …'

'It's okay, Dan,' Meg reassured him calmly. 'We get the picture.'

'And thank you for letting us stay,' added Lauren as Aaron returned and took the remaining chair.

'Very well.' Dan fixed his gaze on Jed. 'I want to start by saying that I'm really grateful to you for agreeing to help us out with this inquiry, even if it was Lauren who put you up to this when she shouldn't have done.'

Lauren opened her mouth to protest but thought better of it when Dan turned his steely gaze on her.

'In the interests of keeping this meeting as brief as possible,' Dan continued, 'I'd prefer to ask questions, Jed, which I'd like you to answer as succinctly as possible, please, rather than you giving us a blow-by-blow account of your whole evening. Is that okay?'

'That's fine,' Jed nodded.

Aaron set a small recording device on the table.

'Okay, can you tell me what time you arrived at The Hanging Man,' Dan began.

'At about five to seven,' Jed replied promptly.

'Were there many people in the pub?'

'There were a couple of groups of people drinking in the lounge bar, who I don't think had anything to do with RAS,

225

but it certainly wasn't crowded. The RAS meeting was being held in the private function room adjacent to the bar. There's one of those zigzag folding walls that you can open out to join the two rooms together, like it was when I went to the karaoke evening there. But that was still pulled almost closed, keeping the RAS members separate from the other drinkers. I got a pint at the bar and then went through to the meeting. There were about twelve people present when I arrived.'

'Did you know any of those present?'

'Tyler Ford was sitting at the far end of a long table, and I saw Mark and Gary there too, but I didn't recognise any of the others.'

'Liam wasn't there?'

'He arrived about two minutes after I did, with another couple of people I didn't know.'

'The total attendance at the meeting was sixteen?'

'Yep, that sounds about right.'

'Was it a formal meeting, with minutes and a written agenda, or informal?' Dan asked next. 'How would you describe it?'

'There was no minutes or agenda that I could see, but Tyler clearly had a mental list of things he wanted to cover in the meeting. Everyone sat around chatting for a while, until Tyler banged on the table to get everyone's attention, then he did most of the speaking. No one took notes.'

'Where were you sitting in relation to Tyler?'

'I was sitting next to Gary on one side of the table, with two others between him and Tyler at the end. I think Gary had saved a seat for me because Tyler beckoned for me to go and sit there. Mark and Liam were on the opposite side of the table to me.'

'What was the first thing Tyler spoke about?'

'He gave a very moving speech about Hal's untimely death and how they were missing a brother in arms. Everyone was very sombre and listening quietly until he got to the end and asked everyone to raise their glasses to their fallen comrade. Everyone stood up and echoed the toast loudly, before downing whatever was in their pint glasses and then banging their empty glasses down on the table. I had planned on sipping my drink slowly so that I stayed alert, but I got frowned at for not downing my pint, so I had little choice but to follow their lead.'

'That's okay; we told you to blend in,' Dan reassured him. 'What exactly did Tyler say about Hal's death?'

'He said that Hal had been murdered late Wednesday evening and that the police were clueless as to who had done it. He wasn't as polite as that, but I'm paraphrasing.'

'That's fine, carry on.'

'Umm … he said that Hal had been viciously stabbed and then put in a car and burnt to a crisp.'

'Were those his exact words?' Dan leant in eagerly.

'Yes, that's what he said.'

Chapter Fifty-two

Meg sensed that Jed had said something important, and she was itching to ask the significance of his statement.

'You're sure Tyler said that Hal was stabbed and *then* put in the car?' Dan insisted.

'Yes,' confirmed Jed.

Dan looked pleased with his response. 'That's interesting, because we didn't release the fact that the victim was stabbed before being put in the car.'

'Does that make Tyler your prime suspect?' Lauren asked, eyes wide.

Dan glowered at her, and she shrunk back slightly in her chair.

Before he could say anything, the waitress arrived with their two coffees. Aaron stirred sugar into his flat white, whilst Dan attempted a sip of his strong black coffee and then thought better of it. It was too hot.

The café was beginning to fill with other people now, which made Dan nervous about being overheard, but the noise levels in the café were also increasing. He coughed. 'Like I said before, no interruptions, please,' he reminded them. 'And we need to keep our voices down. Now, Jed, can you remember anything else that Tyler said?'

'He said that no matter what Hal had done, he didn't deserve to die like that.'

'I wonder what he meant by that?' mused Albert.

Dan looked fit to explode, and Albert held up his hands as if in surrender.

'How was his manner, would you say?' Dan directed his question at Jed, pointedly ignoring the others.

'He seemed genuinely upset by Hal's death, but at the same time there was something slightly odd about the way he spoke about it. He was emotional, and yes, that's natural when your best mate has just been killed, but it was like he knew more than he was letting on.'

'Did any of the others react to this, do you think?'

'I kept looking around the faces of the others, and most of them just looked solemn or upset or angry. But I saw Liam give Tyler a strange look when he said that Hal didn't deserve to die like that.'

'Strange? In what way?'

'He looked at Tyler like he didn't believe a word he was saying.'

'Thank you. Anything else about Hal's murder?'

'Not then, but later in the evening when we were chatting in small groups, there was a lot of speculation as to who could've done it. Liam and Mark were whispering, and I managed to get close enough to overhear them saying something about Tyler leaving the darts that evening to go outside for a fag and then not coming back to finish his game.'

'He left unexpectedly?'

'That's the impression I got.'

'Did they say what time he left the pub?'

'Sorry, no. But it sounded like it was not only before the darts had finished but also well before kicking-out time. According to Liam, it was unusual for Tyler to leave that early.'

'Okay. Going back to the meeting, what did Tyler talk about next?'

'After the toast to Hal, he went on a bit of a rant about the police being likely to prioritise the murder investigation over finding his son, who was still missing. He sounded really pissed off and bitter about that.'

'Did he mention Vikram?'

'I don't think he knew about Vikram being released until one of the others mentioned it. Apparently, this guy, whose name is Callum, lives in the same road as Mia and Vikram, and he told everyone how he'd seen Vikram being brought home in a police car yesterday afternoon. There were a lot of shouts and protests at that. Really vile, racist stuff.'

'That's okay, you don't need to repeat everything they said.'

'Thanks. I honestly thought that some of the members were about to start a riot. Tyler quietened them down and said that they needed to make it clear to Vikram that his sort aren't welcome in Salisbury.'

Dan leant forward. 'Did he say how they were going to do that?'

'He was talking about starting a hate campaign specifically against Vikram, like letters and dog-sh ... excrement through the letterbox, and a protest in the market square.'

'He specifically mentioned letters?' Dan checked, his interest piqued.

'Yeah. He told Callum that he'd have a word with him later about that.'

Dan exchanged glances with Aaron.

'Looks like we've got our secret postman, guv?' Aaron suggested.

'Yes, that seems quite likely if he lives in the same road.'

'Can you enlighten us?' Meg asked, sensing that something had happened that they weren't yet aware of.

Dan hesitated, before realising that the cat was already out of the bag.

'There was a triple nine call during the night,' he explained, 'from Vikram Chopra. Someone had hand-delivered a rather vile anonymous letter to him, and the poor guy was understandably shaken rigid by it. Local police attended but when they realised who Vikram was, they notified me.'

No wonder he's tired and irritable, Lauren thought.

'Thankfully, Vikram had the sense not to handle the letter. I went out to take his statement myself – I've been meaning to go and introduce myself to them since I took over their case – but CSI couldn't attend due to another incident. Viv's over there now with CSI. He'll take any swabs and fingerprints they lift straight to the lab. If we're lucky, we might find Callum's DNA or fingerprints on it, assuming they're in the system. And if Jed's certain about what he heard, then we should be able to charge them.'

'I'm sure about what I heard,' Jed nodded, 'and if you need me to testify, I will.'

'I hope it won't come to that,' Dan said. 'It could put you at risk if the group finds out who the witness is. But just having a witness makes our case that little bit stronger and gives us some leverage during an interview.'

'Tyler specifically said something about sending a message that night,' Jed confirmed.

Dan nodded. 'We suspected from the language used that RAS was probably behind the letter, but it's great that you've confirmed that. Good work.'

'I know I've a bit of a reputation for being a tad racist myself,' Albert said, earning wry grins from Meg and Lauren, 'but sending anonymous hate mail is another thing altogether. I hope you can lock them up for this.'

'So do I,' Dan said with feeling. 'Now, Jed, was there anything else that you saw or heard at the meeting last night that you want to report?'

'Nothing specific. Just that I got a feeling that Tyler was really pissed off at Hal about something. I wouldn't have been at all surprised if he'd murdered Hal himself, but I got the impression, from things other people said, that Tyler doesn't like to get his own hands dirty. It seems to me that he might have put Hal up to abducting Noah, and that he put Callum up to sending the letter to Vikram, so it's equally possible that he put someone else up to murdering Hal.'

'Thanks for that. We'll get Tyler brought in for further questioning. We've got a lot to work to do now, thanks to you.'

'You're welcome. But if you don't mind, I'd rather not go back again.'

'That's fine, we wouldn't want you to do it again,' Dan reassured him.

Chapter Fifty-three

Dan drained the last of his coffee whilst Aaron put his notebook away. 'Right, we've got a busy day ahead of us. Before we go, can I remind you all not to breathe a word of what's just been said here?' He looked at each of them in turn until they nodded their agreement.

'Is there any new information that anyone needs to add?' Meg and Lauren shook their heads.

'In that case, come on, Aaron, we've got work to do.' The two detectives stood up, said their goodbyes and left.

'Well!' spluttered Albert. 'If I'm not mistaken, this case is moving along rather nicely.'

'But there's still an awful lot of unanswered questions,' protested Lauren.

'If you'll excuse me,' Jed interjected, 'I've got a client at the gym in twenty minutes, so I need to scoot too. Listen, I don't blame you for wanting to help Mia to find her son, but this RAS group, they're evil. You really don't want to mess with them, so I'd advise you all to leave it up to DI Dan now. Safer that way.'

He gave Lauren a quick hug, shook Albert's hand and smiled at Meg before leaving.

'What do you think, Meg?' Lauren asked.

'I'm inclined to agree with Jed, that we're best off leaving anything to do with RAS to the police. But there are other aspects of the case that we might be able to help with.'

Lauren nodded her agreement.

'Go on, then. What are all these unanswered questions?' Meg urged.

Lauren showed them a printout of her timeline and the list of questions she'd added to the bottom of it. Then she told them what she'd found out about Cody Johns. Meg and Albert were horrified to hear what he had done to Amelia.

'That poor woman!' Meg exclaimed.

'The scoundrel!' growled Albert.

'Right, let's start with what we do know,' Meg suggested, when they'd recovered their equilibrium. 'We're sure that Hal took Noah from his cot, carried him down the road in a black sports bag and got into his own car, which Amelia was driving. They can't have gone straight to Ludgershall, because Noah was taken between one and one-thirty in the morning, and Rosie said that they didn't arrive in Florence Court until the morning, which I took to mean after she'd got up as she wouldn't have seen anything if she'd still been in bed, would she?'

'Good point,' agreed Lauren, 'but it doesn't take more than half an hour to drive from Laverstock to Ludgershall at night, so where were they for the rest of the time?'

'I did have a thought,' Meg replied. 'When they left Laverstock, Noah was in a black sports bag. But when they arrived at Florence Court, he was in a car seat.'

'Oh my God!' Lauren exclaimed. 'Why didn't I pick up on that? They must have gone somewhere to get a proper child seat!'

'But where could they get one at that time of night?' Meg asked.

'They could have gone to Tesco, which is open twenty-four hours. But that wouldn't have taken all night, so where else did they go?'

Meg couldn't answer that one.

'I think the more important question is where did Hal and Amelia take Noah, after they left Florence Court?' Lauren maintained. 'That's most likely where Noah is to be found now, don't you think?'

'Yes, of course. But how do we pursue that?' Meg asked.

'I have an idea,' Lauren replied, tapping at her screen with her thumbs. 'Rosie said the van was from Enterprise Van Hire.' She read something on her screen. 'Andover is the closest branch, or he could have gone back to Salisbury.'

Meg realised what Lauren was driving at. 'Have you got a phone number for the Andover branch? We'll try them first.'

'Yes, I have. Shall we go and sit in the car? It's too noisy to make a phone call in here.'

'Yes, it's quite busy now, isn't it?' Meg agreed, looking around the packed café.

They made their way to Lauren's car, Meg sitting in the front next to her whilst Albert squeezed into the back, somewhat grumpily.

'It was warmer in the café,' he grumbled.

'It's not that cold,' Lauren answered impatiently. 'It's July, the middle month of summer!'

'British summers aren't like they used to be,' he muttered.

Ignoring him, Lauren asked Meg how she wanted to play this.

'Let me speak to them,' Meg suggested with a glint in her eye. 'I have an idea.'

Lauren put the call on speaker so they could all hear both sides of the conversation. When Meg indicated she was ready, Lauren pressed call.

'Enterprise Car and Van Hire, Andover. How may I help you?' came the disembodied voice of a cheerful young man.

'Good morning,' replied Meg. 'I wonder if you could help me track down someone who rented one of your vans?'

'I'm sorry, we don't give out personal information, for data protection reasons.'

'Oh dear.' Meg allowed her voice to wobble a little.

'What's the problem?' the young man replied.

'Well, you see, a driver in one of your vans blocked my car in my drive and I needed to go to a dentist's appointment. He wouldn't move it until he'd finished loading, and he was positively rude about it. As a result, I missed my appointment. And then, this week, I received a letter charging me for the missed appointment. It's all so upsetting. I didn't know what to do, but my granddaughter's here with me today and she advised me that I should report the driver to the police.'

'Yes, that sounds like a good idea. What date did this happen?'

'It was on Saturday, the third of June.'

'Okay, I've got the screen open on vans out on hire that day. Do you know what type of van it was?'

'It was one of those box-shaped vans. I think they call it a Luton?'

'Okay, that's a three-and-a-half-ton box van. We've got five of those at this branch. Do you have a registration number?'

'Oh no … I didn't think to write it down.'

'Never mind. Where do you live?'

'Florence Court, Ludgershall,' Meg replied, keeping her fingers crossed that the young man wouldn't know that none of the maisonettes there had driveways.

'And the time of day?'

'My appointment was at eleven-thirty.'

'Anything else you can tell me? Like, how long the van was there for?'

'It must have arrived about mid-morning, I think, and it was there until after lunch.'

'Hmm, let me see.' There was a lengthy pause, and the three of them waited impatiently, hoping the young man would come back with something they could use.

'Okay, you're in luck. Four of our vans went out on the Friday for weekend hires, so we only had one available that Saturday morning. Lucky for you, now that I've looked it up, I can remember the bloke who hired it. He was tall, with bleached blond hair and tattooed sleeves. Does that sound like your driver?'

'Yes, that sounds very much like him,' Meg replied, trying not to sound too excited.

'Yeah, I remember him. Walked in without a prior reservation and demanded a box van to take out there and then. Like I said, we only had the one van available, and that was booked to go out at six that evening. I asked him how long he wanted it for, and he told me to mind my own effing business. I explained that he would need to have the van back by five or else I couldn't let him have it. He calmed down then. Told me he needed the van in a hurry to move some stuff; that he only had to pick it up from Ludgershall and take it to Salisbury, and then he'd bring the van straight back.'

Lauren suppressed a squeal of delight, whilst Meg grinned at her.

'Can you let me have the driver's name?' Meg asked.

'Like I said, I'm not supposed to give out personal information. But I guess that if you were to tell the police what I've just told you, they'd be on the phone next asking me for the bloke's information. So, it'll just save a bit of time if I tell you, won't it?'

'That really would be very kind of you.'

'Okay. The driver was Henry Winters, and the address on his driving licence is 503 Devizes Road, Salisbury. I remember thinking that the idiot would've been better off hiring the van from our Salisbury branch.'

Meg repeated the name and address back to him and thanked him profusely, then Lauren ended the call.

Chapter Fifty-four

Lauren fist-pumped the air in delight. 'Not only have we confirmed that Hal hired the van in Andover but, much more importantly, we now know that he took Amelia to Salisbury.'

'Yes, that is good news. If only we had an address in Salisbury,' Meg said dryly.

Lauren's face fell. 'Yeah. But at least it narrows our search a bit.'

'Might it be worth approaching Amelia's parents again?' Meg said thoughtfully.

Lauren cast her mind back to Monday. 'I'm certain Mrs Winters didn't know anything.'

'So why did Hal bring Amelia to Salisbury, then?' demanded Albert.

'Good question. If it wasn't to be nearer to her parents, then presumably it was to be nearer to either Tyler or Hal,' Meg reasoned.

'Oh, I've just had an awful thought!' exclaimed Lauren. 'She must be devastated now that her brother's been murdered!'

'How would she know about that?' challenged Albert.

'I think she would've heard it on either the local radio or TV by now,' said Meg.

'Or seen it online,' added Lauren.

'In which case, might she have contacted her parents after Hal's death? I mean, grief can bring families together,' Meg wondered.

'Or drive them apart,' said Albert with feeling, speaking from personal experience. His relationship with his son, Peter, had been good until his wife had passed away, then everything wrong in Peter's life had suddenly become his fault.

'I guess it depends on what caused the rift in the first place,' Lauren said.

'You've met both Mr and Mrs Winters. What was your impression of them?' Meg asked.

'Mrs Winters came across as quite chatty and confident to me, at first, and she was genuinely upset at not seeing her grandson for so long. But when Hal arrived, she changed like she'd lost all her confidence. Hal was quite horrible to her. But when Mr Winters arrived, he came across as dominant over Hal. I mean, you should've heard the way he demanded to know why Hal was home from work early! It was like Hal was a little boy, not a grown man.'

'I see. If Mr Winters is a bully, then that's probably where Hal learnt his behaviour,' Meg suggested.

'That reminds me about something Viv said. He told me that Mr Winters blamed Tyler for leading their son astray, and RAS for his extreme racist views. But Viv said that Mr Winters was also a racist, and that Hal had probably got his views from his father.'

'They're obviously both bullies and racists,' Meg said with some feeling. 'Hal can't bully his dad, so he takes it out on his mother instead. Which leads me to suspect that the reason for Amelia becoming estranged from her parents is more likely to do with her father than her mother.'

'That makes sense,' Lauren agreed. 'Although isn't it odd that Hal was the one supporting Amelia? Wouldn't he have bullied her too?'

'Not if he knew what the problem was and disagreed with his father. Helping Amelia could be a secret act of rebellion against his father.'

'I say, old gal, not wanting to intrude, but isn't there an awful lot of speculation going on here?' Albert intervened, getting a little bored with the conversation. 'What about a bit of action?' he suggested hopefully.

Meg glanced at her watch and then exclaimed, 'Goodness me, the only action we're going to get is legging it back to the Lodge in time for our lunch!'

Lauren checked her watch and groaned. 'And I've got work in less than an hour.'

Meg and Albert climbed out of the car and set off up Lower Road, then Lauren heaved a sigh of frustration and headed back into the café to grab a sandwich to eat before her shift.

❁

Whilst Maureen Wilkinson was handing over to the incoming late shift, she couldn't help but notice that Lauren was rather distracted.

She asked her to stay behind, and waited until the other staff had dispersed to their various tasks before leaning forward, her elbows resting on her desk, as she studied Lauren with a mixture of concern and irritation etched on her face.

'Did you hear a single word I said, Lauren?' she asked.

'Umm, most of it,' Lauren said sheepishly.

'I seriously doubt that. Do you want to tell me why you're so distracted?'

'I'm sorry, I've got a lot on my mind at the moment.'

'What is it? Is there a problem at home?' Maureen asked, concerned in case Lauren's mother had relapsed.

"No, nothing like that,' Lauren insisted.

'Boyfriend trouble?'

'No ... well, yes ... but that isn't what I was thinking about.'

'Then I'm guessing it's connected to the fact that you and Meg have been going out quite a lot recently. Are the two of you investigating another mystery?'

Lauren's mouth dropped open with surprise.

'I'll take that as a yes,' Maureen said, sighing. 'Lauren, I have no problem with you being friends with Meg, or with you taking her out of the care home when you're off duty. And what you do when you're off duty is entirely your own business. But all of that is on the proviso that it doesn't affect the quality of your work here.'

'Yes, I know. I'm sorry,' Lauren flushed, looking down at her shoes.

'Consider this an informal warning. It won't go on your record, and no one else needs to know about it. But you must be able to do your job effectively when you're at work.'

'I really am sorry, Mrs Wilkinson. I can do better.'

'Very well.' She hesitated. 'Lauren, you're a good carer, and I would hate to lose you. You haven't taken any holiday since you joined us, have you?'

'No.' Lauren was taken aback.

'We have a full complement of staff over the next week. Why don't you take a few days of annual leave?'

Lauren sat up straighter. 'Is that possible?' she gasped, suddenly hopeful.

'I wouldn't have suggested it if it wasn't possible,' Maureen said dryly. 'Now, do you think you can manage to finish this shift without your mind wandering all over the place?'

'Yes, I'll do my best.'

'Very well. You may take Sunday, Monday and Tuesday as annual leave. But I shall expect you back on Wednesday with your mind fully focused on your work.'

'Thank you so much!' Lauren only just refrained from hugging her boss, so delighted was she that she could have a few days to continue the search for Noah.

'Then you'd better get on,' Maureen suggested wryly.

Lauren leapt up and hurried to the door before realising that she had no idea what she was supposed to be doing. As she paused, Maureen calmly informed her that she was working with Taska that afternoon, on the ground floor.

❁

Dan and Aaron were preparing to start their interview with Tyler Ford, who had just been brought in by uniformed officers. He hadn't been difficult to find, as he was at work at B&Q. But he had put up some resistance to being arrested, giving one of the PCs a black eye in the process. All that achieved was another charge on the sheet, one they knew would stick regardless of the outcome of the interview.

Dan signalled to Aaron to start the recording device,

which he did. 'Interview on Saturday the first of July 2023 at thirteen thirty-two. Present are DC Aaron Johnson, DI Daniel Bywater and … please state your name for the tape.'

'Tyler Ford.' He spoke sulkily and without looking at the detectives.

'Tyler, you are still under caution, do you understand?'

'Yeah.'

'You have waived your right to have legal representation. Is that right?'

'Yeah, no point in wasting money,' Tyler said with a scowl.

'You have the right to change your mind. Should you decide you want legal representation, please indicate that clearly to us and we will pause the interview until you have a solicitor present.'

'Yeah, yeah. Just get on with this,' Tyler snarled.

'Do you know why you have been arrested?'

Tyler shrugged.

'You have been arrested on suspicion of the murder of Henry, known as Hal, Winters on Wednesday the twenty-eighth of June this year. Do you understand?'

'No comment.'

'You have also been arrested on suspicion of inciting racial hatred. Do you understand?'

'No comment.'

'You have also been charged with assaulting a police officer. Do you understand?'

'No comment.'

Dan sighed. It looked like it was going to be a very tedious afternoon.

Chapter Fifty-five

Sunday 2nd July 2023

Lauren woke up wondering why it seemed so gloomy for the time of day. She tumbled out of bed and peeked through the curtains. The clouds were a menacing battleship grey, and a persistent downpour reduced visibility to barely two hundred metres, obscuring the normal view from her bedroom. Despite it being July, she shivered.

She found a pair of socks and a cardigan to throw on over her pyjamas before padding downstairs to make some coffee. There was no sign of her mum, who was presumably still asleep. Quietly, she took her coffee back upstairs, opting to do her research from the warmth of her own bed.

She opened her notebook and started searching social media for Amelia Winters. She'd done it before, of course, but this time her focus was on who Amelia's closest friends were. Who might Amelia have turned to, if not her parents?

For obvious reasons, Amelia had not posted anything online since Christmas, and there was very little in the six months prior to that. When trawling back further, Lauren began to realise that Amelia had very few close friends. She eventually found a small tight-knit group of teenage friends who appeared to have done everything together – and had a lot of fun doing it – back in Amelia's schooldays. But only one appeared to have stayed in contact: Abi Purfield. She and Amelia had consistently commented on each other's posts up until July last year.

Lauren started by looking at Abi's social media and discovered that she lived in Hampshire Close. That was in the same housing estate that Amelia had moved to with Cody Johns. Finally, she felt like she was making some progress.

She quickly dressed in jeans and a T-shirt, slipped her feet into a pair of old trainers and threw on a hooded, zipped sweatshirt. She scribbled a note for her mum, leaving it on the hall table when she grabbed her car keys. She was out of the house by ten-thirty. She dashed to her car, glad that she'd managed to park right outside her house last night, the rain now falling in stair rods.

By the time she pulled into Hampshire Close, the rain had slackened slightly, but she was still going to get wet. She twisted round in her seat to rummage in the footwell behind the passenger seat, feeling for her umbrella.

She didn't know which house Abi lived at, so she had parked halfway up the hill. She got out of her car and walked briskly to the nearest front door, her umbrella at least keeping her head dry. She pressed the doorbell and immediately there was a stampede of little feet and an excited clamouring. Eventually, a rather harassed-looking woman in her mid-thirties opened the door, an array of young girls surrounding her. They all looked to be about five or six years old.

'Sorry to take so long,' she said in an apologetic voice. 'My daughter's been having a sleepover for her birthday, so we're all at sixes and sevens this morning.'

'That's okay,' Lauren smiled. 'And which one of you is the birthday girl?'

'Me! Me!' cried a girl with curly brown hair and the biggest brown eyes, jumping up and down excitedly. 'I'm six today. Have you brought me a present?'

'Tamsin, no! You can't ask the lady that!' The poor woman looked quite embarrassed.

'Don't worry,' Lauren reassured the mother before squatting down to the little girl's height. 'Happy birthday to you, Tamsin. I hope you've had a lovely birthday sleepover, and perhaps your mummy will allow you to buy some sweeties with this.' She produced a two-pound coin from her pocket.

'Oh no!' The mother looked even more embarrassed. 'You really don't have to do that!'

Tamsin, meanwhile, had shyly taken the coin and then run off, followed by her friends.

'Tamsin, come back here immediately,' her mother bellowed. The girl crept back down the hall, looking sheepish.

'Haven't you forgotten something?'

'Thank you,' Tamsin whispered before running off again.

Lauren smiled. What a sweet little girl.

'I am so sorry; whatever must you think of us? What can I do for you? You're not selling anything, are you?' A hint of suspicion crept into the mother's voice.

'No, not at all. I'm so sorry to disturb you. An old school friend of mine lives in this road, but now that I've got here, I've forgotten which number she lives at. Do you by any chance know Abi Purfield?' Lauren asked.

'There's an Abi who lives at number eighteen, right at the top of the close.'

'That's great, thank you so much. Good luck with the girls!' Lauren turned and walked back down the bricked driveway as the woman called goodbye and shut the door.

Normally, she'd have walked the short distance to the top of the road, but the rain was getting heavier again, so she ducked quickly into her car. She parked right outside number eighteen, in the curve of the turning area at the head of the cul-de-sac. She sat for a moment, studying the semi-detached house. It was built in the same brick as all the houses in this close, and the matching front doors were both white UPVC with a small high-up semi-circular pane of glass.

Lauren deliberately left her umbrella in the car this time and dashed up to the door of number eighteen, hoping that Abi would A, be in, and B, answer the door quickly. She was lucky on both counts; a woman opened the door a few inches and peered out.

'Yeah?' she asked cautiously.

'Abi Purfield?' Lauren enquired.

'Yeah?'

'I'm so sorry to disturb you when you don't know me, but we're both friends with Amelia Winters and I'm really worried about her.' Lauren trotted out her pre-prepared ruse in an anxious voice. It worked, for the door opened wider to reveal a woman not much taller than Lauren herself, with long straight hair the colour of autumn leaves. She must have been about twenty-three, but she was instantly recognisable as the person she'd seen with Amelia in old Instagram posts.

'Come on in,' Abi said, 'you're getting soaked.'

Lauren stepped across the threshold into a small hallway, feeling chuffed that leaving her umbrella behind had paid off.

'Thank you so much,' Lauren gushed. 'I'm not disturbing you or anything?'

'No, that's okay, my partner's out playing netball this morning. Indoors, obviously, given this rain. I was planning to catch up on some housework while she's gone but, believe me, I'm only too glad of an excuse to get out of doing it! How do you know Amelia?' She cocked her head to one side, studying Lauren carefully as though trying to appraise her.

'I lived a few doors down from her in Andover, until that bastard of a boyfriend broke her arm. We stayed in touch after she moved to Ludgershall, but I haven't heard from her in over a month and that's unusual. That's why I'm worried. I'm just hoping that Cody hasn't found her and done something.'

Abi appeared to accept that. 'Would you like a coffee?' she asked.

'Yes, please.' She followed Abi into the kitchen at the end of the hall. 'You were at school with Amelia, weren't you? She mentioned you quite often.'

'Yeah, that's right,' Abi said, filling the kettle and flicking it on. 'Me, Amelia, Ginny and Kathryn, we were best friends all the way through our time at Salisbury High. The fabulous four, we called ourselves, which sounds kind of silly now. I thought we'd be friends forever, but Ginny and Kathryn went to university after school and never came back to

Salisbury. I went to university too, but only down to Bournemouth to do my nursing degree, then I came back to Salisbury. I work up at the District Hospital. Poor Amelia was the odd one out. That abomination of a father of hers wouldn't let her go to university.'

Lauren wondered what on earth Mr Winters had done for Abi to sound so vehement.

Chapter Fifty-six

Abi poured the drinks and passed one mug to Lauren before leading the way to the long lounge-cum-dining room that ran the depth of the house. She sank onto one end of a dark blue settee, curling her legs up beside her, and indicated to Lauren to take the matching armchair opposite.

'Tell me how you met Amelia,' Abi demanded.

'Well, I live with my parents in Andover, and I met Amelia and Cody when they were moving in, about a year ago. I saw her getting her baby out of the car and I just had to go and say hello. Freddie would've been about three months old then, I guess.'

A shadow crossed Abi's face. 'I used to see Freddie almost every day when they lived on Ramleaze Drive, but I haven't seen him once since they moved away. I bet he's walking and everything now.'

Lauren hesitated. Did Abi not know that Freddie had been taken into care? 'Yeah, he's walking,' she confirmed with her fingers crossed. 'Anyway, I offered to babysit, hoping I could get some hands-on baby experience, but Amelia told me that they never went out in the evenings. I couldn't believe it, but once I saw what a bully her boyfriend was, I understood why.'

'That's Cody,' Abi said grimly.

'Yeah, well, I gradually managed to make friends with Amelia by going round when Cody was at work. I could see she needed a friend.'

'We lost touch after she moved away,' Abi said. 'I think Cody stopped her from going on Instagram, 'cos I never saw any posts from her after she moved.'

'Yeah, he was really controlling. Amelia wasn't supposed to get in touch with past friends or her family or anything. Do you know, he used to check her mobile phone to see who she'd been calling?' Lauren lied glibly, getting thoroughly into her role. She was on safe ground, she thought, seeing as Abi had admitted losing touch.

'That explains why she never called me,' Abi said blankly.

'If it's any consolation, I know she really missed you,' Lauren replied.

'Thank you. So, tell me about what happened in December.'

Lauren stuck to the facts of the case as she knew them, with a little embellishment. Abi nodded. 'How did you keep in touch with her once she'd gone to Ludgershall?'

'She phoned me fairly frequently. It was easier, of course, with her not having Cody checking her calls, but she was still scared stiff of him. She never told me exactly where she lived, for fear Cody might follow me or something.'

'Have you seen Amelia and Freddie since Christmas?' Abi's voice sounded a little strained.

'Amelia and I used to meet up about once a month, at a café in the middle of Ludgershall,' Lauren replied.

There was a lengthy pause as Abi took a long drink of her coffee and appeared to be lost in thought. Then she suddenly looked directly at Lauren. 'That's a load of bullshit, isn't it,' she demanded, her voice icy cold and her eyes narrowed to slits.

Lauren gulped, not quite sure how to answer.

'You tell a very convincing story; I'll give you that. But you haven't got a clue, have you?' Abi gave a hollow laugh.

Realising that Abi had rumbled her, she decided that it was probably best to come clean.

'You're right, of course. And I'm sorry I lied, but I didn't think you'd talk to me unless I could convince you I was a friend of Amelia's.'

'You got that right! Now, tell me who you really are and what the hell you're doing here!'

Lauren started with Sanjeev and told Abi all about Mia and Vikram and Noah, and how she suspected that Amelia's brother, Hal, had abducted Noah. She explained how she and Meg had tracked Amelia from Salisbury to Ludgershall, and how they'd discovered that Hal and

Amelia had taken Noah back to Florence Court before moving out that same day.

'And you say you're investigating this case with one of the residents living in the care home where you work?' Abi scoffed incredulously.

Lauren told her about her friendship with Meg.

'And the police just let you do this, I suppose?'

'Not exactly,' Lauren admitted, before telling her about Dan and Viv.

'It sounds almost as unbelievable as your story about being friends with Amelia,' Abi said, shaking her head.

'What can I do to convince you?' Lauren asked.

'Really, I should just kick you the hell out of here. But I'm curious. Can you bring this old lady to visit? I want to meet her before I decide whether to trust you or not.'

'I can do that,' she replied quickly. 'How about this afternoon?'

'Yeah, that'll work. About two o'clock?'

'I'll be back at two o'clock with Meg,' Lauren promised.

'Very well. And you'd better not be bullshitting me again.'

'I'm not,' Lauren assured her, 'but tell me one thing, how did you know I was lying? What gave me away?'

'For a start, Amelia and I never lost touch, and she's never once mentioned you. And as soon as you said that Freddie was walking, I knew you were a phoney. Freddie was only nine months old when he was taken away from his mother, and he certainly wasn't walking then.'

'Ah,' Lauren realised just how stupid she'd been.

Abi leapt up off the settee and took the mug from Lauren's hand. 'One more thing. Don't you dare go bringing either of those detectives with you. I won't talk to the police because I just know they'll go in heavy-handed, and that's the last thing Amelia needs.'

She saw Lauren's questioning look. 'I might tell you and this other woman what I know, if I decide I can trust you. That's if you even bother to turn up.'

'We'll be here,' Lauren assured her.

'I hope so, because Amelia really needs some help, and I just don't know what to do.'

Lauren arranged to pick Meg up from Britford Lodge at one-thirty and then decided to go and call on Mia and Vikram.

When she arrived in Laverstock, the rain was as persistent as ever and she ran from the car to their front door. Mia opened the door cautiously and then her face lit up on seeing Lauren. 'Oh, have you found Noah?' she cried, beckoning her to come in out of the rain.

'Not yet,' Lauren replied carefully, slipping her wet trainers off in the hall. 'We have a promising lead, but I don't want to get your hopes up too much in case it doesn't pan out.'

'But he's still alive, isn't he?' Mia pleaded, tears appearing in her eyes.

'We believe so, yes.'

'Oh, that's fantastic! Come in and meet Vik. I've been telling him all about you and Meg.' She led the way into the living room.

Vikram rose from the armchair as Lauren entered the room. He was taller than she'd imagined and even more handsome than his photo on his employer's website. His jet-black hair was a little longer now, thick and glossy with a slight wave, and he'd shaved off his beard and moustache, revealing a strong jawline.

'You must be Lauren,' he said warmly, taking her hands in both of his. 'I cannot begin to tell you how grateful I am.'

Mia excitedly told them both to sit down and fussed around getting hot drinks. When they were all settled, Lauren looked at Vik. 'I'm so glad you're out of prison,' she began. 'Meg and I have been convinced all along of your innocence, but it would help if you could tell me your side of the story, as it were.'

'Yes, of course.' He leant forward, elbows resting on his knees, and spoke softly and honestly. His account of the night Noah was taken was virtually the same as Mia's.

'What did you think when you discovered that Noah had been taken?' Lauren asked.

'I didn't know what to think. I couldn't imagine that anyone would do this to us. I suppose I thought that someone must have kidnapped him to demand a ransom, although why they chose us, I have no idea.'

Lauren brought the two of them up to date with the latest progress on the investigation. They had seen the news of Hal's murder on TV but hadn't known that he was the person most likely responsible for taking Noah.

'But, if he's dead, where's my baby?' wailed Mia.

'We believe Hal's sister has Noah.'

'And will she look after him properly?'

'I'm certain of it; she's a mother herself. Her own son is about the same age as Noah.'

'And do you know where she is?' Vikram demanded.

'Not yet, but we're getting closer to finding out.'

'Please, just find our little boy for us,' Vikram pleaded.

Chapter Fifty-seven

When Lauren returned to her car, she saw that she had a text message from Aaron, saying that Tyler had been released from custody. What the hell!

She called him back immediately.

'You got my message then?' he asked.

'What happened?' she demanded.

'Tyler clammed up and wouldn't say anything other than no comment. We interviewed him for three lengthy sessions, yesterday afternoon and evening and again this morning, but he wouldn't budge. We just don't have any substantial evidence yet that he murdered Hal. I mean, we're pretty sure he did it. His alibi is next to non-existent, and it looks very suspicious that he went out for a smoke in the pub car park and suddenly decided not to go back in to finish his darts match afterwards. But it's all circumstantial. CSIs are processing the pub car park as we speak and may have turned something up. But even if it's the proof we need, there's no way we can get the DNA results back in time to charge Tyler before his twenty-four hours are up.'

'That's awful!'

'Yes, I know, but that's one of the frustrations of this job. In the long run, if the evidence proves it was him, we'll get him for it. Meanwhile, I just wanted you to be aware that Tyler is out. Be careful.'

'Thanks, I appreciate that.'

'What have you been up to?' he enquired. 'Have you got anything to tell me?'

Lauren hesitated. On the one hand, she was afraid that involving the police at this stage might just cause Abi to clam up. But Meg had recommended that they tell them about their lead, and if Aaron discovered later that she'd held out on him …

'There is something,' she began.

'You need to tell me!' he said firmly.

Lauren told him a bit about her conversation with Abi without mentioning her name.

'Who is she? We need to interview this witness as soon as possible,' Aaron demanded.

'She's very protective of Amelia, and she's already said she won't talk to the police. I think it would be better if Meg and I could hear what she's got to say and then pass it on to you.'

There was a pause and a scuffling sound as though someone else had grabbed the phone.

'Do I gather that you've found a new witness?' Dan demanded brusquely.

Lauren repeated what she'd said to Aaron.

Dan got straight to the point. 'Do you think she knows where Amelia is?'

'Yes, I believe so.'

'And you think that Amelia's got Noah?'

'Yes.'

'Then you have to hand this over to us, Lauren.'

Lauren pleaded with him to let Meg and her go in first, to prepare Abi for the arrival of the police. Eventually, she gave him Abi's name and address, on the condition that Dan would give them an hour to talk to Abi before coming in. 'But we're coming in at three o'clock, whether you like it or not,' he warned. 'You and Meg need to make Abi understand that she's got to tell us everything. And if I arrive to find she's absconded, then the consequences are all on you.'

✿

When Lauren finally drove away from Mia and Vikram's, she didn't see the white Golf GTI that was parked in a driveway further down the road pull out and follow her. Her mind was too preoccupied. And all the way to Britford Lodge, the rain was so heavy that it was no surprise she didn't spot the same car tailing her.

They held back when she neared Britford Lodge, then continued down to the farm car park where they could turn around. They crawled back up the road and watched in anticipation. Their patience was rewarded when, a short while later, the girl emerged with her elderly friend in tow.

'We might be able to get two birds with one stone,' one occupant said to the other.

Lauren was too busy bringing Meg up to speed on what was happening to notice that she was still being followed. When she indicated to turn into Hampshire Close, the Golf driver paused on the corner to see where they went.

Lauren pulled up in the same spot as before and this time used her umbrella to escort Meg to Abi's front door. It opened before they could ring the bell, and Abi beckoned them to come inside quickly.

Abi studied them as they stood dripping in the hallway. 'I'm surprised to see you,' she admitted. 'I didn't think you'd come back.'

'I promised you, didn't I?' protested Lauren.

'Yeah, but how was I supposed to know you were telling the truth after all the bullshit you gave me earlier?'

'I'm sorry I lied to you, but you know the truth now. Abi, this is Meg Thornton, my partner in investigation.'

Meg shook hands with Abi, and they studied each other for a moment.

'Okay, you'd better come through to the lounge,' Abi said reluctantly.

When they walked in, another woman, about the same age as Abi, was sitting on the settee. She had short brown hair still wet from the rain, or maybe she'd had a shower, and she was wearing a pale blue tracksuit.

'This is my partner, Jenna,' Abi said, sitting down next to her. Jenna nodded briefly at them as Meg and Lauren took the two armchairs, then she looked at Abi. 'Do you want me to stay, Abs, or shall I go and make some drinks?'

'I could do with a coffee.' Abi smiled back at her partner gratefully.

'Can I get you two anything?' Jenna offered, standing up and stretching her lithe body. Lauren and Meg politely asked for a coffee and a tea respectively, and Jenna went out of the room, tactfully closing the door behind her.

Abi stared at Meg. 'Tell me a bit about yourself,' she demanded.

'Very well. I was an English teacher and SENCO for most of my career. That's a special educational needs—'

'Yes, I know,' Abi interrupted.

'I also became deputy head for the last five years before I retired. I was married twice. I divorced the first one after he left me for another woman. My second husband, my soulmate, died of cancer, leaving me a widow. He was a detective chief inspector with Bournemouth CID. He trusted me enough to share most of his cases with me, and occasionally I was able to help him in some small way. I've always liked puzzles and mysteries, so I can't help but investigate when the occasion arises. You might call me a nosy old woman, but I can assure you that I don't miss much, and I still have a very active brain despite this slightly decrepit body.'

Abi nodded thoughtfully. 'And can you vouch for Lauren?' she asked.

'I would trust Lauren with my life. She has been the most invaluable help in our investigations, doing all the things I can't do, like researching stuff on the internet. And driving me around.'

'Very well.' Abi fixed them both with an icy stare. 'You need to understand this about me. I am a very loyal friend, but I can also be your worst enemy. I can't stand people bullshitting me.'

Lauren coloured a little at the criticism but acknowledged the fairness of it.

'I met Amelia when we started secondary school together, and we've been best friends ever since. I wouldn't be talking about her behind her back if I didn't think that she was in desperate need of help. I can't go to the police. It would be like betraying her, so I hope you can find a way to help.'

Lauren was about to speak, but Meg shot her a warning look.

Abi continued. 'I want you to know something of what Amelia's been through in her life so that you can understand why she is where she is now.'

'That would be most helpful,' Meg said encouragingly.

Chapter Fifty-eight

Abi took a deep breath and looked at them both. 'You probably know a little bit about Amelia's family?'

'Not a lot,' Lauren admitted.

'Okay, well, maybe you already know that Amelia's dad and brother are both bullies. But I bet you don't know the full extent of it. Her dad was so overprotective of her that it's amazing she was even allowed to go to school. He wouldn't let her go anywhere outside of school, not even to my house. Not even when my mum called on Amelia's mum to invite her to my thirteenth birthday party.

'Amelia was this little shy girl who couldn't stand up for herself, wouldn't say a word in her own defence. But being with me and Ginny and Kathryn at school, well, that changed her. I like to think that we brought her out of her shell and taught her that life can be fun. We were a pretty rebellious bunch, and I think some of that rubbed off on Amelia. But then she started showing up at school with the occasional bruise.'

'Her dad was hitting her?' Meg asked softly.

'She didn't say as much, but we all guessed what was happening. As we went through our teens, it seemed like the older we got, the more Amelia rebelled against her parents, sneaking out of the house to go places with us. But the bruises got worse too, more of them, more frequently. We all wanted Amelia to tell a teacher about it, but she was terrified of what her dad would do to her. I guess we should've told someone but, like I said, I'm a loyal friend – we all were – and Amelia begged us not to say anything.'

Meg nodded. Sadly, she'd heard similar stories several times during her career and knew all about misguided loyalty. Her friends would've helped Amelia so much more by getting her the help she needed.

'Then we all did our A-levels and everything changed. Ginny went to Cambridge University. She's the clever one; she's still there doing her PhD now. Kathryn went to Birmingham Uni, met a bloke, fell in love and got a good job up there when she graduated. We've kind of lost touch with those two. I also went to uni, but only as far as Bournemouth. I was around some of the time because I did a couple of my modules at Wiltshire College and some of my practical placements at Salisbury District Hospital. But Amelia's dad wouldn't hear of her going to uni, even though she wanted to. He arranged a job for her at the same place he works at, so he was on her back all the time, at work and at home. I think it crushed her. She lost a whole load of weight, and I believe she became anorexic. It was tragic to see, but there didn't seem to be anything I could do.'

'You didn't think of talking to the police or social services?' Meg asked gently.

'I wish to goodness I had,' Abi said bitterly, 'but I was too preoccupied with my nursing course and my new friends. And Amelia kept begging me not to say anything. It sounds pathetic now, doesn't it? I call myself her best friend and I wasn't there when she needed me.'

'Please don't blame yourself,' Meg reassured her. 'It's so much easier with hindsight to know what we should have done. It's never that clear-cut at the time, is it?'

'No, you're right,' Abi heaved a sigh, 'but this is where it gets worse.'

'Worse?' exclaimed Lauren, horrified at the thought.

'Oh, you don't know the half of it yet.' Abi grabbed a tissue from a box on a side table and blew her nose noisily. 'You see, that's when she started dating Cody Johns. He was around their house a lot 'cos he was friends with Hal, and I guess Amelia didn't know any other blokes, what with her father keeping her a virtual prisoner. She really looked up to Cody, but he and Hal were almost as bad as Amelia's dad. All three of them are bullies and thugs. Well, one day, Amelia's dad comes back early from somewhere and he catches Amelia and Cody in bed, umm, you know ...'

258

Meg and Lauren nodded. Their eyes widened with concern.

'He dragged Cody out of bed, punched him and broke his nose, and threw him out of the house.' She stopped and gulped. 'And that's when he r-r-raped his own d--daughter.' She broke down in sobs as Lauren gasped out loud and Meg groaned.

'I didn't know at the time, or I would've reported it, for sure,' Abi said earnestly. 'But I was away in Dorchester on a placement, so I didn't see her for a few months. And, by that time, Amelia was pregnant and living with Cody just down the road from here in Ramleaze Drive. We all assumed she was pregnant by Cody, and she never said anything to suggest that wasn't the case.'

'Do you know now what happened back then?' Meg asked carefully.

'Only the gist of it. Her dad kept her at home and told her employer that she'd quit. Then her parents found out that she was pregnant, and her dad threw her out of the house. She did the only thing she could. She told Cody the baby was his and she went to live with him.'

'Out of the frying pan and into the fire,' whispered Meg.

'Yeah, you could say that. But I think Cody and Amelia were happy together for a little while. I was back living at home by then, and they seemed okay whenever I saw them. Amelia's mum used to sneak up the road to visit her daughter, although neither Hal nor their dad would have anything to do with her.'

'Whatever changed?' asked Lauren.

'Freddie was born. You see, all the Winters family have got this really fine blond hair, and they've all got blue eyes. But Cody is more Mediterranean to look at. Olive skin, dark hair and brown eyes. And Freddie did not take after Cody one little bit.'

'Ah, so Cody suspected that Freddie wasn't his child?' Meg concluded.

'Exactly. There was a huge row when Freddie was about three months old. Cody got the truth out of Amelia and then he stormed round to have it out with her dad. The next thing

I know, Cody and Amelia have moved to Andover, but things just went from bad to worse. Cody was every bit as abusive and controlling as Amelia's dad had been. He wouldn't let her stay in touch with any of her family. Surprisingly, Hal was the one who reached out to her.'

'Hal must have found out what his father had done! That explains why he supported Amelia and eventually helped her to escape from Cody,' Meg surmised.

'Yeah, that's about it.' Abi licked her lips and looked around, puzzled, just realising that Jenna hadn't returned. She stood up. 'I'll just go and give Jenna a hand with the drinks,' she said.

Chapter Fifty-nine

As soon as Abi had gone, Lauren leant towards Meg and whispered, 'Oh my God! This is so much worse than I could've imagined. I can't quite believe—'

She broke off as Abi came back through the door, looking ashen.

'What's up?' Lauren asked.

Meg gasped, being at a better angle to see that a man was following close behind Abi, a knife held against her ribs.

'Sit down,' he ordered, shoving Abi and causing her to fall onto the settee. He stood back so that he could see all three of them clearly, brandishing a large kitchen knife menacingly in front of him.

'Tyler!' exclaimed Lauren in a petrified voice.

'You!' he snorted in derision. 'And the nosy old bag. The wonder sleuths! Ha! What a joke!'

'Where's Jenna?' wailed Abi, tears streaming down her cheeks. 'What have you done with her?' She looked at Tyler beseechingly.

'She's upstairs with my mate Callum, finding out what a real man can do, you fucking pair of lesbos.' He laughed callously at the horrified look on Abi's face.

Just then, footsteps clattered down the stairs and another man entered, presumably Callum.

Meg studied the pair, determined to be able to make a positive identification if she survived long enough. Tyler was just as Lauren had described: big and broad and muscular. Beside him, Callum looked kind of thin and weaselly and a lot less physically threatening. Not that Meg would've liked to cross him, for he had a mean face and was holding a wicked-looking penknife, blade extended, in his right hand.

'Have fun, mate?' Tyler chuckled.

'Nah, she's not my type,' complained Callum in a thin voice, 'but she's tied up nice 'n' tight. She won't be going nowhere soon.'

'Right then,' Tyler looked back at Abi, 'I was most entertained, listening to your little tale of woe outside the door. Shame you had to stop when you did. Why don't you carry on where you left off?'

'What do you want to know?' Abi asked, her voice wobbling as she looked to Meg and Lauren for advice.

'I think he wants to know where Amelia is now,' Meg said calmly. Inside, she was quaking, but she was not going to let this young thug intimidate her.

'Why?' Abi sobbed.

'Why? I'll tell you fucking why!' Tyler growled as Abi cowered under his glare. 'She and her brother took my son away from me. And it wasn't meant to go like that!'

'Tell us how it was meant to go,' Meg suggested, trying to keep Tyler talking.

'You obviously know, so why don't *you* tell *us*?' He jabbed the knife in Meg's direction, and she shifted back into her seat.

'Only if you sit down and stop waving that knife around, before you hurt someone,' Meg replied firmly, thankful for her years of experience as a teacher.

To Lauren's surprise, Tyler and Callum moved to the settee, sitting one each side of Abi. Callum clung onto his penknife still, darting little looks around the room, clearly on edge. Tyler laid the knife on the arm of the sofa next to him and put one arm round Abi's shoulders. She tried to shrink away from him as he hugged her against him. 'We'll listen to what the teacher has to say, won't we, Abi?' he sneered, as Lauren sat frozen with fear.

'I think that you are as much of a bully as Hal and his father, aren't you?' Meg said, keeping a wary eye on him. 'Your bullying drove Mia to leave you. You didn't really care about her, but you hated that she took her son with her.'

'He's my son too,' Tyler growled.

Meg continued, unabated. 'But what really upset you was when she moved in with her new boyfriend.'

Tyler issued a torrent of foul language, which Meg ignored.

'I think you put Hal up to taking Noah for you. What was the plan? I'm guessing that Hal and Amelia were to take Noah and hide him away somewhere for a while. After all, you couldn't have Noah at your place, knowing it was the first place the police would look. I wonder what went wrong. Did Amelia get too attached to Noah and refuse to give him to you? Did Hal refuse to tell you where they were?'

'That bloody double-crossing wanker thought he could pull one over on me,' exploded Tyler, with real venom in his voice.

'And you killed him for that?' Meg asked, one eyebrow raised. 'Well, he certainly can't tell you now, can he?'

'But this little chick can,' said Tyler, hugging the terrified Abi even closer.

Meg noted that he hadn't denied killing Hal.

Whilst all this was going on, Lauren had pulled herself together and was desperately trying to think what she could do. They needed help here, and fast.

She cautiously moved one hand into her pocket and slid her phone out beside her onto the cushion seat, crossing one leg over the other to better shield it from Tyler and Callum's view. She used her thumbprint to unlock her phone, thankful she'd registered both thumbs in her security settings. Then she put it in silent mode; it wouldn't do for a ping to alert them to what she was doing.

She considered calling Viv but wasn't sure whether he would know where she was, whereas Aaron would. Luckily, he was the last person she'd called, so she only had to redial his number. She just had to hope that he would answer it, hear what was happening at their end and put two and two together.

'Tell me, how did you even know we were here?' she asked loudly.

'Huh, wouldn't you like to know?' Tyler sneered.

'Yes, I would,' Lauren retorted, hoping to goad him into replying.

'I've got mates in all sorts of places,' he laughed cruelly. 'You'd be surprised at the different types of people who share the same views as us. A little mole at the nick told me that these two women were going around asking a lot of questions and sharing information with his boss. Wasn't that interesting? Eh?'

'You have someone inside the police force?' gasped Meg.

Lauren felt as though her blood had turned to ice. *Who the hell would do that?*

'Oh yeah, and they gave us your names, your descriptions, where you live ...You wouldn't believe it! Even some of the pigs don't like the bloody immigrants coming here and ruining our country. You'd think we'd be on opposite sides of the fence, wouldn't you, us versus the pigs. But not all pigs are the same.'

'So what if someone told you about us!' Lauren shrugged her shoulders, forcing herself to sound more confident than she felt. 'That still doesn't explain what you're doing here at Abi's house, right now.' She tried to emphasise the last four words, hoping that Tyler wouldn't be suspicious.

Chapter Sixty

Tyler chuckled. 'That was a piece of cake!' He cast a look across at Callum. 'My mate here lives in the same road as the Paki who shacked up with *my* ex and *my* son. I happened to be round Callum's place when I saw you drive up. I didn't even need the pig's description of you; I recognised you from B&Q, didn't I? Callum and I jumped in his car, and when you left, so did we. Followed you all the way to Britford Lodge and then to here, and you never even noticed us, did you?'

Lauren kicked herself for being so unobservant but just hoped that Aaron was listening to all of this. She snuck a look at the time; there was still another ten minutes before Aaron and Dan were due to arrive. She hoped they weren't too far away.

'We followed you up this road,' Tyler continued, 'snuck a look through the window and saw you all cosied up in here. Then we went round the side and found the back door conveniently open. Your lesbo lover,' he looked down at Abi, 'was thinking about screaming, but one press of my mate's blade against her throat persuaded her not to.'

Abi was shaking. 'Please say you didn't hurt her,' she whimpered.

'I don't know. Did we hurt her, Callum?' Tyler taunted.

'Maybe we did, maybe we didn't,' Callum whined nasally.

'Why don't you just tell us what you want now?' Meg intervened.

'What do I want?' Tyler growled. 'I want this bitch to tell me where her bestie is so that I can go and get my son.'

'And then what? You can't imagine that you're going to get away with this, surely?'

'Oh, I think we hold all the aces now.' He removed his arm from Abi, snatched up the kitchen knife and stood up, moving to the doorway in a few quick strides.

'Right, one at a time, on your feet, and don't try anything stupid. You first.' He jabbed the knife in Meg's direction.

'What are you going to do to her?' cried Lauren, as Meg struggled to get out of the softly sprung low armchair.

'Keep your gob shut,' Tyler snarled.

Meg drew herself up straight and Lauren leapt to her side, grabbing hold of her arm, not wanting to be separated for fear of what might happen if they were.

'Nah, you can sit back down and wait your turn.' Tyler pointed the knife threateningly in Lauren's direction, and she sank reluctantly back into her chair. To her horror, she realised that she'd left her phone on the seat. Fortunately, neither of their captors appeared to have noticed. She checked to see that the call was still connected and was grateful to see that it was. At least it hadn't gone through to voicemail or something.

Tyler had been whispering to Callum, who nodded his understanding. Then, he spoke.

'Callum's going to take the old biddy upstairs and tie her up good and proper. She'd only slow us down if we took her with us.'

He nodded at his mate, who stood up and shoved Meg out of the door, none too gently.

Lauren suppressed an anguished cry as she saw her friend being led away. She didn't like the way Callum had grinned wickedly at whatever Tyler had said to him. Please God they wouldn't hurt Meg; she didn't think she could bear it!

'Right, your turn now, bitch!' Tyler waved the knife towards Lauren. 'Go and sit next to Abi.'

Lauren managed to slide her phone back into her pocket before moving across to the settee. She could feel Abi trembling, so she took hold of her hand and gave it a reassuring squeeze.

They sat in silence, watched by a brooding Tyler, until Callum returned.

'She all secure?' Tyler asked. Callum nodded with a sly grin. 'Right, you see them two babies holding hands? Well, go and tie their wrists together.'

Callum smirked as he took a roll of duct tape out of his pocket. Lauren watched helplessly, her stomach roiling with fear as he wrapped the tape round and round their wrists so tightly it almost cut the circulation off. There was no way they could fight back, with her left wrist now bound together with Abi's right.

'Get up!'

Awkwardly, Lauren and Abi struggled to their feet.

'We'll take your car,' Tyler snarled. 'Where's your key?'

'In my jeans pocket,' Lauren replied, reaching with her right hand into her right pocket to get it, thankful that her phone was in the left.

'Uh-uh,' scolded Tyler, darting forward. 'Allow me.' He shoved his hand into her pocket, making her wince and laughing at her discomfort.

'Callum, you go first,' he declared. 'Check the coast is clear. Okay, mate? Unlock the car and get in the driver's side. You two can follow him out, slowly. No shouting or screaming, or I won't think twice about using this knife.'

The trouble was, Lauren believed him.

They left the house. The rain was still pouring down, not that it seemed to bother Tyler. He followed closely behind Lauren, the knife up tight to her spine, so that she didn't dare risk trying to escape.

'Get in the back seat,' he ordered. Lauren stumbled in first and Abi followed as she wiggled across to the other side. Tyler slammed the door and got into the front passenger seat.

'Now, tell me where Amelia is,' he demanded, twisting to look at them.

Abi hesitated, looking at Lauren nervously.

'I think you'd better tell him,' Lauren advised, fervently hoping that Aaron was still listening, if indeed he ever had been. At least if anything happened to them, he'd be able to go and rescue Noah.

'She's at my mum's house,' Abi choked out. 'Not far from here, up the other end of Ramleaze Drive.'

Callum started the car and pulled away smoothly. Lauren was looking out of the windows as they went down the road, thinking that Aaron and Dan should be here by now. Where the hell were they?

⚙

Meg heard them leave and frantically fought to shake loose her bindings. She had to find a phone and call for help! But Callum had done a thorough job with a roll of duct tape; she was strapped to this chair with no hope of moving.

She tried to shout but the tape over her mouth made that impossible.

Frustrated, she wriggled and writhed, trying to edge the chair closer to the desk in the hope of finding a pair of scissors or something. Not that she was sure she could move her hands sufficiently to be of any use, if she ever got there, but she had to do something!

Although the chair was an office one on castors, it had sunk into the carpet and steadfastly refused to budge. Meg's body was aching from the effort, and fear of what might be happening to Lauren was making her tremble.

Chapter Sixty-one

As Callum approached the bottom of Hampshire Close, Lauren spotted a blue Vauxhall Astra parked near the junction. Never had she been so happy to see Viv's car!

As Callum pulled out onto the road running across the bottom of the close, Viv pulled out behind them just as Dan's silver Nissan Juke swung across the front of them from the opposite side, blocking the road. As Tyler swore viciously, marked police cars boxed them in from left and right, leaving Callum nowhere to go. The scene suddenly became chaotic; police officers shouting and pointing tasers, Tyler and Callum swearing, Abi screaming and Lauren crying tears of relief.

As soon as the two thugs had dropped their weapons and been handcuffed by the uniformed officers, Viv had the rear door open and was hugging Lauren. She clung to him with her free right hand and sobbed with the release of pent-up adrenaline.

Aaron opened the other rear door and comforted Abi as Dan supervised getting Tyler and Callum into separate police cars to be taken to the station. Then he came over to the car, concern etched on his face.

'Where's Meg?' he asked anxiously.

'She's back at Abi's house,' Lauren replied, pulling away from Viv's embrace. 'As is Abi's partner. I think they're both tied up somewhere upstairs. If you can separate us, I'll show you.'

It took them several minutes to find something to free Abi and Lauren, not wanting to touch the penknife and kitchen knife now lying on the ground waiting to be processed into evidence. Dan carefully removed the tape, dropping it into an evidence bag. As soon as she could, Lauren was out of the car, sprinting back up the hill towards Abi's house, closely followed by Viv. Her heart was pounding, hoping to goodness that she wouldn't find Meg seriously injured – or worse!

They entered the house and ran upstairs, to find Meg taped securely to an office chair in the small second bedroom, clearly used as a study by the home's occupants. Lauren almost overturned the chair as she enveloped Meg in a bear hug. 'Oh, thank goodness you're okay!' Viv gently pulled her away, promising Meg that they would release her as soon as they could. He too couldn't help feeling relieved that Meg appeared unharmed.

Viv found Jenna trussed up like a chicken, lying on top of the king-sized bed in the master bedroom, and reassured her of her imminent rescue.

Dan arrived and began the painstaking process of gently cutting their bindings free whilst trying to preserve any evidence. Then paramedics arrived, insisting on checking everyone over although, in the end, no one was taken to hospital.

✿

Once Meg had got the circulation back into her arms, which had been tied behind the back of the chair, she felt fine. A little tired and achy, perhaps, and shaken up … but not physically hurt. And she was delighted to see that Lauren and Jenna were also relatively unharmed as Dan escorted them all downstairs.

Abi was waiting in the hall with Aaron, and she threw herself at Jenna, half crying, half laughing in relief. Dan suggested they all sit down, so they made their way through to the lounge. Lauren settled into one of the armchairs again whilst Viv perched on the arm, unwilling to be too far away from her. She checked her phone and was amazed to see that the call to Aaron was still running. She hit end with a sigh of relief.

Abi and Jenna sat huddled together on the settee, with Aaron perched on the other end. Dan led Meg towards the other armchair, but she refused to sit down, fearing that she wouldn't get out of it a second time. She pointed to the dining-room chairs and Dan fetched one from the small table at the far end of the room, positioning it for her before sinking into the armchair himself.

'I don't know where to begin,' he said emotionally, shaking his head.

'Just hold the lecture, please,' begged Lauren. 'We didn't knowingly put ourselves into danger. I had no idea that Tyler and Callum had followed me here.'

'I know,' he said. 'I'm not blaming you. I'm just so grateful that everyone has come out of this unscathed. And I can't believe that you and Meg have cracked this case wide open!'

'We know where baby Noah is,' Lauren said with a grin.

'Yes, I heard. It was a stroke of genius, you calling Aaron so that he could overhear what was happening. We were listening to you in my car on speaker, and relaying everything over the radio to Viv and the two patrol cars. Luckily, we were able to get everyone into position before you left the house, although only just.'

He took a deep breath and exhaled slowly. 'Lauren, will you give me an outline of what's been happening, please? We can take detailed statements later, but I need to get up to speed on the case.'

Lauren explained as succinctly as she could, glossing over much of what had happened to Amelia in the past. There would be a time for that later. When she got to the part about Hal bringing Amelia and Noah to Salisbury, she looked across at Abi and signalled for her to take up the story.

'Hal's idea had been to rent somewhere in Salisbury, but there was nothing cheap enough and immediately available so, in the end, he allowed Amelia to call me. I knew my mum would be happy to help, so I arranged to meet them at her house. I didn't know then that they were bringing a child with them.

'When Amelia got the boy out of the car at my mum's, and told me that he was Freddie, I had a feeling something wasn't quite right. You see, I knew that Freddie had been taken into care because Amelia had been judged to be too emotionally disturbed to look after him, back in December. I couldn't believe they'd have given him back to her when she had nowhere to live.'

'Why didn't you or your mum contact the police when you realised who he was?' Dan demanded. 'There were enough appeals out for Noah. You must have known about his abduction and suspected that the child was Noah and not Freddie!'

'Yes, we saw them, and we read all about the missing child in *The Journal*. But Amelia had convinced my mother that the child with her was Freddie. And even though I had my suspicions, I suppose I just didn't want to believe that Amelia could be involved in something like that. You need to understand that Noah and Freddie are about the same age and they both have blond hair. And I hadn't seen Freddie since he was three months old, so I couldn't be sure that it wasn't him.' She hesitated. 'I think, as time went on, I knew deep down inside that something fishy was going on, from the way that Hal and Amelia were being so secretive. But the problem is, Amelia really truly believes that Noah *is* Freddie. She's got it into her head that she's got her boy back. What could I do? She's my friend. And she's very fragile, you know.'

Chapter Sixty-two

Dan couldn't believe what he was hearing. 'Noah is Mia's child and needs to be returned to his mother,' he said firmly.

'You can't go charging in with a load of armed police,' cried Abi. 'Who knows what she'll do if she thinks you're trying to take her son away from her again? I'm afraid she'll do something stupid!'

'I agree with Abi,' Lauren said earnestly. 'From what she's told me, I think Amelia is suffering from some serious mental health problems, which is hardly surprising given everything she's been through.'

Dan thought for a moment, but he recognised that charging in with all guns blazing – figuratively speaking – wasn't always the best approach.

'Okay, what do you suggest?' he asked, looking at Lauren.

'Would you let Abi and me go in first, to visit Amelia? I can pretend I'm a friend of Abi's.'

'I don't know if that'll work,' intervened Abi. 'She's really paranoid about anyone coming into the house, other than Hal or me.'

'Doesn't she know that her brother is dead?' Dan exclaimed.

'Not yet. I saw the news first and rang Mum. We agreed not to tell Amelia, because we're not sure how she'll react.'

'But hasn't she asked why Hal hasn't been round?' Lauren asked.

'Yes, of course, but so far, we've managed to tell her that he's busy at work. I guess we'll have to tell her soon, though,' Abi said morosely.

'This is a potential powder keg!' Dan muttered to himself.

'If I may suggest something?' interjected Meg.

'Please do!' Dan leant back in his chair. 'I'm hoping your amazing brain can find a way out of this mess.'

'Abi, can you talk to your mother on the phone without Amelia overhearing?'

'I should be able to.'

'Would you be prepared to go into your mother's house on your own?'

'Yes, of course. Why?'

'If you were to break the news to Amelia that Hal has been murdered, I'm assuming she's going to be distraught. If your mother could step in to comfort her, put her arms around her like she might do quite naturally anyway, you could quietly take Noah to the front door. Hopefully, Amelia will be too distracted to notice and, even if she does, she'll just think you're protecting the child. Lauren could be waiting outside to take him from you, with Dan parked just out of sight.'

'Isn't that rather cruel?' protested Abi.

'I'm sorry, but I don't think there's any good way out of this for Amelia,' Meg reasoned. 'The fact is that her brother has been murdered, and sooner or later she's going to find that out. And Noah is not Freddie and needs to be returned to his own mother. Whatever we do, she is going to be distressed by it. The important thing is to minimise the risk of anyone being harmed. You said yourself, with Amelia's current mental state, she's totally unpredictable.'

Meg turned to Dan. 'I'm hoping that you can arrange to have some immediate help in place for Amelia, as I don't think a police cell is the right place for her.'

Dan thought about it and nodded. 'Yes, your idea might work. I'll make some phone calls.'

✿

It took a couple of hours and numerous calls to get everything in place, so Jenna rustled up some tea and cake for everyone whilst they were working on the plan.

Dan's first call was to the superintendent, to get the green light for the operation. She put up some resistance, but eventually Dan convinced her of the merits of this approach, unorthodox though it was. Then he coordinated with all the various police teams that would be required to ensure that this went off without a hitch.

Viv was tasked to liaise with adult mental health services to ensure that a plan was in place to take care of Amelia. First, he got Lauren to brief him on Amelia's backstory so that he could give them an accurate picture. He was appalled when he found out how much she had been through, and he began to understand why both Abi and Lauren were so concerned for her safety.

Aaron was dispatched in Viv's car to take Meg over to Mia and Vikram's house. For one thing, Meg was looking quite exhausted and Dan wanted her out of the action. He overcame her protests by telling her that he needed someone to brief Noah's parents about his imminent rescue and that he could trust her to say the right things. The other reason was that they would need a child seat to transport Noah safely back to his parents, so Aaron was tasked to bring it back with him.

Even Abi was dragged into helping them when Dan asked her to draw a floor plan of the lay-out of her mother's house for the backup officers. Dan reassured her that he sincerely hoped it wouldn't be necessary to send armed officers in, but he had to prepare for every eventuality. Abi reluctantly cooperated.

At last, everything was in place, and they set off in a convoy of cars.

Abi's was the only car to park within sight of the house. Abi nervously got out and walked up the front path to the door, checking that no one was looking out of any of the front windows. She gave Lauren a thumbs-up, and Lauren snuck out of the passenger footwell, where she'd been keeping out of sight. She ran lightly across the lawn and flattened herself against the wall of the house. She knew that armed officers had surrounded the house – not that she could see anyone – and that Dan, Viv and Aaron were not far away. But for this part of the plan, it was just her and Abi.

She'd had to fight for her involvement. Dan had wanted a trained police officer to take her place, and Viv had been adamant that she wasn't going anywhere near the action. But as there had been no female police officer available, and both Abi and Lauren had argued vigorously that Noah would be terrified by the sight of a male officer in uniform, they had reluctantly agreed to let her play her part, on the condition that she did not, at any time or under any circumstances, enter the house.

Abi rang the doorbell and entered her mum's house, as pre-arranged. When the door closed, Lauren crept as close as she could, ready to take Noah and run, if necessary. After a period of anxious waiting, there was an unearthly wail that seemed to go on forever. Lauren bit her nails, wondering if she should go in or not.

Suddenly Abi appeared at the front door, clutching a toddler in her arms, who was also screaming and sobbing. The poor little mite must be so confused!

Lauren took him from Abi as gently as she could and hugged him close against her chest, murmuring reassuring words into the top of his head. Abi silently handed over a bedraggled-looking cuddly rabbit, its blue jacket streaked with dirt. Tears were streaming down her cheeks as she turned and went back inside.

Lauren made her way slowly down the path to the waiting car, which had now pulled up, soothing Noah as she went. Viv jumped out to open the door for her, and she fastened Noah into his car seat before climbing into the back seat next to him. She held out the cuddly toy rabbit to the now sullen child, and he snatched it from her, hugging it tightly. Then she fastened her own seat belt and nodded to Viv, who had returned to the front passenger seat, that they were ready to go. As Aaron pulled away, Lauren could see two paramedics hurrying up the path to the door to Abi's mother's house. At least Amelia would be going to hospital for a psychiatric evaluation, and not the police station.

Chapter Sixty-three

When they arrived in Laverstock, Lauren carried Noah straight into the lounge, where Mia and Vikram were waiting side by side on the settee holding hands. The anxiety on their faces magically transformed when they saw Noah. As Lauren carefully handed him to his mother, he stretched out his arms to her, beamed a radiant smile and babbled, 'Mama, Mama, Mama.'

There wasn't a dry eye in the room.

Meg, Lauren and Viv slipped quietly out of the house, shutting the front door to leave the reunited family in peace. Aaron and Dan were waiting for them on the pavement, Dan's car pulled up behind Viv's.

'Well done,' Dan murmured as he leant in to give Meg a kiss on the cheek. 'Your plan worked perfectly.'

'Thank you,' she replied, blushing slightly. 'What happens now?'

'Aaron and I are going to take you back to Britford Lodge for a well-earned rest.'

'But what about my statement?' she asked.

'That can wait until tomorrow morning,' Dan insisted.

'What about mine?' asked Lauren.

'That can also wait until tomorrow,' said Viv, taking her hand and looking at her lovingly. 'You and I have something else to discuss tonight.'

Lauren's heart gave a gigantic flip, and her stomach trembled like a jelly. Viv moved closer and pulled her into his embrace.

'I love you,' he whispered into the top of her head. She looked up and he bent his head so that their lips touched, tentatively at first and then passionately.

'Get a room already,' teased Aaron, and they reluctantly moved apart, looking embarrassed.

'About time,' muttered Dan, opening the front passenger door and helping a beaming Meg into his car. Straightening up, he looked Viv in the eyes. 'I shall see you at briefing, eight o'clock sharp tomorrow morning.'

'Don't you need me to help with the interviews this evening, guv?' Viv asked.

'I think Aaron and I can handle those.'

They watched as Dan ran round to the driver's door and Aaron climbed into the back.

'What now?' Lauren whispered, as they watched Dan's car disappear round the corner.

'Where were we?' asked Viv, pulling her in for another kiss.

✿

Later that evening, Viv and Lauren were snuggled up on the sofa at her house, telling Bekka about their day, when Viv's phone rang. He sighed and looked at the screen.

'It's Dan,' he said, sounding surprised. He stood up and moved to the window, listening intently for what seemed like an age. Lauren was hoping that nothing had gone wrong. Perhaps Tyler had escaped, or something equally as dreadful?

'Okay, guv, I'll be in as soon as I can. Don't you worry, I can manage everything.'

He ended the call and turned around.

'Don't tell me Dan wants you to go into work, not at this time of the evening?' Lauren exclaimed, looking concerned at the serious expression on Viv's face.

'You have to expect callouts at all sorts of unreasonable times if you're dating a detective,' he warned her.

'But what the hell has happened?'

'Dan's been called up to the hospital.'

'Oh no! Why? What's wrong?'

'Well, I don't know that anything is wrong as such. Not unless you consider his wife about to give birth as being a problem!' he grinned.

'What? Katie's in labour? Oh, you beast!' She threw a

cushion at him. 'For a minute there, you had me really worried.'

'Gotcha!' He sank down beside her and slipped an arm around her shoulders.

'I was serious about having to go into work,' he said. 'Apparently, Katie's been having niggling pains all day, but she didn't want to tell Dan while he was busy with the case. When he phoned her to let her know he was going to be late home, she broke the news that he was about to become a dad. By then, her pains were every five minutes, so he dashed home and took her straight up to the maternity unit. They reckon the baby should be born this side of midnight, barring any complications. Obviously, Dan's going to stay with her; that's why he's asked me to go in. I need to take over the interviews with Tyler and Callum.'

Lauren hugged him. 'I'm so excited for Dan and Katie,' she said, her eyes shining brightly as she gazed into his. 'I guess I will just have to get used to you being called out at all sorts of unreasonable times, seeing that I am definitely going to be dating this particular detective for a long time to come.'

Viv pulled her into his chest and whispered in her ear. 'And I guess I'll just have to get used to you sticking your nose in where it doesn't belong.' He took the sting out of his words with a passionate kiss.

Epilogue

Two weeks later

It was a sunny Sunday afternoon, and Dan was standing in the conservatory at Britford Lodge cradling his baby daughter in his arms. His wife, Katie, was sitting on a small settee next to Lauren, with Meg and Albert on matching cane armchairs.

'Who wants to hold her first?' he asked.

'Me!' clamoured Lauren, as Albert nearly choked at the thought of holding a baby that small. Meg was content to bide her time, watching as Dan carefully positioned the precious bundle into Lauren's eager arms.

'Have you two finally decided on a name?' Lauren asked, staring in awe at the baby's perfect little face and huge blue eyes.

'We have,' smiled Katie. 'She's called Meghan Elizabeth Bywater.'

'Meghan?' Meg looked at Dan questioningly.

'It was the closest we could get to Meg plus Lauren,' he explained with a twinkle.

'Oh, that is the sweetest thing!' exclaimed Lauren.

A tear glistened in Meg's eye as she nodded. 'That's lovely,' she agreed. 'And Elizabeth?'

'After my mother,' said Katie, a little sadly. 'I just wish she could be here to see this little one. She so badly wanted to be a grandmother.'

Dan placed a hand on Katie's shoulder and squeezed it gently. 'Katie's mum passed away the year before we got married,' he explained.

'I'm sure she would have been over the moon,' Meg said sympathetically.

'But she'll have a substitute granny in you, Meg, won't

she?' grinned Lauren, chuffed to bits as baby Meghan wrapped her tiny fingers around one of hers. 'As well as her Aunty Lauren.' She nuzzled her nose close to the baby's.

'I think I'm probably old enough to be her great-grandmother,' said Meg, beaming. 'But it's an honour I would be delighted to bear, if you will allow me?'

'Of course,' said Dan, pulling another of the cane armchairs over so that he could sit down. 'She'll have Nanny Carol – that's my mum – and Great-granny Meg. What more does a child need?' He caught Lauren's eye. 'Not forgetting Aunty Lauren,' he added hastily, 'to add to the other aunts and uncles she's got. I have a feeling she's going to be spoiled rotten.'

No one could argue with that.

'I say,' said Albert, after a lull in the conversation, 'are we allowed to ask if there are any updates on the case?' He was tired of all this cooing over a baby.

'You do realise that I'm still on paternity leave?' said Dan.

'Eh, what?' demanded Albert.

'Paternity leave. It's an entitlement for all dads now,' he explained.

'Didn't happen back in my day,' grumbled Albert.

'Then it's a good thing that times change, isn't it?' chipped in Meg. 'I think it's great that fathers get to spend time with their young offspring. It's not just the mother who needs to bond with baby, you know.'

'Exactly,' said Dan, 'although my two weeks are almost up. I'll be back at work tomorrow morning.' He grimaced. 'But not to worry, I've been keeping in touch with Viv by phone.'

'Daily,' muttered Katie.

'And he's kept me up to speed.'

'Come on then: spill the beans!' demanded Albert.

'Very well. As you know, Hal and his sister, Amelia, abducted baby Noah and took him, in the first instance, to Amelia's maisonette in Ludgershall. Tyler has finally confessed to putting Hal up to doing it, but only after his mate Liam dropped him right in it. Liam was present on an evening when Tyler was ranting about wanting to get his son away from his mother's … umm … coloured partner. Apparently, Liam told him to just go ahead and do it, and Tyler explained that he couldn't because he'd be the first person the police would suspect. That's when they hatched the plan for Tyler to set up a cast-iron alibi and for Hal to abduct Noah for him. Liam told us all of this in his statement, leaving Tyler without a leg to stand on. The actual abduction took place pretty much as you two had worked out.' He nodded at Lauren and Meg.

'We were able to track Hal's car using ANPR, which helped fill in a few blanks. They went straight from Laverstock to Tesco on Southampton Road, where they bought the car seat and a lot of other paraphernalia they needed for Noah, then parked up in a lay-by near Middle Wallop for the rest of the night.'

'Whatever for?' put in Albert.

'We'll probably never know, with Hal dead and Amelia too disturbed to talk to us. But I suspect they didn't want to risk waking any of the neighbours by arriving in Ludgershall in the middle of the night.'

'Why didn't they just stay in Ludgershall?' asked Meg. 'Why risk bringing Noah back to Salisbury?'

'Apparently, that was the plan agreed with Tyler. He wanted to have his son near enough to visit easily.'

'But from what Jed told us, Tyler clearly didn't know where Noah was. What went wrong?'

'Tyler says that Hal refused to tell him where Noah was. I suspect that, by the time they arrived in Salisbury, Hal had realised there was a problem with his sister believing that Noah was Freddie.'

'Is that why Tyler killed him?'

'He says it was an accident … that he met Hal outside the pub that Wednesday night and challenged him over Noah's whereabouts. He says Hal drew the knife, they struggled, and Hal ended up being the one stabbed. The evidence doesn't bear that out at all, though. CSI eventually found the knife, which only had Tyler's fingerprints on it. And Hal was stabbed multiple times, which is not something that happens accidentally.'

'I assume Tyler's been charged with murder?'

'Among other things, yes,' Dan confirmed.

'What about the black sports bag?' asked Meg. 'Did they ever find that?'

'Yes. When Hal and Amelia couldn't find a place to rent, he dumped all her belongings from the van into a lock-up garage. Luckily, Abi's mother overheard where that was, when Amelia was asking Hal to fetch various things for her. We went through everything and found a nearly brand-new black sports bag, with a baby blanket and a dummy still inside it. Forensic examination proved that Noah had been inside the bag. And the dummy had a residue of honey and morphine on it.'

'Morphine!' gasped Meg. 'That's why Noah never cried!'

'Exactly. They were lucky they didn't accidentally kill him, to be honest. But a doctor has checked Noah thoroughly and given him a clean bill of health, so there's no harm done.'

There was a moment's solemnity at the thought of what might have happened.

'What about the other members of RAS?' Meg asked.

'We've been able to charge Liam for his part in the conspiracy, and Callum for sending racist hate mail to Vikram in addition to his part in terrorising you. And thanks to your friend Jed, we now know exactly who the other members of RAS are, so we can monitor their activities in the future. Although I suspect with Hal dead and three of their members in custody, the group might even fall apart.'

'And what's being done about that bloody incompetent DI who was in charge of the case before you?' Albert wanted to know.

'DI Barnes is currently on gardening leave. He was due to retire next year anyway. With a little encouragement, he's agreed to take early retirement.' Dan gave a wry smile.

'Did you find the insider that Tyler said had been passing on information to him?' asked Meg.

'Yes, it was PC Thomas, who was working with Barnes' team. We've suspected for some time that RAS were getting advance information about police raids and such like, which is why we've never managed to pin anything on Tyler Ford until now. Thomas confessed when we challenged him, and he's been dismissed.'

'Is that everything?' asked Meg. 'Lauren, you've been remarkably quiet. Haven't you got any questions?'

'Umm, actually, I knew all of this already,' she said, a little sheepishly.

'What? What?' exclaimed Albert, bristling with indignation.

'Viv's been keeping me up to date, but I promised him I wouldn't say a word to anyone. And I haven't.'

'Good for you, girl,' smiled Meg, pleased that her young friend was learning that trust works both ways.

'And I trust none of you will repeat anything I've just said,' said Dan, directing his gaze at Albert. 'The case hasn't come to court yet, and we don't want to jeopardise the prosecution, do we?'

'Oh no. Absolutely not!' agreed Albert.

'There is one thing that Dan hasn't told you …yet,' said Katie, looking at her husband encouragingly.

'Oh, I … umm …' Dan seemed strangely lost for words.

'Well, spit it out, man,' demanded Albert.

'The super is bringing in another DI to replace Barnes because, unfortunately, neither of our detective sergeants has passed their inspector's exams yet. But there's been a bit of a restructure and they're promoting me to DCI.'

There was a chorus of congratulations, with none looking prouder than Meg.

THE END

I'd be very grateful if you could take the time to RATE and REVIEW on Amazon, Goodreads or the site where you purchased this book. (PS: you don't need to have bought the book on Amazon to leave a review.)

You can also check out my website for details of other books in the series:

https://www.wendyboynton.co.uk

If you enjoyed reading this book … watch out for
my next one!

COMING SOON

The Mystery of the Missing Bequest

The Salisbury Murders: Book Four

When an elderly resident passes away naturally, the only mystery is what happened to his three leatherbound stamp albums containing a valuable collection. These were left as a specific bequest in Patrick's will to his lifelong friend Sophie, but they have gone missing.

Jack Harris, former resident of The Cedars, was Patrick's friend. Convinced the albums have been stolen, he calls in Meg and Lauren to investigate. They quickly identify a list of suspects, but their greatest challenge is working out how the albums were smuggled out of Victoria House unseen. Their case soon becomes complicated when their prime suspect is murdered!

Believing that the likely thief was either blackmailed or bribed into stealing the albums, Meg and Lauren investigate Patrick's and Sophie's families. The former believes the inheritance was rightly theirs; the latter could have wanted Sophie's fortune for themselves. The difficulty is: are any of them telling the truth?

Now working with three octogenarians – Meg, Albert and Jack – Lauren has her work cut out balancing the investigation, her mother's latest health scare and her love life. Her determination to find the missing albums leads her into a dangerous situation, and when she goes missing, DCI Dan and DS Viv must do everything in their power to find her. Will Lauren survive her terrible ordeal?

Glossary of Abbreviations

A&E:	Accident and Emergency
ABH:	Actual bodily harm
A-levels:	Advanced levels (school exams)
ANPR:	Automatic Number Plate Recognition
CCTV:	Closed circuit television
CID:	Criminal Investigations Department
CSI:	Crime Scene Investigator
DC:	Detective Constable
DCI:	Detective Chief Inspector
DI:	Detective Inspector
DNA:	Deoxyribose-nucleic acid (genetic material)
DS:	Detective Sergeant
GCSE:	General Certificate of Secondary Education (school exams)
GP:	General Practitioner (doctor)
LGBTQ:	Lesbian, gay, bisexual, transgender and questioning
NA:	National Action
NVQ:	National Vocational Qualification
O-levels:	Ordinary levels (school exams, replaced by GCSEs)
PC:	Police Constable
RAS:	Radical Action Salisbury
SENCO:	Special Educational Needs Co-ordinator
SIO:	Senior Investigating Officer